LIBRARY IN A BOOK

CAPITAL PUNISHMENT

THE FACTS ON FILE LIBRARY IN A BOOK SERIES

Each volume of the Facts On File Library in a Book series is carefully designed to be the best one-volume source for research on important current problems. Written clearly and carefully so that even the most complex aspects of the issue are easily understandable, the books give the reader the research tools to begin work, plus the information needed to delve more deeply into the topic. Each book includes a history of the subject, biographical information on important figures in the field, a complete annotated bibliography and a carefully designed index—everything the researcher needs to get down to work.

LIBRARY IN A BOOK

CAPITAL PUNISHMENT

Stephen A. Flanders

Bibliographic materials prepared by
Caroline M. Brown, M.L.S., Rutgers University

Facts On File
New York • Oxford

LIBRARY IN A BOOK: CAPITAL PUNISHMENT

Copyright © 1991 by Stephen A. Flanders

Facts On File, Inc.   Facts On File Limited
460 Park Avenue South Collins Street
New York NY 10016   Oxford OX4 1XJ
USA   United Kingdom

Library of Congress Cataloging-in-Publication Data
Flanders, Stephen A.
   Capital punishment / by Stephen A. Flanders : bibliographic materials prepared by Caroline M. Brown.
       p.   cm. — (Library in a book)
   Includes bibliographical references and index.
   Summary: Reviews the history and current status of the death penalty in the U.S., focusing on the legal and ethical issues of its use by the criminal justice system.
   ISBN 0-8160-1912-6
   1. Capital punishment—United States—Juvenile literature.
   [1. Capital punishment.]   I. Brown, Caroline M.   II. Title.
III. Series.
KF9227.C2F53   1990
345.73'0773—dc20
[347.305773]   90-42868

A British CIP catalogue record for this book is available from the British Library.

Text design by Ron Monteleone
Jacket design by Nadja Furlan-Lorbek
Composition by the Maple-Vail Book Manufacturing Group
Manufactured by the Maple-Vail Book Manufacturing Group
Printed in the United States of America

10 9 8 7 6 5 4 3 2 1

This book is printed on acid-free paper.

CONTENTS

——

Contents

ACKNOWLEDGMENTS

The author would like to thank the following organizations and individuals for their assistance: Henry Schwarzschild at the Capital Punishment Project of the American Civil Liberties Union; Leigh Dingerson at the National Coalition to Abolish the Death Penalty; Watt Espy at the Capital Punishment Research Project; the NAACP Legal Defense and Education Fund; the Sprague Library at Montclair State College; and Eleanora von Dehsen and Nicholas Bakalar at Facts On File.

INTRODUCTION

The purpose of this book is to provide a one-stop source for information about capital punishment. The first part of the book is an overview of the topic. It is designed to give the reader a basic perspective of the many issues pertaining to the death penalty. It includes a general introduction, a chronology of major events, a summary of important court cases and a biographical listing of key individuals.

Once acquainted with the subject of capital punishment, the reader can turn to the second part of the book for a comprehensive guide to reference materials on the subject. A broad spectrum of resources is identified for use in further research. At the end of the book are a listing of acronyms used throughout and a description of federal and state court systems. Also included are two appendices that furnish basic statistical information on the death penalty.

The status of capital punishment in American society is constantly changing. This book is current through December 31, 1989. Readers are encouraged to consult the reference sources in the second half of the book for developments subsequent to this date.

PART I

OVERVIEW OF THE TOPIC

CHAPTER 1

INTRODUCTION TO CAPITAL PUNISHMENT

In 1972 the Supreme Court halted executions in the United States. Four years later, the Court authorized their resumption. Between 1977 and the end of 1989 120 prisoners were put to death. The nation's death row population now numbers more than 2,250 inmates. Capital punishment, or the death penalty, has again become a basic fact of American criminal justice.

In simple terms, capital punishment is the lawful taking of a person's life after conviction for a crime. However, the use of death as a punishment is highly controversial. It has raised difficult legal and ethical issues. The debate over capital punishment continues to be waged in both the courts and the political arena.

This chapter consists of seven sections. American ideas of justice are deeply rooted in the long tradition of Western culture. Historical Background traces the development and use of capital punishment since earliest times. The next section, Capital Punishment in America, reviews the status of the death penalty in the United States today. Capital Punishment and the Law examines the criminal justice system that administers the death penalty and the main legal issues which have arisen over use of the sanction. The major areas of disagreement concerning the death penalty are addressed in The Capital Punishment Debate. The relationship of the religious community to this debate is discussed in Capital Punishment and Religion, and the international status of capital punishment is assessed in Worldwide Perspective. The final section, Future Trends, considers possible developments in the years ahead.

3

Two notes are important. Abolitionism normally is used to describe the movement in America to end slavery. In the context of capital punishment, the term refers to opposition to use of the death penalty. Conversely, retentionism signifies support for maintaining the sanction in effect. Court cases throughout the chapter in bold print are reviewed in detail in Chapter 3.

HISTORICAL BACKGROUND

The infliction of death for the purpose of retribution has been a facet of human existence since earliest times. Even before the emergence of organized societies, individuals killed to avenge wrongs done to them and their families. These killings were acts of private retribution. There was no code that specified wrongful conduct or the penalties such behavior would incur.

The first criminal laws were an outgrowth of this practice of personal justice. These laws evolved as a means of codifying the compensation one individual or family owed another in order to right a personal wrong. The idea that this restitution involved a punishment imposed on behalf of the society as a whole, however, was yet to come.

As more-organized social structures developed, wrongs or crimes were divided into public and private offenses. Public offenses, such as witchcraft and blasphemy, were punished by the state while private offenses still were answered by acts of personal retribution. This split system of justice eventually yielded to a unified scheme in which private retaliation was replaced by a concept of public justice. Behind the shift was an emerging recognition that every crime committed by any member of society was harmful to the interests of the entire society. With the public-private distinction removed, the individual relinquished the right to personal revenge. In return, the state assumed responsibility for the punishment of all crimes, including personal offenses such as murder. Personal vengeance had given way to lawfully derived and administered death sentences.

Capital punishment was common throughout the ancient world. Death sentences were imposed for a wide variety of offenses. One of the earliest recorded sets of laws known to Western society, the Babylonian Hammurabi Code (ca. 1700 B.C.), decreed the death penalty for crimes as minor as the fraudulent sale of beer. Egyptians were killed for disclosing sacred burial places. The Athenian leader Draco in the seventh century B.C. fashioned a criminal code which prescribed the death sentence for most offenses. The severity of this code gave rise to the word draconian.

4

Socrates' suicide several hundred years later to escape execution for the crime of irreverence is among the most famous events in Western intellectual history. The Torah, the law of the Hebrews, authorized death for over a dozen offenses. Jesus Christ was crucified under the laws of the Roman Empire.

The Middle Ages and Renaissance saw little change in the widespread use of capital punishment. Death was the standard penalty for major crimes across Europe. The methods of execution frequently were cruel and barbaric, often involving some form of torture. The condemned were subjected to such ordeals as burning at the stake or being crushed under heavy stones. Minor offenses normally merited corporal punishment, such as branding or flogging.

The reign of King Henry VIII was illustrative of this period. Apart from the famous beheadings of several of the monarch's wives, as well as of Sir Thomas More, over 70,000 executions took place during the first half of the 16th century in England. Over the next several centuries, Great Britain continued to add to its already large number of crimes punishable by death. By 1780, the British criminal law contained 350 capital crimes. The statutes were known popularly as the "Bloody Code." Interestingly, the actual number of executions throughout this era dropped substantially. The reasons for this decline included the reluctance of judges and juries to convict persons of minor offenses that required the death penalty.

The emphasis on reason and humanity that marked the 18th century Enlightenment brought about a transformation in the way capital punishment was viewed. The extensive use of the death penalty and the brutal manner in which it was administered were denounced by such leading thinkers as the French philosophers Montesquieu and Voltaire. In 1764, the Italian jurist Cesare Beccaria greatly advanced the entire field of criminal justice when he published his *Essay on Crimes and Punishment*. Widely translated and read, his book had an immediate and dramatic impact.

Beccaria criticized the use of torture, the imposition of harsh penalties for minor offenses and the archaic state of the criminal law in general. He argued that the certainty of punishment was much more important to deterring crime than the severity of the sanction. He favored incarceration and hard labor for persons convicted of capital crimes.

Beccaria's writing served as the theoretical foundation for the major reforms in criminal law which occurred in the late 18th and early 19th centuries. In England, his ideas were taken up by the philosopher Jeremy Bentham, who advocated a complete revision of the British criminal code. Bentham's proposals, such as a reduction in the number of designated capital crimes, were presented to Parliament by another preeminent legal reformer, Sir Samuel Romilly. Although neither lived to see the result, their efforts sparked a reform movement that brought the number of capital crimes in Britain down to four by the mid-1800s.

The American colonies inherited the British system of law. Each of the colonies had its own criminal code, reflecting the distinctive circumstances of its founding. In early Puritan Massachusetts, the list of capital crimes included witchcraft, blasphemy and adultery. In contrast, the Quaker influence in Pennsylvania limited the death penalty to crimes of murder and treason. Paralleling the trend in criminal law in the mother country, the number of capital offenses in each of the colonies increased throughout their development. By the time of the American Revolution, all of the colonies had severe criminal laws. Legal historians, noting the relatively low rate of executions across the colonies, point out that these criminal codes were far harsher in word than in practice.

Americans in the first years of the nation were familiar with the new ideas on criminal justice taking hold in Europe. Beccaria's book had been published in New York City in 1773. In 1787 Dr. Benjamin Rush, a signer of the Declaration of Independence and surgeon general to the Continental Army, delivered an address at the home of Benjamin Franklin in Philadelphia. Rush called for an end to public executions as part of an overall reform of the criminal justice system. The same year he helped found the Philadelphia Society for Alleviating the Miseries of Public Prisons.

The society was instrumental in the development of the prison system in the United States. In 1790 the Walnut Street Jail in Philadelphia was converted into the nation's first modern penitentiary. The emergence of penal institutions had a major impact on the use of capital punishment. Historically, one of the reasons societies had relied so heavily on the death penalty was that other punishment options did not exist. The new prison facilities, funded by the state and manned by professional staffs, changed this. For the first time, confinement became a realistic alternative punishment for many crimes.

Rush was the first prominent American to publicly urge the abolition of the death penalty. He published several influential essays in which he maintained that capital punishment was indefensible on either rational or religious grounds. Rush was joined by other legal reformers, most notably the state's attorney general, William Bradford, in a campaign to modernize Pennsylvania's criminal code. In 1794 the state became the first political entity to differentiate among degrees of homicide when it made first-degree murder its only capital offense.

Other states followed suit in a general movement to update the criminal law. Over the next two decades, state penitentiaries were constructed, and the number of capital offenses were cut considerably. While the efforts of those opposed to capital punishment helped make these reforms possible, the primary impetus for their implementation was the perceived need to curb excesses in the criminal justice system. The death penalty itself was widely accepted and remained in effect throughout the country.

Capital punishment in the United States has undergone many modifications since the early 1800s. Its use gradually has become more limited and constrained. However, the death penalty has endured as a basic fact of American jurisprudence. The debate over capital punishment throughout American history has been characterized by the struggle of a relative handful of groups and individuals to change the nation's broad and consistent support for the sanction. The level of opposition has varied greatly. More often than not, its strength and success have been affected by other historical events.

The first concerted nationwide campaign against the death penalty took hold in the 1830s and 1840s. The movement initially formed around a desire to halt public executions. Public hangings of the time normally drew large crowds. Disturbed by the drunkenness and riots that often accompanied these events, legislatures in five states had passed laws providing for private executions by 1835. A growing antigallows sentiment over the next 15 years caused another 10 states to enact similar measures.

This sentiment was fueled by a new generation of abolitionist leaders. Many had been inspired by the ideas and writings of the politician and lawyer Edward Livingston. In the early 1820s, Livingston had drafted a new criminal code for the Louisiana Assembly that eliminated capital punishment. Although his proposals were not approved, his arguments against the death penalty were published and read throughout the nation.

The abolitionist cause was joined by such prominent reformers as Robert Rantoul Jr. and John L. O'Sullivan and the writers John Greenleaf Whittier and Walt Whitman. The period also saw the formation of the first abolitionist organizations, most notably the American Society for the Abolition of Capital Punishment. The movement was effective in communicating its message to the American public. Written appeals, speeches, lectures, meetings and debates were all part of the effort to generate understanding and support for abolitionist goals. Supporters William Cullen Bryant, editor of the *New York Post*, and Horace Greeley, founder of the *New York Tribune*, used their newspapers to reach a nationwide audience.

The campaign met with limited success. Maine implemented what was in effect a moratorium on executions in 1837. Ten years later, abolitionist forces achieved their most important victory to date when Michigan became the first state to completely abolish capital punishment. The sense that the movement was gaining momentum was short-lived. Although Rhode Island and Wisconsin repealed their death penalty statutes in the early 1850s, the attention of the country had turned elsewhere. After 1846, abolitionist activity faded as the Mexican War, the growing struggle over slavery and the Civil War dominated the national agenda.

The diminished abolitionist movement made little real headway in the decades following the Civil War. Led by the dedicated reformer Marvin H. Bovee, opponents of capital punishment were able to persuade many state legislatures that mandatory death sentences for certain crimes should be replaced by discretionary sentencing procedures. By the 1890s, 21 states had switched to discretionary capital sentences. The abolitionists had believed that, given the option, courts would be more lenient in their sentencing patterns. In practice, the actual number of executions did not drop as juries continued to impose the death sentence.

The Progressive Era around the turn of the century witnessed a burst of renewed abolitionist activity. In 1897 Congress approved a measure submitted by representative Newton M. Curtis (R, N.Y.) that reduced the number of federal capital offenses to four. The first years of the 20th century saw a rejuvenation of abolitionist organizations. The ranks of capital punishment opponents included representatives from the new field of penology. The development of a more scientific approach to understanding criminal behavior contributed to the general inclination of the time for criminal law reform. Between 1907 and 1917, eight states repealed captial punishment, bringing the total number of abolitionist states to 12, or one-quarter of the Union.

Abolitionist gains were halted by America's entry into World War I. Historians believe a series of sensational crimes in the years just after the war caused the reinstatement of the death penalty in four states. Members of the law enforcement community moved to the forefront of efforts to retain capital punishment.

Since the early 1920s, an interesting pattern has emerged in the debate over capital punishment. Certain kinds of events have tended to build support for the death penalty and others to generate opposition to the sanction. Not surprisingly, public support for capital punishment has been highest in the aftermath of particularly horrid or brazen crimes. Conversely, controversial executions have led to an upsurge in abolitionist activity.

In 1924 the renowned lawyer Clarence Darrow, an ardent foe of capital punishment, undertook to defend two young men, Nathan Leopold and Richard Loeb, accused of killing a neighborhood child. His stirring plea against their execution, which ultimately resulted in terms of life imprisonment, inspired abolitionists across the country. The following year Darrow, Sing Sing prison warden Lewis E. Lawes and other leading opponents of the death penalty formed the American League to Abolish Capital Punishment. Membership picked up dramatically two years later following the execution of the Italian-born anarchists Sacco and Vanzetti. Supporters of the two men, alleging their murder convictions were politically motivated, fought an unsuccessful six-year legal battle to reverse their sentences. Their executions sparked worldwide protests. A picture secretly taken by a news photographer during the electrocution of murderess Ruth Snyder in 1928 also raised many doubts as to the wisdom of capital punishment.

This revitalized abolitionist activity was quickly matched by growing cries for greater use of the death penalty. These pleas were driven by widespread alarm over a rise in violent crime. The St. Valentine's Day Massacre in 1929 became a symbol of the gangster violence of the Prohibition period. The kidnapping murder of the Lindbergh baby in 1932 led to both federal and numerous state statutes making kidnapping a capital offense. In the wake of violent crime sprees in their states, Kansas and then South Dakota legislators restored the death penalty.

As the United States entered World War II, the federal government and 42 of the 48 states authorized capital punishment. This status did not change for almost 20 years. During this time, there was no real debate over the merits of the death penalty as the nation was preoccupied with the difficult challenges of the war, its cold war aftermath and the conflict in Korea. The executions of Julius and Ethel Rosenberg for espionage in 1953 met with opposition, but at issue were their death sentences rather than the death penalty itself.

The catalyst for resumed abolitionist efforts was the publication in 1954 of *Cell 2455 Death Row* by California death row inmate Caryl Chessman. The book, which characterized the prison system as a virtual school for crime and condemned the death penalty as little more than an act of vengeance, provoked a sympathetic response. Chessman, who published two more books about death row before his eventual execution in1960, became a celebrated author and an international cause célèbre. His case served to galvanize a new affiliation of organizations and individuals opposed to capital punishment.

The territories of Alaska and Hawaii ended the death penalty in 1957. The following year, Delaware became the first state in 40 years to abolish capital punishment. In 1959 the American Law Institute, in its Model Penal Code, proposed significant changes in the way capital punishment was administered in the criminal justice system. Campaigns were mounted to eliminate the death penalty in California, New Jersey, Ohio and Oregon.

In each state, however, abolitionist forces were unable to convince a majority of the public that the death penalty should go. Law enforcement organizations and officials, political figures and others in favor of retaining capital punishment frequently cited statistics showing a steady increase in violent crime. In 1961 Delaware restored the death penalty after a series of highly publicized murders of elderly citizens. The same year Congress added skyjacking to the list of federal capital offenses.

Historically, opponents of capital punishment had worked to eliminate the practice through the legislative repeal of death penalty statutes. To even the most optimistic abolitionist, though, it was increasingly evident there was little chance capital punishment would be ended through the legislative process in the foreseeable future. During the early 1960s, a major switch in tactics on the part of the abolitionist movement occurred. This shift was led by a small group of lawyers at the NAACP's Legal Defense and Education Fund (LDF). The new strategy was to move the struggle over capital punishment to the judicial arena.

The LDF was established in 1939 as a nonprofit organization to litigate civil rights issues and provide legal services to the poor. Fund lawyers were deeply involved in the civil rights movement, particularly in the South, where they frequently represented black defendants accused of capital crimes. Firsthand experience with the criminal justice system had convinced many of the attorneys that the death penalty ultimately was unworkable and wrong.

By 1965 the LDF, under director Jack Greenberg, had launched a nationwide legal attack on capital punishment. The immediate goal was to block every execution in America thorugh a combination of lawsuits, appeals and other court actions. At the same time Fund lawyers, headed by law professor Anthony G. Amsterdam, undertook a series of test cases designed to challenge the constitutionality of the death penalty. The hope was that the Supreme Court would consent to hear one or more of these cases, rule the death penalty unconstitutional and thus outlaw capital punishment in the United States.

The LDF was subsequently joined by the American Civil Liberties Union (ACLU) and other legal organizations committed to ending the death penalty. Within two years, a coordinated series of legal actions across the country had achieved a freeze on executions in the United States. For the first time since the federal government started keeping statistics in 1930, no one was put to death in 1968. The moratorium continued over the next four years as the courts struggled to resolve the different legal challenges raised against capital punishment.

The legal campaign to have the death penalty declared unconstitutional seemingly had succeeded in 1972. In **Furman v. Georgia,** the Supreme Court struck down the nation's capital punishment laws. The Court found that the statutes as written permitted the death penalty to be imposed in an arbitrary and capricious manner in violation of the Eighth Amendment's ban on cruel and unusual punishment. Most significantly, though, the Court did not go so far as to rule that capital punishment itself was unconstitutional but only that the haphazard way in which it was administered was constitutionally impermissible.

The decision met immediate criticism. President Richard Nixon and California Governor Ronald Reagan were two of the most outspoken of the many political figures across the nation who denounced the ruling as an unwarranted intrusion on the prerogatives of the legislative branch of government. The Supreme Court was characterized as thwarting the will of the majority as expressed through its elected representatives. The Court, it was argued, had usurped to itself the right to make rather than interpret law.

Many states moved quickly to amend their capital punishment laws to conform to the procedural guidelines outlined in the **Furman** judgment. In 1976 the Supreme Court held that the new statutes provided sufficient safeguards to insure that the death penalty was employed in a constitutionally acceptable manner. The Court's ruling in **Gregg v. Georgia** reinstated capital punishment in America. The nation's first execution in 10 years took place in January 1977 when Gary Gilmore was put to death in Utah by a firing squad.

The last 15 years have seen the Supreme Court consistently reaffirm its reasoning in the **Gregg** decision. The debate over capital punishment also has moved to the center of the political arena. The death penalty was a major issue in the 1988 presidential campaign. A national coalition of organizations opposed to capital punishment continues to fight the sanction, but neither courts nor legislatures seemed inclined to overturn the death penalty. As the United States enters the 1990s, capital punishment remains a fixture of the criminal justice system.

CAPITAL PUNISHMENT IN AMERICA

This section beings with a summary of the current status of capital punishment in the United States. The Death Penalty Today reviews the basic facts of the sanction: the laws that authorize its use and the offenses for which it may be imposed; the numbers of death sentences and executions; and the methods employed to execute convicted criminals. The remaining parts then address the different sides in the debate over capital punishment, public attitudes toward the death penalty and the extent of the issue's impact in the political process.

THE DEATH PENALTY TODAY
Death Penalty Statutes and Offenses

Thirty-seven states and the federal government authorize the death penalty for the commission of certain crimes. In most states, only murder is a capital offense. In order for a specific murder to warrant the death penalty, the Supreme Court requires that two conditions must be met. It must be a first-degree murder and one or more aggravating circumstances must be present.

Crimes of murder normally are divided between two degrees. First-degree murder involves the deliberate and premeditated taking of a life. Other acts of murder, such as crimes of passion, are classified as second-degree. Aggravating circumstances refer to those aspects of a crime that increase its severity but are apart from the essential elements of the offense itself. Torture committed in conjunction with a murder would be an example.

Aggravating circumstances are defined in the applicable death penalty statute. Circumstances considered for murder include:

- The crime was particularly vile, atrocious, or cruel.
- There were multiple victims.
- The crime occurred during the commission of another felony.
- The victim was a police or correctional officer in the line of duty.
- The offender was previously convicted of a capital offense or violent crime.
- The offender directed an accomplice to commit the murder or committed the murder at the direction of another person.

The death penalty is imposed most often for murders committed during the course of another major felony. These homicides are usually termed felony-murders. In most states, there is no need to prove intent to commit these homicides on the part of the killers. The law assumes that persons who engage in serious felonies are responsible for the consequences of their actions and the dangerous situations they create. Defendants who kill, even accidently, in the course of another felony may be found guilty of first-degree murder. It is only necessary to show the offender intended to commit the original crime.

Historically, many states held accomplices to a felony-murder equally liable for the crime, even if they did not participate in the actual homicide. In 1982 the Supreme Court, in **Enmund v. Florida,** prohibited states from sentencing to death accomplices to a felony-murder unless it was shown the accomplice took part in the killing, intended that the killing occur or was involved in the employment of lethal force.

A few states still have death penalty statutes for crimes not involving homicide, such as kidnapping and child rape. However, recent Supreme Court decisions linking the death penalty to offenses involving the death of the victim make it extremely unlikely anyone will ever be sentenced under these laws.

Federal law provides for the death penalty only for air piracy (skyjacking) involving homicide, murder committed in conjunction with certain drug offenses and specified crimes under the Uniform Code of Military Justice (UCMJ). The UCMJ applies to members of the armed forces.

At the time the Supreme Court invalidated the nation's capital punishment laws in 1972, federal statutes authorized the death penalty for six offenses. The states that passed new death penalty measures following the **Furman** decision amended their capital sentencing procedures to conform to the guidelines established by the Court. These laws subsequently were found acceptable. The federal government, however, has yet to enact legislation to revise its pre-**Furman** statutes, most of which still remain on the books, and they are widely considered to be unconstitutional and unenforceable.

In 1974 Congress passed the Air Piracy Act, which made homicide resulting from an aircraft hijacking a capital offense. No one has been charged under the statute. Legal experts also believe that this law would not withstand constitutional review.

A number of bills providing for a comprehensive revision of federal death penalty procedures have been introduced in Congress since 1974. Legislative hearings have been held and several measures have been endorsed by the Senate Judiciary Committee, but to date no bill has gained the necessary congressional backing to become law.

Against a backdrop of public concern over illegal drugs, Congress added a death penalty provision to its ominibus antidrug bill approved in October 1988. The legislation, which conformed to key Supreme Court rulings on capital punishment, marked the end of a protracted effort to get a death penalty measure through Congress. Sponsors suggested the law could serve as a precedent for other capital punishment bills. The death penalty provision targeted major drug traffickers, or "kingpins," who committed murder in the course of a drug transaction. It also authorized the death penalty for anyone killing a law enforcement officer in the course of a drug-related crime.

After the **Furman** ruling, Congress did not amend the UCMJ, which permitted the death penalty for 13 offenses. In 1983 the Court of Military Appeals, the nation's highest military tribunal, overturned the death sentence of a soldier convicted in 1979 of rape and murder. The appeals court found that the UCMJ's capital sentencing procedures did not meet constitutional requirements.

As a consequence, President Ronald Reagan in 1984 signed an executive order which remedied the legal defects in the UCMJ. In November of the same year, the first person was sentenced to death under the new regulations. Appeals in this and several subsequent cases are still pending.

A series of spy cases involving current and former members of the military in the mid-1980s led to calls in Congress for the death penalty for armed forces personnel engaged in espionage. Legislation authorizing the sanction for military personnel convicted of espionage in peacetime was added to the 1986 Department of Defense Authorization Act and signed into law by President Reagan.

Death Sentences and Executions

Since the reimposition of capital punishment in 1976, murder has been the only crime for which the sanction has been imposed. More than 20,000 homicides potentially punishable by the death penalty take place in America each year. Statistical studies reveal, though, that only a small percentage of those who commit a capital offense are sentenced to death. In the 1970s the ratio of murders to death sentences was 117:1. This ratio became even more pronounced in the 1980s.

Over 2,250 persons are now on death row across the country. Four states—California, Florida, Georgia and Texas—account for roughly half of the death sentences handed down in the United States since 1973. The single largest death row population, now approximately 300, is in Florida. Within the four states, as elsewhere in the nation, juries in rural counties are more likely to impose the death penalty than those in urban areas.

Men are more likely to be sentenced to death than women. Almost 99% of those currently awaiting execution are male. In general, death row inmates come from the poorest segments of society. Well over half are unskilled. A similar number were unemployed at the time they committed their crimes. As a percentage of the nation's total population, racial minorities are disproportionately represented on death row. This is particularly true for blacks, who make up about 40% of the current death row population.

A similar disparity is found when the frequency with which the death sentence is imposed is measured against the race of the murder victim. A person who kills a white faces a greater percentage chance of receiving the death penalty than a person who kills a black. When the race of the defendant is included, the disparity becomes even larger. Blacks who murder whites are statistically much more likely to be sentenced to death than whites who murder blacks.

All of the death sentences handed down since 1973 have been in state or military courts. No one has been sentenced to death under federal law subsequent to the Supreme Court's landmark **Furman** ruling. The last federal execution took place in 1963. Although several soldiers are currently under death sentence, no member of the military has been executed since 1961.

Only a very small percentage of those sentenced to death following the **Furman** decision have actually been executed. As of December 31, 1989, 120 persons had been put to death in the United States since the resumption of executions in 1977. Forty percent of those executed have been black.

In 1988, state courts added 296 defendants to the death row population. A Justice Department report the same year found that of every 30 persons sentenced to death in the previous decade, 10 had left death row and one was executed. The primary reason for departing death row was having a sentence legally voided because of an unconstitutional statute or otherwise reversed.

In most states, governors have the power to grant clemency to those on death row. In practice, though, this authority is used sparingly. Since 1973, slightly more than 50 death sentences have been commuted by state executive action.

Since 1982, the number of prisoners on death row has more than doubled. The burgeoning death row population poses difficult questions. Unless executions increase dramatically, death row will continue to expand at an accelerating rate. It is questionable, though, whether American society would long remain comfortable with the volume of executions necessary to significantly reduce the size of the death row population.

Methods of Executions

For over a century, the uniform method for exeucting persons in America was hanging. The only exceptions were spies, traitors and deserters who could face a firing squad. In 1888 New York directed the construction of an "electric chair." It was believed the newly harnessed power of electricity would prove a more scientific and humane means of execution. The first electrocution took place in that state in 1890. Similar reasoning led to the introduction of the gas chamber in Utah in 1924. Death was brought on by asphyxiation from lethal fumes.

The continuing desire for a less painful, error-free means of execution led to the development of the lethal injection method in the 1970s. Initially approved in Oklahoma and Texas in 1977, this method involves injecting a combination of a sedative and a fatal chemical agent into the condemned prisoner's bloodstream. The sedative is meant to make the execution painless. A lethal injection was first used to carry out a death sentence in 1982.

The American Medical Association (AMA) went on record in 1980 as opposing the participation of any physician in an execution by lethal injection. A doctor's involvement was seen as a contradiction of the professional responsibility under the Hippocratic Oath to save life. As it now stands, no state that employs lethal injection requires a physician be present. The deadly solution is normally administered by medically trained technicians.

The most commonly approved methods of execution in the United States today are lethal injection, electrocution and the gas chamber. Idaho and Utah allow for execution by shooting while hanging has been retained by Delaware, Montana and Washington. Since the resumption of capital punishment in 1977, the vast majority of executions have been by electrocution. A relative handful have been by lethal injection and only two by gas and one by firing squad.

The last public execution in America occurred in 1936. Executions now are attended only by the public officials involved, the invitees of the condemned and a small number of designated witnesses, most often including representatives from the press. Photos and other visual or audio records of the proceedings are not allowed.

OPPOSITION TO THE DEATH PENALTY

Opposition to capital punishment in America goes back to the first years of the nation. Early abolitionists raised many arguments against the death penalty that remain part of the debate over the issue today. The 1830s and 1840s saw the formation of the first organizations dedicated to the abolition of capital punishment. Although inactive for long periods when the nation was preoccupied with other issues, abolitionist groups such as the American League to Abolish Capital Punishment were the mainstay of efforts to eliminate the death penalty until the early 1960s.

At this point, the battle over capital punishment switched from state legislatures to the courts. The NAACP Legal Defense and Education

Fund took the lead in seeking the elimination of the death penalty through the judicial system. Over the last 30 years, LDF attorneys have participated in numerous Supreme Court cases concerning capital punishment. The organization continues in the forefront of litigation against the sanction. It maintains up-to-date information on death sentences and executions nationwide and provides counsel to indigent death row inmates.

Since the mid-1960s, the American Civil Liberties Union has had a major role in the abolitionist movement. In addition to its involvement in legal matters, the ACLU's Capital Punishment Project issues policy statements and news releases, pamphlets, reports and other information and education resources. Representatives from the ACLU are active in public debates and at legislative sessions and clemency hearings.

In 1976, following the restoration of capital punishment by the Supreme Court, the Capital Punishment Project helped organize the National Coalition Against the Death Penalty (NCADP). Formed as a resource, coordination and support agency for a nationwide campaign against capital punishment, the coalition now numbers over 120 national, state and local organizations. Its membership includes legal, religious and civil rights groups.

A substantial number of the members are religious organizations. Most of the nation's major religious denominations have voiced their opposition to capital punishment. Many civil rights groups have long condemned what they view as the discriminatory manner in which the death penalty is disproportionately imposed on minorities in general and blacks in particular.

In recent years, Amnesty International has had an increasingly important role in the debate over capital punishment in the United States. The international human rights organization, which has been active in abolitionist activity since its founding in 1961, releases an annual report on executions worldwide. In 1980 the organization called for the creation of a presidential commission to study the death penalty in America. Amnesty International published its own critical report on the subject in 1987. In the same year, it launched a worldwide campaign to end capital punishment in the United States.

SUPPORT FOR THE DEATH PENALTY

In the 19th century, the leading proponents of capital punishment were members of the Protestant clergy. The most prominent was George B. Cheever, who wrote several influential tracts justifying the death penalty in Biblical terms. Outside of certain fundamentalist religious circles, similar arguments are not part of the public debate today.

Since the early 1900s, the law enforcement community has played a key role in efforts to retain the death penalty. Police officials, district attorneys and judges have emphasized strongly the deterrent value of the sanction. Organizations such as the International Association of Chiefs of Police and the National District Attorneys Association, as well as state and local law enforcement groups, have lobbied extensively in favor of capital punishment measures.

There is a network of conservative organizations, such as the Washington Legal Foundation, which advances the retentionist position in such forums as the courts and legislative hearings. The academic and intellectual communities also have their defenders of capital punishment, the best known of whom is the philosopher and teacher Ernest van den Haag. The death penalty in America at the present, however, is in no real jeopardy of widespread revocation, and there is no formal, coordinated national movement on behalf of its retention.

PUBLIC ATTITUDES

Americans overwhelmingly approve of capital punishment. This support, which opponents of the death penalty readily grant, is reflected in the fact that 37, or roughly three-quarters, of the states currently have death penalty statutes. These laws have all been enacted since 1973. In most instances, capital punishment bills have been passed by the state legislatures. In the five states which held public referenda on the death penalty, voters in four favored capital punishment by a substantial margin. The only exception was Kansas, where voters rejected a reimposition of the death penalty in 1987.

Public opinion polls consistently document the high levels of support for capital punishment. This support has increased significantly over the past 25 years. In the mid-1960s, the population was almost evenly divided between those who favored and those who opposed the death penalty for murder. By the mid-1970s, Americans advocated the death penalty for murder by a margin of two to one. In 1985 the percentage had risen to 75%, or three to one. Support for the death penalty is now at its highest point since formal studies on American attitudes about capital punishment were first conducted prior to World War II.

Attitudes about capital punishment are based on individuals' values, convictions and, to a lesser degree, experiences and perceptions. The data about the relationship between demographic factors and a given position on the death penalty are imprecise. In very general terms, men and those more affluent tend to support capital punishment more than women and the less affluent. The region of the country, size of the community, educational level and type of occupation, though, seem to have no real bearing. More conclusive is the fact that whites strongly favor the death penalty while blacks are more divided on the issue.

Social scientists are wary of generalizations about why Americans support capital punishment. The most commonly advanced theory is that the average citizen is deeply concerned about the steady rise in the nation's crime rate. Sensational crimes are extensively covered by the print and broadcast media. Many individuals have had a direct experience with violent crime. Support for the death penalty is seen as an expression of the desire to deal firmly with the violence and lawlessness in American society.

Opponents of capital punishment cite what is known as the "Marshall hypothesis." Supreme Court Justice Thurgood Marshall has argued that those who favor the death penalty are frequently uninformed about the actual nature and use of the sanction in America. It is Marshall's contention, shared by many abolitionists, that as the public becomes more educated about the issue, the general attitude will change from support to opposition. Abolitionists also note the relatively high levels of support for alternatives to capital punishment. Recent polls have indicated that a slight majority of those surveyed would endorse life imprisonment without parole as a substitute for the death penalty.

THE DEATH PENALTY IN POLITICS

Capital punishment first became a national political issue in the 1960 presidential campaign. The movement to spare California death row inmate Caryl Chessman had raised the level of public discussion on the issue. Of the major candidates canvassed on the subject during the primary season, only Senator Hubert H. Humphrey (D, Minn.) went on record as opposing the death penalty.

Lyndon B. Johnson's administration became the first, and only, presidential administration to recommend ending the death penalty for federal crimes. Attorney General Ramsey Clark, in testimony before Congress, called on the Untied States to join the growing worldwide trend toward abandonment of the sanction. All of the presidential administrations since, however, have supported capital punishment.

Most political figures and public officeholders endorse capital punishment. The relatively few public figures who oppose the death penalty are normally found on the more liberal end of the political spectrum while those who are more conservative are often its staunchest advocates. Political analysts believe that when the death penalty becomes an issue in a campaign, the candidate favoring capital punishment almost inevitably will benefit.

Most often, the death penalty has not been a dominant issue in major campaigns. The 1988 presidential race was an exception. Then Vice-President George Bush, the Republican nominee, campaigned extensively on his advocacy of the death penalty for the killers of law enforcement officers. He contrasted his position with the strong abolitionist stance of his Democratic opponent, Massachusetts Governor Michael S. Dukakis. Political experts agree that Bush's active support of capital punishment contributed to his eventual victory.

Since coming to office, President Bush has continued to press for extending the death penalty to those who murder police officers in the line of duty. His proposed legislation must be acted on by the Congress. The Senate has two of the leading figures in the debate over capital punishment. Both Edward M. Kennedy (D, Mass.), a strong opponent of the death penalty, and Strom Thurmond (R, S.C.), as adamantly in favor of the sanction, sit on the Senate Judiciary Committee, where capital punishment bills are first reviewed.

State legislatures have been the primary battlefield in the political fight over capital punishment. State legislators, who are responsible for fashioning the criminal codes that address most homicide offenses, are more immediately and directly affected by the views of their constituents on capital punishment. In recent years, the most intense political debate over the death penalty has been in New York. The governor of the state, Mario Cuomo, is the most prominent, and effective, opponent of capital punishment in public life today. In each of his first seven years in office, Governor Cuomo has successfully vetoed measures that would restore the death penalty in New York.

CAPITAL PUNISHMENT AND THE LAW

Capital punishment is inseparable from the law. The law defines the death penalty, authorizes its use and specifies the circumstances under which it can be applied. This section contains two parts. The first, Criminal Justice System, explains how capital punishment actually functions within the law in America. Legal Issues then addresses the difficult questions of law that have dominated the debate over capital punishment for the last quarter century.

CRIMINAL JUSTICE SYSTEM

Capital punishment cannot exist outside of a criminal justice system. A person may kill another to avenge a wrong, but this is an act of private revenge. The idea of punishment implies there is an established standard of behavior to which persons are able and expected to conform. It suggests, as well, that society has both a means to determine whether a person has violated this standard and penalties to be applied depending on the infraction. The basic judicial system required to impose a punishment is necessarily the product of an organized society.

In a modern political state, such as the United States, the rules governing unacceptable behavior are specified in the law. In America, the law has two components. The first is statutory law. This refers to the statutes, or laws, which are enacted by a legislature. These laws reflect the public policy wishes of the people as expressed by their elected representatives. What crimes are and the penalties for these crimes are defined by the statutory law.

This law, however, does not function in a vacuum. The courts modify and shape the law as they apply it in specific cases. The legal rules fashioned by courts in the process of deciding cases is known as common law. This second component of American law evolves over time as judges refer to prior cases and the precedents set by other justices to help them determine the appropriate ruling to make in a given instance.

America also has two distinct sets of laws. Each state has its own unique body of laws passed by its legislature. Historically, the preponderance of criminal activity has been a matter for state law. State criminal codes address offenses such as murder, rape and kidnapping—all of which have merited the death penalty in a majority of states at one time or another. Federal law, which is enacted by the U.S. Congress, traditionally has dealt with crimes that cross state lines or that directly affect the national government. In this context, for example, Congress has at different times made air piracy, espionage and the assassination of the president federal capital offenses.

The courts are where determinations of guilt or innocence are made and punishments meted out to the convicted. Corresponding to the distinction between state and federal law, there are state and federal court systems. These court systems are described in greater detail in Appendices B and C. The important point to note is that each judicial system has trial courts and appeals courts. The overwhelming majority of capital cases today are heard in state trial courts.

The fact that a person has been convicted of a capital crime and sentenced to death by a trial court does not mean that the law has taken its full course. Capital punishment statutes provide for an automatic review of every death sentence by a state appeals court. If this court upholds the death penalty, the defendant still has two other possible avenues of appeal. The first is postconviction proceedings in the state court system.

Normally, these appeals culminate in a ruling by the state's highest court. However, if federal questions of law are involved, the defendant has the right to petition the federal courts for review. Appeals based on issues of federal law have the potential to reach the Supreme Court. This entire appeals process may, and almost invariably does, extend over a number of years. The average time in the United States from the date of conviction to the date of actual execution is now approximately eight years.

There are three other important elements of the criminal justice system as it pertains to capital punishment. In criminal trials, the government's case is presented by a prosecuting attorney. Prosecutors have a substantial amount of discretion in the performance of their duties. A criminal proceeding has a number of key decision points. These include what charges to bring, whether to plea bargain and what sentence, if any, to offer a defendant in return for a guilty plea. The choices a prosecuting attorney makes in a potential capital trial have a direct impact on the likelihood of a person facing a possible death sentence.

The ability of the prosecutor to influence a capital proceeding is balanced, at least theoretically, by the defendant's right to legal representation. It is a basic tenet of American jurisprudence that each person accused of a crime is entitled to a defense counsel. The capabilities of the defense attorney can have a major bearing on the outcome of the trial.

Finally, there is the penal system. Prisons fulfill several obvious roles in the administration of capital punishment. The area in prisons where inmates are held pending their execution, commonly known as death row, has held a certain fascination in American culture and lore. Since the 1930s, executions in America have been carried out within the relative privacy of prison walls. Less readily apparent is the fact that the development of modern penal institutions has provided society a range of possible punishments for serious crimes. It would not be possible, for instance, to advocate mandatory life sentences in lieu of the death penalty if appropriate confinement facilities were not available.

LEGAL ISSUES

The debate over capital punishment for the last 25 years has been waged primarily in the judicial system. In a series of court cases extending over this period, the Supreme Court has effectively set the parameters of capital punishment in America today. Summaries of the most significant Supreme Court decisions are provided in Chapter 3. Presented here are the basic issues that have driven the legal struggle over the role of capital punishment in American society.

The most basic legal controversy centers on whether capital punishment is inherently constitutional. This issue raises an even more fundamental legal question. How is the constitutionality of any given law determined? Since the early 19th century, the Supreme Court has exercised a power of judicial review or what in essence is the authority to strike down statutes it deems unconstitutional. The Court has the final say as to whether a legal measure conforms to the Constitution. Two elements normally are necessary for the Supreme Court to declare a law unconstitutional. The first is a clear and convincing argument that the law violates a specific constitutional provision. Historically, the Court has been reluctant to rule against the expressed will of the legislative branch of government without a compelling reason to do so. Second, the constitutional provision must be applicable to the law in question.

Most of the constitutional challenges to the death penalty have been based on one or more of the first ten amendments. When these amendments, the Bill of Rights, were added to the U.S. Constitution in 1791, it was with the understanding that they applied only to federal law. State laws were beyond their reach.

As legal challenges to capital punishment mounted in the 1960s, one of the first issues that had to be resolved was whether the Bill of Rights could appropriately be applied to state death penalty statutes. The answer was found in the Fourteenth Amendment. This amendment, which was passed in 1868 in the aftermath of the Civil War, stipulates that states shall not "deprive any person of life, liberty, or property, without due process of law." In the 100 years since its enactment, the Supreme Court has gradually interpreted this due process clause as extending all the due process guarantees in the Constitution, the first ten amendments included, to state laws. In other words, the Supreme Court was empowered to review state laws for adherence to the fundamental individual rights articulated in the Bill of Rights.

In 1972, in **Furman v. Georgia,** the Supreme Court did precisely this when it held that the nation's capital punishment laws, both federal and state, were in violation of the Eighth Amendment. The Court found that the arbitrary and capricious way in which the death penalty was administered constituted cruel and unusual punishment. The Court, however, did not rule that capital punishment itself was unconstitutional. Only the random and freakish employment of the death penalty, and not the sanction itself, was ruled constitutionally indefensible. Many states revised their death penalty statutes to respond to the objections voiced in the **Furman** decision. Four years later, in **Gregg v. Georgia,** the Court reinstated capital punishment, holding that the new death penalty statutes contained safeguards which would insure the sanction's use in a rational and fair manner.

Capital Punishment

Since 1976, the Supreme Court has declined to reconsider the basic legality of capital punishment itself. Instead, the Court has concentrated on narrower constitutional questions: what crimes merit the death penalty and which members of society, if any, are ineligible to receive a death sentence.

The Supreme Court has emphasized that a punishment must be proportionate to the crime committed. In applying this standard to the death penalty, the Court has overturned capital punishment statutes that allowed the death sentence to be imposed for rape and kidnapping. The Court indicated that the death penalty was a disproportionate and excessive response to offenses which did not involve the death of the victim. In apparently linking the death penalty to crimes involving homicide, the Court has raised doubts as to the constitutionality of capital punishment for offenses such as espionage and treason. Whether the death penalty is disproportionate for all nonhomicidal crimes has yet to be litigated.

Another tenet of American jurisprudence that has guided the Supreme Court's thinking on the death penalty is the belief that punishment should be related to the culpability of the defendant. Within a legal context, culpability implies the ability to exercise and take responsibility for one's conduct. There is widespread consensus in American society that juveniles are not sufficiently mature or informed to be held fully accountable for their actions. The debate has been waged over the age at which a juvenile may be considered an adult for the purposes of a capital trial. In a series of controversial decisions on this issue, the Court effectively has set 16 as the minimum age at which a person can be held responsible and executed for capital offenses.

The Court likewise has ruled that it is unconstitutional to execute persons who are insane. The development of guidelines governing the execution of the mentally retarded has proved to be more difficult. The degree of mental retardation and its impact on a person's ability to act responsibly are difficult to measure. The Court essentially has held that if a mentally impaired person is unable to distinguish right from wrong and behave accordingly, then that individual is not subject to the death penalty.

The constitutionality of different methods of execution also has been litigated. In 1890 the Supreme Court decided that the use of the newly invented electric chair was not cruel and unusual punishment. Interestingly, the federal government in 1925 substituted electrocution for hanging because it was viewed as more humane. The 1920s also saw several unsuccessful challenges to the introduction of the gas chamber. Proponents of lethal gas defended it as a swift and painless means of execution.

More recently, inmates facing death by lethal injection sought unsuccessfully to block the procedure on the novel grounds that the Federal Drug Administration had not approved the fatal drugs to be used.

The Supreme Court has consistently taken the position that a given method of execution is not unconstitutionally cruel if it does not involve torture, barbarism or the infliction of unnecessary pain and suffering. Opponents of capital punishment maintain that any form of capital punishment, no matter how humane in intent, is by its very nature a kind of torture. Moreover, executions do not always go as planned. Many abolitionist publications contain graphic accounts of botched executions which caused evident pain and suffering to the condemned.

Legal experts agree that the last sweeping challenge to the death penalty was eliminated in 1987. In **McCleskey v. Kemp,** the Supreme Court turned aside arguments that capital punishment in the United States was administered in a racially discriminatory manner. These arguments were based on statistical evidence which showed that blacks were significantly more likely than whites to receive the death penalty for similar crimes. The Court accepted the general accuracy of the information but found that broad statistical studies were insufficient to prove racial discrimination in a given specific case. **McCleskey** raised a line of questioning that goes to the very core of the American criminal justice system. In its decision, the Supreme Court indicated that in order to establish that racism had played a part in a person receiving a death sentence, it was necessary to prove actual discrimination in the case at hand. As several of the dissenting justices pointed out, that was easier said than done. In their view, the wide discretion provided prosecutors, judges and juries frequently served to mask the institutional racism that still infects the criminal justice process. How was it possible to prove that a certain prosecutor was more likely to offer a plea bargain agreement to a white defendant than to a black? The majority acknowledged this problem but suggested that short of changing the entire American system of justice, which was both unreasonable and undesirable, the best answer was to surround the administration of capital punishment with extensive procedural safeguards.

The net effect of the Supreme Court's major rulings on capital punishment has been twofold. It is clear that the death penalty, at least from a legal perspective, is here to stay. After affirming that capital punishment is itself constitutional, the Court has gone on to define more precisely the circumstances and conditions under which it may be imposed. The Court as it is currently constituted has shown no inclination to reverse this course. In dealing with the various broad constitutional challenges to the administration of the death penalty, the Court has gradually removed the remaining legal obstacles to a full resumption of executions in the United States. It is generally agreed that there are few if any remaining legal arguments against the death penalty that will affect more than a relative handful of death row inmates.

In recent years, a great deal of the legal debate over capital punishment has centered on procedural questions. There are several reasons for this. First, and most importantly, has been a growing recognition throughout the entire criminal justice system that the death penalty is substantively different from other criminal sanctions. This has meant an enhanced focus on the procedural safeguards necessary to insure that capital punishment is administered in a fair and appropriate way. Secondly, as broad or far-reaching constitutional challenges to the death penalty have been progressively whittled down since 1976, defense lawyers have increasingly turned to challenging the death sentences of their clients on technical or procedural grounds.

The Supreme Court has long taken the position that death is different from other punishments. The irrevocable nature of the death penalty has caused the Court to pay particular attention to procedural safeguards in capital cases. As early as 1932, the Court ruled that an indigent defendant had the right to a lawyer in a capital trial. Since the reinstatement of the death penalty in 1976, the Court has insisted on clear and objective standards to guide the administration of capital punishment.

In response to Supreme Court rulings, death penalty statutes across the nation share several traits. They all require a bifurcated, or split, trial proceeding. The bifurcated trial separates the determination of guilt or innocence from the decision as to what penalty will be imposed. This is done to insure a convicted defendant has an opportunity to present mitigating evidence prior to sentencing. Death penalty statutes also all require an automatic review of every death sentence by an appeals court.

The Court has effectively barred mandatory capital punishment laws, holding that automatic death sentences for certain crimes do not allow for individualized consideration of all the circumstances involved in a specific case. This same reasoning has led the Court to maintain that trial courts must permit defendants to introduce a wide range of evidence concerning mitigating factors on their behalf.

The most contentious legal issue today concerns the use or misuse of the appeals process. The sheer volume of death penalty appeals threatens to overwhelm the criminal justice system. This volume can partly be attributed to the steady growth in the size of the death row population. It is also due to a deliberate strategy on the part of many opponents of capital punishment. It is their hope that by paralyzing the appeals courts with an excess of legal actions, the nation will eventually conclude capi-

tal punishment is unworkable. This may well occur. Efforts by the Supreme Court to streamline the handling of death sentence appeals have
proved unsuccessful to date. A number of leading legal figures, most
notably retired Supreme Court Justice Lewis F. Powell Jr., have suggested that if a solution cannot be found, then the death penalty should
be abandoned.

THE CAPITAL PUNISHMENT DEBATE

The debate over capital punishment has ranged across philosophy, religion, criminology and the law. Abolitionists base their opposition to capital punishment on several core themes: its tendency to brutalize society;
the inevitability of caprice and bias in its application; its disproportionate
imposition on minorities and the less advantaged; and the inescapable
risk of executing the innocent. Proponents maintain that death is the
appropriate punishment for certain crimes. The death penalty is said to
protect society by incapacitating dangerous criminals and deterring others from similar offenses.

The debate is often complex. This section summarizes the main arguments for and against capital punishment.

DETERRENCE

Deterrence is the idea that punishments imposed by society for criminal
activity discourage its members from engaging in such behavior. Advocates of capital punishment contend that fear of death deters people from
committing serious crimes. The average person will think twice before
running the risk of possible execution. In addition, the death penalty
alone is viewed as a severe enough sanction to keep professional criminals
from taking part in violent acts.

Deterrence is the most frequently made and widely accepted argument
in favor of the death penalty. It has generated intense debate and controversy. Opponents of capital punishment have attacked the deterrent value
of the death penalty on a number of grounds.

They note first that there is no conclusive evidence the death penalty
has any impact on the rate of violent crime. At the least, capital punishment is no more effective a deterrent than prolonged incarceration. Abolitionists stress that with deterrence, the certainty of punishment is much
more important than the severity. Any fear of death is diminished, they
contend, by the long delays in capital trials, the fact death sentences are
carried out in private and the relatively low number of executions.

Abolitionists cite statistics showing that in a majority of murders the killer knew the victim. A rational consideration of future penalties has little or no bearing on situations where murders occur as a result of family quarrels or other emotional disturbances. Proponents respond that the death penalty is not applicable to these kinds of homicide but to premeditated first-degree murder. Crimes such as killing a police officer are those which are said to be deterred by capital punishment.

Numerous studies have been conducted to gauge the actual effectiveness of the death penalty as a deterrent. Most often, murder rates are examined in states that have abolished capital punishment. The rate of murders committed in the years prior to abolition is compared to the rate in subsequent years. The problem with this methodology is that many other variables can be involved. A general rise in the crime rate, a change in a state's demographics or new types of violent crime, such as gang wars, may appear to complicate the picture. Experts agree that the studies to date have not been able to ascertain the deterrent value of capital punishment.

Finally, abolitionists argue that even if the deterrent effect of the death penalty were established, this would not in itself justify retaining capital punishment. They point out that if, as retentionists say, the specter of electrocution or lethal injection deters murder, then logically it should follow that burning at the stake or drawing and quartering would be even more effective in discouraging potential killers. But society has long renounced these methods of executions as barbaric. From the abolitionist perspective, if society can forego the deterrent value of these means of executions, it can also do without more modern, but still uncivilized, ways of putting people to death.

PROTECTION

Both advocates and opponents of capital punishment agree that society has a right to protect itself from criminal activity. The debate is over the appropriateness of the death penalty as one of the means of protection.

Proponents claim that in imposing the death sentence for certain offenses, the law is sending a clear message about types of behavior that will not be tolerated. Capital punishment is a statement by society that it is willing and able to protect itself from brutal, violent crimes. The educational value of the death penalty also is noted. By defining murder as a capital offense, for example, the law serves to develop a general abhorrence for the crime.

Abolitionists maintain that the selective and often arbitrary way in which the death penalty is administered undercuts any message its use may be meant to deliver. They contend that death sentence statistics reveal that the criminal justice system disproportionately singles out the less advantaged members of society for execution. The wealthier, more educated and more socially connected rarely, n receive the death penalty. In their view, the message conveyed is that America has two standards of justice.

The death penalty also is advanced as a means of protecting society from violent, habitual offenders. Opponents counter that the rate of recidivism, or return to criminality, among convicted murderers released from prison is very low. Moreover, dangerous individuals are just as incapacitated by life imprisonment without parole as by death.

RETRIBUTION

Retribution refers to the penalty a society exacts for wrongful behavior. It is the idea that persons should pay for their crimes.

The criminal law of a society reflects its value system or moral code. Proponents of capital punishment believe that the law should place less value on the life of a convicted murderer than on the life of an innocent victim. The law recognizes the necessity of this kind of distinction, justifying killings committed in self-defense or during the arrest of a dangerous felon. They conclude the state has the right and duty to execute certain grievous offenders in order to uphold and preserve greater societal values.

Proponents insist there is no valid substitute for the death penalty. More serious offenses should be met by more severe penalties. If varying lengths of imprisonment are used to punish all crimes, then society risks losing sight of the distinction between murder and misappropriation of funds. Proponents emphasize that retribution is not revenge. The individual desire for revenge has been replaced in modern society by a concept of lawful punishment. It is important that the penalty for a crime fulfill society's sense that justice has been served. For certain horrid infractions, only the execution of the offender will satisfy the public that justice has been attained.

Opponents of the death penalty agree that retribution is an essential part of justice. However, the penalties imposed by a society should not be based on vindictive or bloodthirsty motives. In a civilized community, the brutal nature of violent crime should not determine the limits of appropriate punishments. They contend very long periods of confinement will meet society's need for justice.

In an argument that parallels their attack on the deterrent value of capital punishment, abolitionists stress that the death penalty is not imposed in an uniform manner. Society is not protecting higher values or distinguishing between the relative seriousness of different offenses if it executes one person for murder but spares another for the same crime.

PROPORTIONALITY

Retribution involves the issue of proportionality. In simple terms, the sentence should fit the crime. As for capital punishment, is death ever warranted as a penalty? If so, are there only certain crimes which merit its imposition?

Opponents of capital punishment obviously would answer the first question no and describe the second question as irrelevant. From the abolitionist perspective, an eye for an eye or a life for a life is neither a sound nor workable principle of criminal justice. Punishments should correspond to the moral culpability of the offender, not the harm suffered by the victim.

Moral culpability, though, as advocates of capital punishment point out, is related under the law to the impact a crime has on a victim. A person who commits murder is guilty of a more serious offense than an individual who merely injures another. Proponents maintain that death is the only form of retribution that matches the grievousness of certain crimes.

Proponents are in agreement that murder deserves the death sentence. There is less consensus as to whether the death penalty should be inflicted for nonhomicidal offenses. In recent years, American law has increasingly connected capital punishment to crimes involving the death of the victim.

BARBARITY

Abolitionists strongly believe that capital punishment in any form is barbaric. The infliction of death, they maintain, has no place in an enlightened society. An execution, no matter how swift and painless, is still psychological, if not physical, torture. As opponents also observe, no method of execution is foolproof. In recent years, there have been instances of botched electrocutions resulting in even more painful ordeals for the condemned. In other cases, prisoners apparently suffered during the injection of lethal drugs.

It is alleged that capital punishment brutalizes a society. Executions are seen as a form of institutionalized violence. Use of the death penalty accustoms a society to violence and hardens its members to the suffering of others.

Proponents counter that it is violent, wanton crime that tears apart the social fabric. Abolitionists are criticized for seeming at times to be concerned with the punishment of criminals but indifferent to the impact their actions have on society. The fact a given punishment may cause a prisoner anguish is not sufficient reason to abandon its use. Capital punishment supporters have pointed out that the substitute often recommended for the death penalty, life imprisonment without parole, is also a form of psychological torture.

PUBLIC OPINION

Public opinion surveys consistently show high levels of support for capital punishment. Should this matter in the decision whether to retain or abolish the death penalty?

Many opponents of capital punishment believe it should not. They argue that public policy should lead public opinion on issues of justice and the law. Capital punishment should be eliminated on the merits of the arguments against it. It is suggested that opinion polls actually reveal a fear of rising crime rates more than they reflect inherent support for the death penalty. If the public were more informed about capital punishment, then the sanction's popularity would diminish significantly.

Proponents characterize these views as elitist and self-righteous. The elected representatives of the people should determine the appropriateness of a given punishment and not self-appointed arbiters of right and wrong. Public opinion polls document the widespread majority support behind the enactment of death penalty laws in state legislatures across the nation. Death penalty advocates also accuse abolitionists of hypocrisy. They note that in the 1960s, when surveys indicated an almost evenly divided public on the issue of capital punishment, abolitionists were quick to cite the results.

A number of abolitionists, while sharing the perception the public is uninformed about capital punishment, stop short of discounting the importance of public opinion to the functioning of the criminal justice system. They see their role as educating and persuading a majority of Americans that the death penalty is defective and wrong. As this occurs, they expect the nation to abandon capital punishment.

IRREVERSIBILITY

The risk of executing an innocent person is generally considered the strongest practical argument against capital punishment. Abolitionists condemn the death penalty for its irreversibility. The death sentence, once carried out, is irrevocable. If society executes an innocent prisoner, there is no way to undo the error. In contrast, imprisonment always leaves the possibility of overturning a wrongful conviction.

The possibility that innocent persons may be sentenced to death exists. In 1987 professors Hugo Adam Bedau and Michael L. Radelet, both strong opponents of capital punishment, published in the *Stanford Law Review* a detailed study of death sentences in 20th century America. They concluded that, between 1900 and 1985, 349 persons were incorrectly convicted of capital offenses and 23 innocent prisoners were actually executed. Abolitionists cite these figures in general, and the instances of persons wrongly sentenced to death since 1973 in particular, as proof that no amount of procedural safeguards can insure innocent persons will not be executed.

Proponents make two points in rebuttal. First, the extensive safeguards now surrounding a capital trial in fact do work. The recent instances in which it was found that innocent persons had been sentenced to death are taken as evidence of the effectiveness of the criminal justice system in catching such errors. However, even the theoretical possibility of an innocent prisoner being put to death is not grounds for abandoning capital punishment. Advocates of the death penalty maintain that society cannot place its concern for the wrongly condemned person above its legitimate and compelling interest in administering the death sentence for heinous crimes.

FAIRNESS

One of the most complex aspects of the debate over capital punishment is the question of fairness. The issues involved go to the very structure and nature of the American criminal justice system.

Abolitionists charge that the death penalty is not applied in an even remotely impartial manner in the United States. Because the way it is administered is so fundamentally unfair, the practice of capital punishment should be discontinued. Moreover, abolitionists assert that the discretion built into the criminal justice system makes it impossible to ever achieve a truly consistent and unbiased use of the sanction.

Opponents of capital punishment point first to the fact that the death penalty is disproportionately imposed on the less advantaged members of society. The poor, the uneducated and the socially unacceptable are more likely to face execution than those of more privileged backgrounds.

Abolitionists contend that justice is not blind where the death sentence is concerned. Juries are less sympathetic to persons from society's lower strata. Those of lesser means do not have access to the same quality of defense counsel. Key procedural issues may be overlooked by an inexperienced or overworked public defender.

The problem of the uneven distribution of justice becomes even more pronounced in the case of racial minorities. Blacks in particular make up a much larger share of the death row population than their percentage of the population as a whole. Abolitionists cite these statistics as evidence that the racism which still infects American society is manifested in harsher penalties for blacks than for whites. Most importantly, because the criminal justice system allows district attorneys, judges and juries great latitude in determining the fate of a given prisoner, there is no way to guarantee that bias or prejudice does not play a part in the decision made.

Many advocates of the death penalty acknowledge the issues of fairness raised by use of the sanction. They argue that the procedural safeguards built into the process for capital cases, such as bifurcated trials and appellate review, have answered these concerns.

Furthermore, proponents reject the idea that allowing the criminal justice system the discretion necessary to reach an individualized determination in each case results in unfair verdicts. This assertion is seen as an attack on a fundamental principle of American jurisprudence. If it were true, then all punishments arrived at under current procedures, and not just death sentences, potentially would have to be abandoned as fatally flawed. Rejecting the notion that capital sentences are inherently unfair, proponents stress the need for full enforcement of the safeguards already in place.

EXPENSE

The issue of expense is the most recent addition to the debate over capital punishment. It is commonly assumed that it costs less to execute a person than it does to imprison that individual for life. The reverse, however, is true.

The costs of capital cases have soared in recent years. There are several reasons for this: Capital trials take longer to litigate; a second penalty phase is required if a guilty verdict is returned; a protracted appeals process normally follows all death sentences; and death row facilities where defendants often await execution for many years require more money to staff and maintain. The result is that capital cases are significantly more expensive than trials for serious felonies where the death penalty is not applicable. Incarceration of a prisoner for 40 years is substantially less costly than going through the full legal process necessary to put a person to death.

Many localities are having difficulty meeting the costs involved in capital cases. Recognizing the growing concern over the availability of funding for the criminal justice system, the abolitionist movement has argued that capital punishment does not make economic sense. Instead of dedicating scarce resources to executing a relative handful of prisoners, it would be more worthwhile to sentence capital offenders to long prison terms and use the money saved to fully fund efforts such as victim-assistance programs.

Many advocates of the death penalty label these arguments insincere. In their view, the high costs of capital punishment are due to the inor-

33

dinate number of appeals filed by abolitionist legal groups as part of their campaign to block executions. Other proponents accept that the procedural safeguards involved in capital trials are necessarily more expensive but insist that capital punishment's importance to the administration of justice is such that it should be underwritten regardless of the cost.

CAPITAL PUNISHMENT AND RELIGION

Capital punishment and religion have been linked since the first use of death as a sanction. The earliest laws and criminal codes were religious in nature. Throughout much of Western history, many religious offenses were punishable by death. As recently as the 18th century, witchcraft was a capital crime in the American colonies. The differentiation between civil and religious crimes is a comparatively modern development. As Western societies evolved, gradually the idea took hold that religious offenses were not properly the province of a civil government. In the United States, the First Amendment to the Constitution established a clear separation of church and state.

Although religion has no formal role in the governance of the nation, American institutions are deeply rooted in the Judeo-Christian tradition. American law has been shaped and formed by religious influences. The relationship of organized religion to public policy in the American experience has been an advisory one. Religious leaders have spoken from a position of moral authority in the public debate over questions of right and wrong, crime and punishment and justice and mercy.

In the 19th century, the major religious denominations uniformly supported the notion of capital punishment. Members of the clergy, particularly from the Congregationalist and Presbyterian denominations, publicly opposed efforts to abolish the death penalty. They based their arguments mainly on the Bible. Genesis 9:6, "Whosoever sheddeth a man's blood, so shall his blood be shed," was frequently cited as evidence of God's instruction to punish murder by death.

By the middle of the 20th century, this kind of literal Biblical interpretation no longer had much force in an increasingly secular American society. Reflecting the growing concern over social issues, many churches became active both in the civil rights movement and in efforts to help the disadvantaged and needy. While the New Testament does not explicitly condemn capital punishment, some contemporary theologians have insisted on the incompatability of human execution with Jesus Christ's message of forgiveness and redemption. The death penalty is called a fundamental departure from this message and from Christianity's commitment to the sanctity and dignity of human life.

Certain religious groups, such as the Quakers, have long opposed capital punishment within the context of an overall pacifism. Within the last 30 years, representative organizations of almost all of the nation's major denominations have issued statements calling for an end to the death penalty. Many religious groups are active in the abolitionist movement.

A number of more conservative religious organizations continue to endorse capital punishment. These include Mormons, Jehovah's Witnesses and certain fundamentalist Christian and orthodox Jewish groups.

WORLDWIDE PERSPECTIVE

The trend worldwide is toward a gradual decrease in the use of the death penalty. The United Nations has become increasingly active on the issue of capital punishment. Although the organization has not taken a formal abolitionist position, many studies, reports and resolutions have called on member nations to progressively restrict the number of offenses for which the death penalty may be imposed. In 1971 the General Assembly adopted a resolution that articulated an ultimate goal of eliminating capital punishment in all countries.

This goal is far from realized. As of May 1986, 28 countries had abolished capital punishment. Another 18 countries had limited its use to exceptional circumstances, such as treason in wartime. Roughly two-thirds of the world's nations, or 129 countries, retained the death penalty for ordinary crimes. The most common capital offense is murder. Although a number of these countries have not carried out executions in recent years, it is generally agreed there is no tangible international movement toward widespread abolition.

The first two nations to end capital punishment were Venezuela (1853) and Portugal (1867). As opponents of the death penalty often point out, all of the major Western democracies, except for the United States, have subsequently abandoned the sanction. In Europe, only Greece and Turkey impose the death sentence for ordinary crimes. The British Parliament voted a five-year moratorium on executions in 1965 and made the ban permanent in 1969. British Commonwealth members Australia, Canada and New Zealand likewise no longer permit capital punishment. France halted use of the guillotine in 1977 and abolished the death penalty four years later.

Latin America has a long abolitionist tradition. Ecuador, Costa Rica and Uruguay, along with Venezuela, had foregone the death penalty by the end of the 19th century. Most of the other Latin American nations have joined their ranks, many in the last 30 years. Chile, Cuba, Guatemala and Paraguay continue to authorize capital punishment.

Elsewhere, the death penalty is widely in effect. The nations of Eastern Europe, while under communist governments, provided for capital punishment for a variety of offenses. Until recently, the Soviet Union defined certain economic crimes, such as profiteering, as capital offenses. The dramatic changes taking place in much of the communist world apparently are having an effect on the administration of justice there, including greater constraints on the death penalty.

One communist nation in which this is not the case is China. The execution of persons involved in the 1989 Tiananmen Square uprising illustrated that government's continuing reliance on the death penalty to suppress political dissent as well as to punish ordinary criminal activity. Although not sanctioned elsewhere for political crimes, capital punishment remains part of the criminal law throughout Asia. Japan inflicts the death penalty for a range of homicide offenses.

All but a handful of the African nations have death penalty statutes. South Africa has one of the highest judicial execution rates in the world. The same is true of the Middle East, where only Israel has terminated capital punishment. Islamic fundamentalism has led to more severe death penalty laws in a number of countries. The powerful influence of Islamic justice was revealed in February 1989 when the Iranian leader, Ayatollah Khomeini, called for the death of the British author Salman Rushdie for the alleged crime of blasphemy in one of his novels, causing Rushdie to go into hiding even though he did not live in Iran.

FUTURE TRENDS

The debate over the death penalty in America has spanned the nation's history. It is not likely to end soon. The issue of capital punishment does not lend itself to compromise. Recent experience indicates that neither side in the controversy would accept a resolution of the issue which did not basically conform to their position. When the Supreme Court struck down the nation's death penalty laws in 1972, proponents of the sanction campaigned extensively for new capital punishment statutes. Four years later, the Court's decision upholding the new laws led to the formation of a national coalition of abolitionist groups.

There is scant likelihood the Supreme Court will reverse its 1976 ruling and declare capital punishment unconstitutional. Three Reagan administration appointments to the highest bench have given the Court a more conservative cast. Both of the sitting justices who categorically oppose the death penalty are in their eighties. It is conceivable that President George Bush will have an opportunity to add to the conservative majority.

In the near future, capital punishment will probably vary little from its current status. The number of death sentences and executions will neither rise nor decline significantly. Similarly, the breakdown of states with and without the death penalty is basically set. At the state level, capital offenses will continue to be confined to crimes involving murder. Congress took the first step toward a resumption of federal executions when it authorized the death penalty for drug-related homicides in 1988. However, the long time period involved in capital trials and appeals means it will be years before a federal execution could actually occur.

Death row will continue to expand. Even if executions were to increase to the highest annual rate recorded since the government started keeping such statistics, 199 in 1935, this would only slow the steady expansion of the death row population. It is almost certain such a level of executions would be widely condemned.

The future of capital punishment ultimately may come down to the question of expense. A single capital trial now costs in the millions of dollars. The enormous volume of appeals in capital trials is straining both federal and state court systems. Unless workable solutions are found to the practical difficulties involved in the administration of the death penalty, American society eventually may decide to significantly restrict or even abandon capital punishment.

CHAPTER 2

CHRONOLOGY

This chapter is a chronological account of the significant events in the evolution of capital punishment in America since the early 1920s. It incorporates entries drawn from a broad spectrum of legal, political, social and cultural developments. Events outside the United States which had an impact on capital punishment within it or which were significant worldwide are included.

The chronology is divided into yearly increments. Within each section, individual entries are preceded by the specific date on which they occurred. The format for entries features two cross-referencing techniques: Court cases in bold print are addressed in greater detail in Chapter 3, and dates in parentheses at the end of an entry indicate related items within the chronology.

As described in Chapter 1, the modern debate over capital punishment dates back to the mid-18th century. The roots of the current controversy over the death penalty in America can be traced to the 1920s. The chronology begins with the marked increase in abolitionist activity during this period brought on by a series of highly publicized and controversial murder trials. Although this effort made little headway at the time, many of the organizations, ideas and tactics which emerged played a major role in the struggle over capital punishment in later decades. The relative scarcity of chronology entries from the late-1930s to the mid-1950s reflects the nation's preoccupation during this time with World War II and its aftermath.

1924

February 8: A gas chamber is used for the first time in the execution of Gee Jon, a convicted tong-murderer, in Nevada. Although electrocution remains the mode of execution in most jurisdictions, five other states in the next two years construct similar facilities.

September 10: In a case which gained nationwide attention, Richard A. Loeb and Nathan F. Leopold Jr. are sentenced to life imprisonment in Chicago for the murder of a neighborhood child. Their attorney, Clarence Darrow, had argued the execution of the two young men would serve no useful purpose. The verdict encouraged opponents of capital punishment across the country.

September 19: The *New York Times*, in a significant departure from its historical support for capital punishment, publishes an editorial which suggests the death penalty has become unworkable.

1925

January 31: President Calvin Coolidge signs a measure substituting electrocution for hanging in federal death sentences.

February 12: A bill that would reinstate capital punishment is defeated in South Dakota.

July 20: The American League to Abolish Capital Punishment is formed in New York City by Clarence Darrow, Lewis E. Lawes and other leading opponents of the death penalty. In its first year, the league enrolls over 1,000 members nationwide and establishes affiliates in several states.

August 23: Nicola Sacco and Bartolomeo Vanzetti are executed in Massachusetts for two 1920 murders. The case, which commanded worldwide interest, had precipitated an unprecedented six-year legal battle over their guilt or innocence. The executions contribute to an upsurge in abolitionist activity and lead to the formation of the Massachusetts Council for the Abolition of the Death Penalty.

1928

January 12: Ruth Snyder and Henry Judd Gray are electrocuted at Sing Sing Prison in New York for the murder of her husband. A photo taken of Snyder during the execution by a newsman with a concealed camera causes many to question capital punishment.

1929

February 14: In what would become known as the St. Valentines Day Massacre, seven gangsters are shot by members of a rival organization. The event contributes to growing public unease over violent crime.

April 30: The death penalty is abolished in Puerto Rico.

1931

April 6: In a statewide referendum in Michigan, a bill that would reinstate the death penalty is defeated.

December 31: The federal government begins to publish annual statistics on executions in the United States. It is reported 155 persons were executed in 1930.

1932

March 1: The baby son of Charles A. Lindbergh is kidnapped from his home in Hopewell, New Jersey. The body of the infant is found in nearby woods two months later. The incident leads Congress to pass a federal kidnapping statute, popularly known as the Lindbergh Act, that makes the crime a capital offense. Similar "Lindbergh laws" are enacted in over 20 states by the end of the decade. (April 3, 1936)

March 13: Kansas reinstates the death penalty following a series of violent crimes by Clyde Barrow and Bonnie Parker, Charles "Pretty Boy" Floyd and others.

November 7: In a decision related to the Scottsboro Boys case, the U.S. Supreme Court rules in *Powell v. Alabama* that failure to provide counsel to a defendant in a capital case violates constitutional due process protections.

1936

April 3: After a sensational trial, Bruno Richard Hauptmann is executed in New Jersey for the kidnapping murder of the Lindbergh baby. (March 1, 1932)

August 14: In the last public execution in the United States, a crowd of 20,000 watches as Rainey Bethea is hanged in Owensboro, Kentucky.

1937

January 4: The American League to Abolish Capital Punishment initiates a drive to seek state laws preventing the execution of minors.

May 21: In Galena, Missouri, approximately 500 persons pay an admission fee to the gallows to view the execution of Roscoe Jackson. It is the last execution in America that general spectators are allowed to attend.

1939

October 11: The National Association for the Advancement of Colored People (NAACP) forms a Legal Defense and Education Fund to provide legal assistance to the poor and to challenge racial segregation in the courts.

1944

November 13:   Pope Pius justifies the use of capital punishment.

1945

January 31:   Private Eddie D. Slovik is executed by firing squad in the European theater of operations. He is the only U.S. soldier put to death for desertion during World War II.

1946

January 19:   President Harry S. Truman and the War Department limit imposition of the death penalty by military courts-martial.

October 1:   An international military tribunal at Nuremberg, Germany sentences 12 former Nazi leaders to death. In subsequent "Nuremberg trials," an additional 25 German war criminals receive the death penalty.

1947

January 13:   The U.S. Supreme Court, in *Louisiana ex rel Francis v. Resweber*, rules that a second attempt to execute an individual after a malfunctioning electric chair had halted the first try does not constitute cruel and unusual punishment under the Eighth Amendment.

1948

February 5:   The Supreme Soviet approves a decree abolishing capital punishment in the Soviet Union. (January 12, 1950)

May 22:   Caryl Chessman is sentenced to death in California for a kidnapping crime he insists he did not commit. Chessman in time becomes a famous death row author and symbol of resistance to capital punishment. (April 17, 1954; July 10, 1955; October 6, 1957; May 2, 1960)

July 14:   The U.S. Army ends mandatory death sentences for murder and rape.

October 19:   The United Nations Human Rights Commission rejects an amendment proposed by the Soviet Union to the International Bill of Rights which would ban the death penalty in peacetime.

November 12:   An international tribunal in Tokyo sentences seven Japanese leaders, including wartime Prime Minister Hideki Tojo, to death.

1950

January 12: *Tass* reports the revival of the death penalty in the Soviet Union for treason, espionage and sabotage. (February 5, 1948)

May 24: Austria abolishes the death penalty.

1951

May 26: The British Royal Commission on Capital Punishment submits a report critical of the practice.

1952

November 31: The November issue of the *Annals of the American Academy of Political and Social Science* is dedicated to research on the issue of capital punishment. The conclusion in all of the articles and reports is that the death penalty is ineffective and unwise.

1953

June 19: Julius and Ethel Rosenberg are put to death for furnishing information about the atomic bomb to the Soviet Union. They are the first U.S. civilians executed for espionage.

1954

April 17: *Cell 2455 Death Row* by California death row inmate Caryl Chessman is published. Chessman characterizes the prison system as a school for crime and condemns the death penalty as a meaningless act of vengeance. (May 22, 1948; July 10, 1955; October 6, 1957; May 2, 1960)

1955

July 10: A second book by Caryl Chessman, *Trial by Ordeal*, is released. His writings bring the author first national and then international attention. Chessman's case becomes a rallying point for abolitionist activity across the country. (May 22, 1948; April 17, 1954; October 6, 1957; May 2, 1960)

1957

June 6: Hawaii, which had not executed anyone in over 25 years, abolishes the death penalty for all crimes.

June 30: Arthur Koestler's *Reflections on Hanging*, a highly critical study of the death penalty, is published in the United States.

Chronology

October 6: The third and last book of death row author Caryl Chessman, *The Face of Justice*, is published. (May 22, 1948; April 17, 1954; July 10, 1955; May 2, 1960)

1958

April 2: Delaware Governor J. Caldo Boggs signs into law a bill that abolishes capital punishment. The state is the first to eliminate the death penalty in 40 years. (December 18, 1961)

October 27: The season premiere of the television series "Omnibus" is a documentary critical of capital punishment.

1959

January 4: The New York Committee to Abolish Capital Punishment is established.

1960

February 18: California Governor Edmund G. Brown announces he will call a special session of the state legislature to consider elimination of the death penalty. Brown links the issue of capital punishment to the case of death row inmate Caryl Chessman.

March 10: The California legislature rejects Governor Edmund G. Brown's abolition bill and adjourns from special session.

April 6: The UN Economic and Social Council calls on Secretary General Dag Hammarskjold to study the effect of the death penalty on crime.

April 9: The death penalty is backed by Vice-President Richard M. Nixon and opposed by Senator Hubert H. Humphrey in replies to a questionnaire sent to major presidential contenders by the Union of American Hebrew Congregations.

April 26: In response to mounting demands that he grant clemency to Caryl Chessman, Governor Edmund G. Brown states the California constitution bars him from doing so.

May 2: After a protracted 12-year legal struggle, the internationally renowned death row author Caryl Chessman is executed at San Quentin, California. (May 22, 1948; April 17, 1954; July 10, 1955; October 6, 1957)

1961

January 28: In a study conducted at the request of the Governors Board of the American Bar Association (ABA), the American Bar Foundation finds that long delays in carrying out death sentences weaken public confidence in the law. The study urges uniform postconviction procedures.

April 1: A pioneering law article by Los Angeles attorney Gerald Gott-lieb is published in the spring issue of the *Southern California Law Review*. In the article, "Testing the Death Penalty," Gottlieb suggests the tradi-tional abolitionist tactic of persuading state legislatures to end capital punishment has met with limited success. He argues that the death pen-alty instead should be attacked through the court system on the grounds it violates the Eighth Amendment's prohibition of cruel and unusual punishment.

May 6: The Soviet Union broadens its death penalty statutes to in-clude large-scale embezzlement of state property and counterfeiting.

August 12: Capital punishment is ended in Bolivia under its new con-stitution.

November 1: New Zealand abolishes the death penalty for all crimes except treason.

December 18: Delaware legislators override a veto by Governor Elbert N. Carvel to reinstate the death penalty. (April 2, 1958)

1962

May 31: Nazi war criminal Adolf Eichmann is executed in Israel.

1963

March 14: Georgia raises the minimum age for execution from 10 to 17.

March 15: Victor Feuger is hanged in Iowa for kidnapping. He is the last federal prisoner executed in the United States.

October 21: In a dissent to a U.S. Supreme Court decision to refuse to hear the case of *Rudolph v. Alabama*, Justice Arthur J. Goldberg, joined by Justices William O. Douglas and William J. Brennan Jr., contends there are substantive reasons to consider whether the Eighth and Four-teenth Amendments to the Constitution permit the death penalty for a convicted rapist who neither took nor endangered human life.

1964

May 2: Attorney Marvin Belli charges that of 23 verdicts by Dallas juries entailing death sentences, seven were given after only four to seven minutes of deliberation.

November 4: In a statewide referendum, Oregon voters approve aboli-tion of the death penalty by a margin of 455,000 to 302,000.

Chronology

1965

March 5: Vermont ends the death penalty except for a second conviction for murder.

March 12: West Virginia legislators vote to eliminate the death penalty for all crimes.

March 17: The National District Attorneys Association urges the abolition of capital punishment.

June 1: New York Governor Nelson Rockefeller signs into law an abolition bill. However, the measure retains the death penalty for killing a law enforcement officer in the line of duty.

June 20: The American Civil Liberties Union (ACLU) announces a nationwide drive to end capital punishment.

November 8: Great Britain abolishes the death penalty for a trial period of five years. (Dec 18, 1969)

1966

April 24: The NAACP Legal Defense and Education Fund (LDF) announces an extensive survey on the use of the death penalty for rape convictions in the South. (May 3, 1968)

June 29: The Lutheran Church in America urges the abolition of capital punishment.

November 9: Colorado voters reject a proposal to terminate capital punishment in the state.

1967

April 12: California carries out its first execution in four years.

April 13: The NAACP LDF and ACLU challenge the constitutionality of Florida's death penalty laws in federal court. The court temporarily halts executions in the state pending its review of the class action suit.

June 2: Luis Jose Monge dies in Colorado's gas chamber. Soon after, mounting legal challenges to the constitutionality of the death penalty bring about a moratorium on its use. Monge becomes the last person executed in the United States until 1977.

June 27: Charging there is a disproportionate number of blacks on San Quentin's death row, the NAACP LDF files a class action suit in federal court in San Francisco to block executions in the state.

July 5: A federal district court stays all California executions while it considers the NAACP LDF claim that the state's death penalty law is unconstitutional.

August 10: The NAACP LDF, contending that attorneys often stop representing death row inmates when a case has gone beyond state court appeals, urges a federal district court in California to order hearings on the contention that the legal rights of the inmates have been violated.

August 25: A federal court in San Francisco cancels the blanket stay of executions in California and rules appeals for each inmate must be considered separately.

November 27: In response to a suit brought by the ACLU, a California superior court rules the state's death penalty does not constitute cruel and unusual punishment even in cases where murder has not been committed.

1968

May 3: NAACP LDF director Jack Greenberg releases statistics showing 90% of persons executed in the South for rape since 1930 were black. (April 24, 1966)

June 3: The U.S. Supreme Court, in **Witherspoon v. Illinois,** holds that persons who oppose the death penalty cannot automatically be excluded from juries in capital cases.

July 2: The Johnson administration asks Congress to abolish the death penalty for all federal crimes and to reduce to life imprisonment the sentences of federal prisoners on death row. Attorney General Ramsey Clark urges the United States join over 70 other nations that have abandoned capital punishment.

September 13: The National Council of Churches issues a policy statement calling for the abolition of capital punishment.

October 30: Truman Capote, at odds with ABC-TV over the scheduling of his documentary, "Death Row, USA," demands the program be aired prior to a pending U.S. Supreme Court decision on whether protracted delays in capital cases constitute cruel and unusual punishment. ABC ultimately decides not to broadcast the film.

November 18: The California Supreme Court rules the state's death penalty is constitutional, rejecting arguments the law does not provide sufficient standards by which judges and juries should decide who receives a death sentence.

November 26: A U.S. appeals court rules that North Carolina's provisions for imposing the death penalty are unconstitutional.

December 31: The Federal Prisons Bureau reports that 1968 marks the first year without an execution since statistics were first collected in 1930. NAACP LDF director Jack Greenberg describes the current legal moratorium on capital punishment as a "de facto national abolition of the death penalty."

1969

February 15: A Gallup Poll survey finds growing support among whites for the death penalty for murder and opposition by a majority of blacks.

March 3: The National Urban League urges abolition of the death penalty throughout the United States.

March 31: New Mexico becomes the 13th state to abolish or severely limit capital punishment. The death penalty is retained only for killing a police officer or jail guard.

April 4: The U.S. Supreme Court hears arguments in the case of William L. Maxwell, a black man sentenced to death for rape in Arkansas in 1962. The case is expected to produce a landmark decision on the constitutionality of the death penalty. (June 2, 1970)

December 18: Great Britain makes permanent its ban on capital punishment for all crimes except treason. (November 8, 1965)

1970

January 31: The American Psychiatric Association, in a brief to the U.S. Supreme Court, claims the threat of the death penalty may incite certain persons to crime rather than deter them.

March 25: President Richard M. Nixon calls for the death penalty to curb the rise of bombings in cities.

June 2: The U.S. Supreme Court sends the case of *Maxwell v. Bishop* back to a lower court for procedural review, in effect postponing a decision on the constitutionality of the death penalty. The action leaves intact a judicial freeze that has halted all executions in the United States for the past three years. (April 4, 1969)

October 8: Congress enacts legislation that makes it a capital offense to cause a fatality by a bombing.

October 15: The Justice Department, in a friend-of-the-court brief, notifies the Supreme Court it does not support pending constitutional challenges to capital punishment.

December 11: Setting an important precedent, a federal appeals court in Virginia holds that the death penalty for rape when the victim's life is neither taken nor endangered is unconstitutional.

December 29: Arkansas Governor Winthrop Rockefeller commutes the death sentences of all 15 death row inmates in the state to life imprisonment.

1971

January 7: The U.S. National Commission on Reform of Federal Criminal Laws, headed by former California Governor Edmund G. Brown, issues a series of recommendations, including abolition of capital punishment.

January 16: The Vatican announces its abolition of the death penalty.

January 20: The World Council of Churches Central Committee, meeting in Addis Ababa, Ethiopia urges the nations of the world to eliminate capital punishment as a violation of the "sanctity of life."

May 3: The Supreme Court rejects two major constitutional challenges to the death penalty. Neither an absence of clear standards to guide the imposition of the death sentence nor the common practice of allowing a single jury to determine both guilt and penalty are found to be unconstitutional. The court does not address the basic constitutional question of whether the death penalty constitutes cruel and unusual punishment, thus the nationwide moratorium on executions remains in effect.

May 25: The Connecticut legislature defeats a measure to abolish capital punishment.

June 28: The U.S. Supreme Court, setting aside the death sentences of 39 persons, including mass murderer Richard Speck, announces it will hear several cases during its next term on the constitutionality of capital punishment.

September 24: Faced with the likelihood that only seven justices will be on the bench when its new term begins in early October, the Supreme Court postpones scheduled hearings on capital punishment.

October 5: A federal magistrate in Boston rules that convicts in Massachusetts may not be kept on death row for more than 10 days prior to their scheduled executions.

October 9: Pennsylvania Governor Milton Shapp and eight former governors from around the country file a friend-of-the-court brief with the U.S. Supreme Court that argues the death penalty does not deter murder.

Chronology

1972

January 17: The New Jersey Supreme Court in a 6–1 vote rules the state's capital punishment statute as currently written is unconstitutional.

January 26: A bill calling for the death penalty for drug pushers is defeated in the Georgia legislature.

February 18: The California Supreme Court, in *People v. Anderson*, rules that the state's death penalty is unconstitutional. Among those whose sentences are changed to life imprisonment by the decision are Sirhan Sirhan, convicted assassin of Senator Robert F. Kennedy, and mass murderer Charles Manson. California Governor Ronald Reagan charges that the court has set itself "above the people and the legislature."

February 23: A California superior court judge releases black militant Angela Davis on bail, holding that the statutory ban on bail in capital cases had been invalidated by the California Supreme Court decision.

April 2: A UN inquiry into the death penalty indicates that many governments are reluctant to abolish capital punishment. Replies from 69 countries reveal that 75% still employ the death penalty, although few people are sentenced to death and even fewer executed.

April 26: The United Methodist Church at a convention in Atlanta, Georgia adopts a doctrine of social principles that includes opposition to capital punishment.

June 25: Governor Ronald Reagan leads a successful drive to place on the November ballot a proposed amendment to the California constitution that would restore capital punishment.

June 29: In a landmark decision in **Furman v. Georgia,** the U.S. Supreme Court rules that the death penalty as imposed under current statutes is unconstitutional. The court finds that the arbitrary and capricious manner in which the death penalty is applied constitutes cruel and unusual punishment. The decision spares over 600 persons on death row. In his dissent, Chief Justice Warren Burger notes that states could retain capital punishment by altering their laws to conform to the court's ruling.

June 29: At a news conference, President Richard Nixon criticizes the Supreme Court decision and urges retention of the death penalty.

November 7: A referendum to restore the death penalty is approved by a large margin of California voters.

November 22: A Gallup Poll finds that public support for capital punishment is at its highest point in nearly two decades. Fifty-one percent of the persons questioned favored the death penalty for persons convicted of murder.

December 6: The National Association of Attorneys General approves a resolution recommending the death penalty for violent crimes. The association notes that while the Supreme Court outlawed the death penalty in its present form, it did not rule the sanction itself cruel and unusual punishment.

December 8: Governor Reuben Askew signs into law a measure making Florida the first state to reinstate capital punishment since the Supreme Court decision in **Furman v. Georgia.** The bill authorizes the death penalty for premeditated murder and the raping of a child under 11.

1973

February 12: The American Bar Association (ABA) votes to recommend a one-year delay on actions to reinstate state death penalty statutes on the grounds the issue remains unsettled in the wake of the Supreme Court decision in **Furman v. Georgia.**

March 14: President Richard Nixon in his State of the Union message advocates the imposition of the death penalty for a number of violent crimes.

July 26: The Florida Supreme Court upholds the state's new capital punishment statute. The law provides for a separate sentencing procedure for capital crimes and automatic appeal of all death sentences.

December 31: By the end of 1973, 23 states have enacted new death penalty statutes since the Supreme Court struck down capital punishment laws in June 1972. A total of 44 prisoners await execution across the nation.

1974

March 13: The U.S. Senate approves legislation to reinstate capital punishment for a variety of serious crimes.

April 11: The House Judiciary Committee is unable to complete action on death penalty legislation, already approved by the Senate, before the end of the current session of Congress.

November 21: The National Conference of Catholic Bishops speaks out against capital punishment in a reversal of the traditional Roman Catholic Church stand supporting the death penalty as a legitimate means of self-protection for the state.

December 31: An additional six states by year's end have approved new capital punishment laws.

1976

April 28: A Gallup Poll shows that 65% of Americans favor the death penalty for convicted murderers, 28% are opposed, and 7% are undecided.

July 2: The Supreme Court rules that the death penalty is not inherently cruel or unusual. In its landmark decision in **Gregg v. Georgia** and two related cases, the court upholds the constitutionality of the new statutes in Georgia, Florida and Texas. In **Woodson v. North Carolina,** the court rules that mandatory death penalty laws which do not allow for differences in defendants and circumstances are unconstitutional.

July 6: Canada abolishes capital punishment for all but traitorous military crimes.

August 14: The Southern Christian Leadership Conference passes a strongly worded resolution against capital punishment.

November 2: Convicted murderer Gary Mark Gilmore, denied a new trial in Utah, says he will not appeal and wants to be executed by firing squad as scheduled on November 15.

November 15: Gary M. Gilmore's execution is delayed by legal maneuvers and two unsuccessful attempts at suicide.

November 28: The Law Enforcement Assistance Administration reports that 285 persons were sentenced to death in 1975, bringing the death row population at the end of the year to 479.

1977

January 12: The U.S. Supreme Court rejects motions filed by abolitionist groups which seek to postpone the execution of Gary M. Gilmore scheduled for January 17.

January 17: Gary M. Gilmore is executed by firing squad in Utah State Prison. It is the first execution in the United States since 1967. In what is to become a common practice, opponents of the death penalty conduct a vigil outside the prison.

February 15: The ABA rejects a proposal calling for an end to capital punishment.

June 6: The Supreme Court rules that states may not make the death penalty mandatory for the murder of a police officer. Citing its decisions in July 1976, the court holds that judges and juries must be allowed to consider mitigating circumstances.

June 29: In **Coker v. Georgia,** the Supreme Court finds that the death penalty for rape is unconstitutional. Citing the Coker decision in a summary opinion, the Court holds that the death sentence for nonhomicidal kidnapping is cruel and unusual.

August 3: A federal appeals court in New Orleans reverses a Texas court ruling that TV cameramen can film executions of condemned prisoners.

December 8: Amnesty International announces a campaign for abolition of the death penalty.

1978

January 2: Results of a study conducted by the Center for Applied Social Research show that murderers of whites are far more likely to be sentenced to death than murderers of blacks.

April 22: The National Legal Aid and Defender Association announces it will not hold future conventions in states that have adopted the death penalty.

July 3: The Supreme Court, in **Lockett v. Ohio,** requires that every person convicted of a capital offense be permitted to offer a broad range of extenuating evidence prior to sentencing.

December 23: Spain abolishes the death penalty except for military crimes committed in time of war.

December 31: Opponents of capital punishment hail the absence of executions in 1978 but note there are 475 persons on death row.

1979

February 13: The American Bar Association calls on the Supreme Court to provide free counsel to persons who are appealing their state death sentences in federal court.

May 25: Convicted murderer John A. Spenkelink is electrocuted in Florida. He is the first person executed in two years and only the second since the Supreme Court restored the death penalty in 1976.

May 31: President Jimmy Carter rebukes U.S. Ambassador to the UN Andrew Young for comparing the execution of John A. Spenkelink to the executions in Iran.

Chronology

1980

February 12:   Theodore R. Bundy is sentenced to death for the kidnapping murder of a 12-year-old girl. (January 24, 1989)

April 14:   Norman Mailer wins the Pulitzer Prize for *The Executioner's Song*, a fictionalized account of the last nine months of Gary M. Gilmore, the first person executed in the United States after a 10-year moratorium in 1977.

April 22:   The Parliamentary Assembly of the Council of Europe condemns capital punishment in peacetime and recommends the European Convention on Human Rights be amended to make it illegal.

May 19:   In **Godfrey v. Georgia,** the Supreme Court sets aside death penalty statutes that are excessively broad or vague.

May 26:   Amnesty International calls for the creation of a presidential commission on capital punishment.

July 22:   Delegates to the annual meeting of the American Medical Association (AMA) proclaim that physicians should not participate in the execution of prisoners.

November 13:   The Roman Catholic Bishops of the United States object to the fact that the death penalty is more likely to be exercised unjustly against the poor who cannot afford adequate defense but uphold the principle of the state's right to impose capital punishment.

1981

March 15:   A Gallup Poll reveals that two-thirds of all Americans, the highest percentage in 28 years, favor the death penalty for murder. Reflecting the level of support, 35 states have enacted new death penalty statutes since the Supreme Court invalidated current capital punishment laws in 1972.

May 4:   The U.S. Supreme Court for the first time extends constitutional protection against double jeopardy beyond the question of guilt to the sentence itself, ruling in *Bullington v. Missouri* that a defendant who had received a life sentence at a first trial could not be sentenced to death on retrial.

August 9:   Justice Department statistics show that more than half the prison inmates awaiting execution in 1980 were in Georgia, Florida and Texas.

August 28:   The Food and Drug Administration (FDA) rejects a request by five condemned prisoners to use federal drug regulations to block their execution by lethal injection. (October 15, 1983; March 20, 1985)

September 30: France abolishes capital punishment.

December 9: In its annual report, Amnesty International characterizes the death penalty in the United States a violation of human rights.

1982

July 2: The Supreme Court determines, in **Enmund v. Florida,** that death is an excessive and disproportionate punishment for a defendant who aided and abetted in the commission of a murder but who neither killed, attempted to kill or intended to kill the victim.

August 22: The number of prisoners under death sentence in the United States exceeds 1,000.

December 7: Charlie Brooks is executed by a combination of sedatives and drugs in Texas. He is the first person put to death by lethal injection.

1983

January 15: In the first instance of a pontiff speaking out against capital punishment, Pope John Paul II condemns the death penalty in an address to the Vatican diplomatic corps.

May 9: Associate Supreme Court Justice Lewis F. Powell Jr., in a speech delivered in Georgia, says that unless Congress and the courts can find a speedier way to handle death penalty appeals, states should abolish capital punishment.

July 6: In **Barefoot v. Estelle,** the Supreme Court holds that petitions for review in capital cases must raise issues that are at least "debatable among jurists of reason" and establishes guidelines for lower federal courts handling death penalty appeals.

October 11: The Court of Military Appeals, the nation's highest military court, strikes down procedures used for sentencing members of the armed forces to death. The court notes the president can remedy the constitutional defects without new legislation. (January 31, 1984)

October 15: A federal appeals court panel orders the FDA to weigh evidence that drugs used for executions by lethal injection can cause "torturous pain." (August 28, 1981; March 20, 1985)

1984

January 23: The Supreme Court, in **Pulley v. Harris,** rules that a state may carry out the death penalty without first conducting a "proportionality" review to insure the sentence is in line with other sentences imposed in the state for similar crimes.

January 31: President Ronald Reagan signs an executive order during the month designed to correct defects in the administration of the death penalty under the Uniform Code of Military Justice. (October 11, 1983)

November 1: Margie Velma Barfield, who was convicted of killing her fiance and who confessed to killing three other people by poisoning, is executed by lethal injection in North Carolina. She is the first woman put to death in the United States in 22 years.

1985

March 20: The Supreme Court rules that the FDA is not required to approve the drugs used to execute prisoners by lethal injection. (August 28, 1981; October 15, 1983)

July 26: Reflecting concern over a string of recent spying cases involving Navy personnel, Congress approves a measure that would permit execution of military personnel for peacetime espionage.

September 11: Charles Rumbaugh, convicted of committing robbery and murder when he was 17, is executed by lethal injection in Texas. The execution is the first in more than two decades for a crime committed by someone under age 18.

November 13: A study conducted by the ACLU asserts that since 1900 343 persons were wrongfully sentenced to death in America, 25 of whom were actually executed.

November 28: The latest Gallup Poll shows that American support of capital punishment for a variety of serious crimes has increased sharply over the last seven years. Seventy-five percent of Americans now favor the death penalty for murder.

1986

January 10: James Terry Roach, who was 17 when he took part in the murder of a teenage couple, dies in South Carolina's electric chair despite international protests against the execution of offenders for crimes they committed while juveniles. Mother Teresa and UN Secretary General Javier Perez de Cuellar are among those pleading for mercy.

February 23: President Ronald Reagan signs a measure under which members of the armed forces convicted of espionage in peacetime could be executed.

April 15: Amnesty International reports there were more than 1,125 documented executions worldwide in 1985.

May 5: The Supreme Court holds that dedicated opponents of capital punishment may be barred from juries in capital cases regardless of whether the move increases the likelihood of conviction.

May 13: New York City Mayor Ed Koch calls for a federal law imposing the death penalty on those convicted of wholesale narcotics dealing.

June 26: In **Ford v. Wainwright,** the Supreme Court rules that the Eighth Amendment bars the execution of the presently insane. The Court requires states to establish procedures for determining sanity that meet minimum due process standards.

November 26: New Mexico Governor Toney Anaya, who leaves office in a few weeks, commutes the death sentences of all five persons awaiting execution in the state.

1987

February 18: Amnesty International announces it is opening a worldwide campaign against the death penalty in the United States.

April 23: In a controversial decision, the Supreme Court finds that Georgia's capital punishment law is constitutionally applied despite a wide statistical disparity in the imposition of death sentences between whites and blacks. The ruling in **McClesky v. Kemp** ends what opponents had called their last sweeping constitutional challenge to capital punishment.

June 15: The Supreme Court annuls a Maryland law that provided for the use of "victim impact statements" at death sentence hearings. The decision in **Booth v. Maryland** is denounced by victims rights groups.

June 23: The Supreme Court strikes down the last vestiges of the mandatory death penalty in the United States, holding that state laws making executions compulsory for murders committed by prisoners serving life terms without parole are unconstitutional.

September 26: Pope John Paul II appeals for clemency in the case of Paula R. Cooper, an 18-year-old Indiana woman facing execution for a murder she committed when she was 15. (July 13, 1989)

November 1: A study published in the *Stanford Law Review* by professors Hugo Adam Bedau and Michael L. Radelet finds that 349 innocent persons were convicted and 23 actually put to death in 20th century America.

1988

March 15: Willie Jasper Darden, a convicted murderer whose case attracted worldwide attention, is executed in Florida.

June 29:   Addressing the issue of juvenile executions, the Supreme Court rules in **Thompson v. Oklahoma** that a state may not impose the death sentence for crimes committed by persons when they were less than 16 years old unless the state has specifically legislated the death penalty for such minors.

July 31:   The Justice Department reports that of every 30 persons sentenced to death since capital punishment was reinstated in 1976, 10 left death row and one was executed.

August 1:   The movie *The Thin Blue Line* by filmmaker Errol Morris is released. The documentary film examines the possible innocence of Randall Dale Adams, on death row in Texas for the murder of a police officer. The movie brings national attention to the case, and Adams is subsequently released.

September 25:   Republican candidate George Bush favors capital punishment and Democratic candidate Michael S. Dukakis opposes it in their first presidential election debate.

October 12:   In the second presidential election debate, CNN newsperson Bernard Shaw asks Democratic candidate Michael S. Dukakis if he would still oppose the death penalty if Mrs. Dukakis were raped and murdered. Dukakis answers he would. The appropriateness of the question generates considerable controversy.

November 22:   Congress adjourns after passing a comprehensive drug bill which includes the death penalty for homicides connected to drug-related crimes.

1989

January 24:   After numerous appeals and delays, serial killer Theodore R. Bundy is electrocuted in Florida. (February 12, 1980)

February 6:   In his annual message before the midyear convention of the American Bar Association, Supreme Court Chief Justice William H. Rehnquist urges reform of the system by which death sentences are reviewed in federal courts. Calling for changes to speed up the appeals process, he notes that the elapsed time between the commission of a capital crime and the date of execution averages eight years nationally.

February 14:   The Ayatollah Khomeini calls for the execution of British author Salman Rushdie for commiting blasphemy in his novel *The Satanic Verses*. Rushdie goes into hiding, and the incident strains already poor relations between Iran and the West.

June 14: The Chinese government begins executing individuals who participated in events culminating in the massacre in Tiananmen Square. The executions provoke worldwide condemnation.

June 23: The Supreme Court rules that indigent inmates on death row do not have a constitutional right to a lawyer to assist them in a second round of appeals.

June 26: In **Penry V. Lynaugh,** the Supreme Court rules that execution of the mentally retarded is not precluded by the Eighth Amendment, but the Court requires states to establish clear standards for considering mental retardation as a mitigating factor. In a separate decision, the court holds that the execution of a defendant who committed a capital offense at age 16 is not unconstitutional.

July 13: The Indiana Supreme Court bars the execution of Paula R. Cooper for a murder she committed when she was 15 years old. Her death sentence had drawn appeals for leniency from a number of groups around the world. (September 26, 1987)

August 16: Louisiana Governor Buddy Roemer commutes to life imprisonment the death sentence of Ronald Monroe. The case had attracted national attention because of the possibility it was her estranged husband, and not Monroe, who had killed a woman in 1977.

September 21: A special committee of federal judges established by Supreme Court Chief Justice William H. Rehnquist submits its findings on the judicial system's handling of death penalty cases. The panel, headed by retired Supreme Court Justice Lewis F. Powell Jr., recommends imposing strict limits on the multiple appeals filed by death row inmates. Chief Justice Rehnquist formally transmits the panel's proposal to the Senate Judiciary Committee for consideration.

October 5: Fourteen of the nation's most senior federal judges forward an unusual letter to the Senate and House Judiciary Committees. The letter notes that the proposal submitted by Supreme Court Chief Justice William H. Rehnquist for reform of the appeals process in death penalty cases does not reflect the views of the entire federal judiciary on the issue.

December 31: Sixteen persons were executed in the United States in 1989, an increase of 5 over the previous year. The total for the decade was 117.

CHAPTER 3

COURT CASES

Since the 1960s, the judicial system has played a central role in the debate over capital punishment. This chapter provides summaries of what are generally considered the most significant court cases concerning the death penalty to date. These cases addressed the major issues of capital punishment: the constitutionality of the death penalty; the relationship of punishment to the crime committed; the procedures to be followed in capital trials; the execution of juveniles, the insane and the mentally retarded; and the question of racial discrimination in the application of the death sentence. Reflecting their broad relevance and the important questions of law involved, all of these cases ultimately were decided by the Supreme Court. Each case is presented in the same format: Background, Legal Issues, Decision and Impact. Court cases in bold print are discussed separately within the chapter.

WITHERSPOON V. ILLINOIS (1968)

BACKGROUND: William G. Witherspoon was convicted in 1960 for the murder of a Chicago police officer. An Illinois law specified that persons could be excluded from serving on a jury for a capital crime if they opposed or had "conscientious scruples" against the death penalty. This "scrupled juror" rule was invoked by the prosecutor at Witherspoon's trial to dismiss any prospective member of the jury who voiced misgiving about capital punishment. Witherspoon contested his conviction and challenged the constitutionality of the procedure by which Illinois selected juries in capital cases. After Illinois courts rejected his appeals, the Supreme Court granted his request for review.

LEGAL ISSUES: Witherspoon's counsel maintained that—in violation of the Sixth Amendment—the question of his client's guilt or innocence had not been determined by an impartial jury. His argument rested on the contention that jurors without scruples against capital punishment were more inclined to vote for guilt than were those with qualms about the sanction. He asked the Court to overturn Witherspoon's conviction on the grounds it was obtained from a biased or "prosecution prone" jury.

The attorney general of Illinois responded that a state had a right to insure that jurors were able to meet their responsibilities under the law. In defense of the scrupled juror statute, it was alleged that jurors who opposed capital punishment would be reluctant to convict a defendant of a capital offense out of concern the death penalty would be imposed. It was also noted there was no substantive evidence that "death qualified" juries were more likely to convict.

DECISION: In a decision announced June 3, 1968, the Supreme Court did not specifically address Witherspoon's claim that his conviction was the result of a biased jury. As Justice Potter Stewart noted in his majority opinion, available data was "too tentative and fragmentary" to conclude that such juries were more likely to find a defendant guilty. The Court instead focused on the narrower question of Witherspoon's punishment. Justice Stewart declared that the Constitution did not permit jury selection procedures which in effect produced a "hanging jury." The Court reversed Witherspoon's death sentence, ruling in his case that the systematic exclusion of jurors who had merely voiced ambiguous feelings about the death penalty had deprived him of his constitutional right to an impartial hearing. The Court concluded that an appropriate inquiry had to be conducted to determine a potential juror's level of opposition to capital punishment before that person could be excluded from jury duty. Only those persons who indicated they would automatically vote against imposition of the death penalty could legitimately be disqualified.

IMPACT: Witherspoon was the first time the Supreme Court significantly limited the ability of state governments to impose the death penalty. The decision raised the hopes of abolitionists who looked to the Court to eventually outlaw capital punishment. The immediate impact of the *Witherspoon* ruling, because it applied retroactively, was to open a new avenue of appeal for many of the approximately 430 persons under death sentence nationwide at the time. However, it was quickly recognized that the ruling left their convictions intact, and many states moved to implement new, constitutionally acceptable jury selection procedures with the intent of resentencing their death row inmates. These efforts were superseded in 1971 when the Court held, in **Furman v. Georgia,** that the nation's death penalty statutes as written were unconstitutional.

After the restoration of the death penalty in 1976, the Court returned to the issue of juror selection at capital trials in a number of subsequent decisions. That same year the Court stated in *Davis v. Georgia* that the exclusion of even a single juror in violation of the principles determined in *Witherspoon* invalidated the death sentence imposed. The rules for determining whether a juror could be excluded from the sentencing phase of a capital trial were further clarified in *Adams v. Texas* (1980) and *Wainwright v. Witt* (1985). Jurors could not be excused for their views on capital punishment unless those views would prevent or significantly impair the performance of duties as outlined in their oath and instructions. In 1986 the Court again considered the question of jury bias in the determination of guilt and innocence first raised in *Witherspoon*. The Court found, in *Lockhart v. McRee*, that the practice of striking jurors who were unequivocally opposed to the death penalty from the guilt phase of a capital trial did not abridge a defendant's Sixth Amendment rights, even if it were established that "death qualified" juries were somewhat more "prosecution prone" than average juries.

FURMAN V. GEORGIA (1972)

BACKGROUND: In 1965 the NAACP Legal Defense and Education Fund (LDF) launched a campaign to have the death penalty declared unconstitutional. By 1967 a series of legal challenges to death sentences across the nation had succeeded in halting all executions while the courts grappled with the difficult constitutional issues involved. After the Supreme Court ruled against several major challenges to capital punishment in May 1971, many in the abolitionist legal movement worried the moratorium on executions was about to end.

However, the following month the Court announced it would review four cases to determine whether the death penalty constituted "cruel and unusual punishment in violation of the Eighth and Fourteenth Amendments." In two cases, *Aikens v. California* and *Furman v. Georgia*, the defendants contested their death sentences under state law for murder. *Jackson v. Georgia* and *Branch v. Texas* questioned the constitutionality of the death penalty for rape. Underscoring LDF arguments about racial discrimination in the imposition of capital punishment was the fact that in each of the four cases the defendant was black and the victim was white.

LEGAL ISSUES: LDF lawyers, who represented three of the defendants, presented a progression of interconnected arguments against the death penalty. They noted the Supreme Court's understandable reluctance to overturn well-established death penalty statutes in forty-one states but urged the Court to do so because the laws violated the cruel and unusual punishment clause of the Eighth Amendment. They called on the Court to continue its practice, first articulated in 1958, of viewing the Amendment's prohibition on cruel and unusual punishment within the context of "evolving standards of decency." Acknowledging that the existence of the death penalty in so many states suggested its use was acceptable to contemporary society, they contended the public tolerated the sanction only because it was so infrequently imposed. A mere fraction of those who committed capital offenses were ever put to death. Those who were executed were disproportionately the poor, the disadvantaged and minorities. They concluded that it was cruel and unusual to randomly single out a relative handful of persons for a penalty which society would not condone if evenhandedly and extensively applied.

Attorneys for the states responded that the people, through their elected representatives, should decide what penalties a state might employ. There was no clear and compelling reason for the Court to impose its judgment on legislative bodies. By any measure of contemporary standards, the death penalty could not be construed as cruel and unusual punishment. The idea that Americans in reality opposed capital punishment was characterized as an attempt to explain away the fact that the federal government and the majority of states had death penalty laws. If there were discriminatory practices in the actual imposition to the death sentence, then the issue was not capital punishment but equal protection under the laws as guaranteed by the Fourteenth Amendment. The small number of executions represented the care with which the death penalty was used.

Recognizing the importance of the pending Supreme Court decision, numerous groups filed friend-of-the-court briefs. These included arguments against capital punishment from a range of civil rights and religious organizations.

DECISION: The case from California had subsequently been dismissed after the California Supreme Court ruled the state's capital punishment statute unconstitutional in February 1972. The remaining three cases, officially reported under the name *Furman v. Georgia*, were decided on June 29, 1972. In a brief general opinion, the Court declared that imposition of the death penalty in these cases would constitute cruel and unusual punishment.

In a departure from normal practice that reflected the disparate views of the justices on the issues involved, there was no majority opinion which explained the Court's reasoning. Instead, each of the five justices who voted for abolition wrote a separate concurring opinion. Justices Brennan and Marshall believed capital punishment in general was prohibited under the Eighth Amendment. The other members of the majority did not address the constitutionality of capital punishment itself but rather the way in which current laws caused the death penalty to be imposed. Justices Douglas, Stewart and White agreed that the nation's capital punishment statutes resulted in cruel and unusual punishment because of the arbitrary and capricious manner in which the death penalty was imposed.

Each of the dissenting justices likewise issued a separate opinion. The general conclusion was that the majority had gone too far in trying to find a judicial solution to the troubling aspects of capital punishment. As a consequence, the Court through judicial review had encroached upon the powers constitutionally provided to legislatures.

IMPACT: At the same time it announced its *Furman* decision, the Supreme Court issued orders which similarly reversed the death sentences in over 100 other capital cases under appeal. The effect of *Furman* was to render the nation's capital punishment laws, as written, unconstitutional. The ruling spared from execution the approximately 630 persons on death row across the country.

The *Furman* decision provoked widespread reactions. Although abolitionist groups hailed the landmark judgment, the prevailing response was negative. Political leaders nationwide, most notably President Richard Nixon and California Governor Ronald Reagan, strongly criticized the Court's action. Many stated their intention to find a way to reinstate capital punishment.

In his dissent, Chief Justice Burger noted that the lack of a clear majority consensus on the ultimate constitutionality of the death penalty meant the full scope of the *Furman* ruling was unclear. He suggested that legislatures could enact capital punishment measures tailored to satisfy the objections stated in *Furman* by "providing standards for juries and judges to follow in determining the sentence in capital cases or by more narrowly defining the crimes for which the penalty is to be imposed." Over the next several years numerous states followed this course in amending their death penalty laws. In 1976, in **Gregg v. Georgia,** the Supreme Court restored capital punishment by upholding the constitutionality of the revised statutes.

GREGG V. GEORGIA (1976)

BACKGROUND: In 1972 the Supreme Court struck down the nation's capital punishment laws. These statutes had allowed juries in capital cases an essentially unrestricted discretion to determine whether a person received the death sentence. The Court found in **Furman v. Georgia** that the resulting arbitrary and capricious manner in which the death penalty was imposed violated the Eighth Amendment ban on cruel and unusual punishment.

By 1976, 35 states had enacted death penalty measures that attempted to conform to the guidelines established in the **Furman** decision. That same year the Supreme Court agreed to review five cases that challenged the constitutionality of the new laws in several states. Its ruling would possibly determine whether capital punishment would be reinstated in the United States. Two of the cases concerned mandatory death sentences and are reviewed separately in **Woodson v. North Carolina.** The other three cases, *Gregg v. Georgia, Profitt v. Florida* and *Jurek v. Texas,* involved defendants convicted of murder.

LEGAL ISSUES: In **Furman,** the Supreme Court had stopped short of concluding that capital punishment itself was unconstitutional. This left open the possibility that death penalty statutes could be designed that would pass judicial scrutiny. The states argued that they had implemented procedures that met the Court's requirement for clear sentencing standards in capital cases. These included a "bifurcated," or split, trial proceeding in which guilt or innocence was determined during a first phase and the sentence then imposed during a separate second phase. Juries were provided certain criteria to follow in deciding which convicted capital offenders would receive the death penalty.

Attorneys for the defendants contended neither these nor any other procedures ultimately would ensure capital punishment was administered in a rational and fair way. They asserted the Court should take the final step of declaring the death penalty itself unconstitutional, alleging the sanction was no longer compatible with contemporary standards of decency and as such was a violation of the Eighth Amendment ban on cruel and unusual punishment.

DECISION: In a historic judgment delivered on July 2, 1976, the Court ruled that capital punishment did not invariably violate the Constitution and upheld death penalty laws which set objective standards for juries to follow in their sentencing decisions. The Florida, Georgia and Texas statutes were found to be within constitutional limits. The Court chose to present its basic reasoning in *Gregg v. Georgia*, making it the lead case in the decision.

The seven members of the majority were unable to agree on an opinion. In the Court's ruling, Justices Stewart, Powell and Stevens noted that passage of new death penalty measures by so many states after **Furman** undercut the argument society no longer endorsed the sanction. The different majority opinions in general indicated the Court would uphold capital punishment laws which met several key conditions: clear standards to guide juries in their sentencing decisions; consideration of any mitigating factors prior to sentencing; and automatic review of each death sentence in a state appellate court

IMPACT: Although *Gregg v. Georgia* reinstated the death penalty, the ruling did not overturn **Furman**. Instead, the decision reflected the Supreme Court's judgment that the defects previously identified in the administration of the death penalty had been remedied. More than 460 persons had been sentenced to death under post-**Furman** statutes, and *Gregg* cleared the way for a resumption of executions. The first execution in 10 years was carried out in 1977.

On the same day the *Gregg* decision was released, the Supreme Court determined in **Woodson v. North Carolina** that mandatory death sentences were unconstitutional. Together, **Furman** and **Woodson** made it clear the Court would not consent to giving a capital jury either too much or too little discretion in arriving at a sentence. Other states consequently moved to amend their death penalty laws to conform to the guided-discretion statutes approved in *Gregg*.

The 7–2 vote in *Gregg* suggested the Supreme Court was not likely to significantly modify its core stance on capital punishment in the forseeable future. In subsequent decisions, the Court has focused on further defining the circumstances when the death penalty is a constitutionally acceptable punishment.

WOODSON V. NORTH CAROLINA (1976)

BACKGROUND: The Supreme Court in 1972 ruled death penalty statutes that did not contain specific sentencing standards were unconstitutional. Relying on the precedent established in **Furman v. Georgia,** the North Carolina Supreme Court overturned the provision of that state's capital punishment law which granted the jury tremendous leeway on when to impose the death penalty. In 1974 the North Carolina legislature attempted to resolve the question of sentencing procedures in capital trials by passing a new statute that made the death penalty mandatory for first-degree murder. The state's highest court subsequently upheld death sentences two defendants had received under the new law following their murder convictions. The defendants appealed, and in 1976 the U.S. Supreme Court agreed to hear their case, *Woodson v. North Carolina*, as part of a broad review of the constitutionality of various state capital punishment laws enacted in response to the **Furman** decision.

LEGAL ISSUES: The basic question before the Supreme Court was whether mandatory death statutes provided a constitutionally acceptable response to the rejection in **Furman** of unbridled jury discretion in sentencing decisions. Attorneys for the states involved argued mandatory sentences would prevent arbitrary and freakish inconsistencies in the imposition of capital punishment. Defense lawyers countered that mandatory statutes did not take into account the unique circumstances of a given case and would still result in indiscriminate sentencing patterns. They further contended there was no workable way to address the concern raised in **Furman** and called on the Court to abolish capital punishment outright.

DECISION: The Supreme Court announced its decision in *Woodson v. North Carolina* on July 2, 1976, the same day it delivered its landmark **Gregg v. Georgia** ruling. The Court declared North Carolina's capital punishment law unconstitutional because it did not provide "objective standards to guide, regularize, and make rationally reviewable the process for imposing a sentence of death." In a companion case, *Roberts v. Louisiana*, the Court struck down that state's mandatory death penalty statute for similar reasons.

The 5–4 majority in *Woodson* stressed the fact that since the early 19th century the United States had gradually moved away from mandatory sentences. An automatic death sentence was seen as inconsistent with "evolving standards of decency" and consequently constituted cruel and unusual punishment under the Eighth Amendment. The Court stated that "particularized" consideration had to be given to the relevant aspects of a convicted defendant's character and record before a death sentence could be imposed.

IMPACT: In its simultaneous release of the **Gregg** and *Woodson* decisions, the Supreme Court staked out a carefully defined position on capital punishment. In **Gregg**, the Court found that the death penalty per se was not unconstitutional and upheld death penalty statutes that provided for guided jury discretion in sentencing decisions. With its ruling against mandatory sentences in *Woodson*, the Court, in effect, had endorsed a "bifurcated" or split trial process in capital cases where conviction and punishment were determined in separate hearings.

Woodson established the important precedent that a defendant was entitled to an individualized sentencing determination. In later decisions the Supreme Court extended this principle to include a defendant's right to present a broad range of mitigating evidence prior to sentencing. The Court continued to rule against mandatory death sentences. The following year, in *Harry Roberts v. Louisiana*, a Louisiana statue that mandated the death penalty for persons convicted of killing a police officer was overturned. The Court did not accept the argument that the process of convicting a person of a special and narrowly drawn category of crime could serve as a substitute for "particularized" consideration. In 1987 the Court effectively ended mandatory death sentences in the United States when it nullified, in *Sumner v. Shuman*, a Nevada law that required the death penalty for murders committed by prisoners serving life sentences without possibility of parole.

COKER V. GEORGIA (1977)

BACKGROUND: Anthony Coker escaped from a Georgia correctional institution where he was serving consecutive life sentences for murder, rape and kidnapping. He subsequently raped an adult woman during an armed robbery. Georgia's death penalty statutes authorized capital punishment for rape if one or more of the following aggravating circumstances was present: The defendant had previously been convicted of a capital offense; the rape occurred during the commission of another capital felony (including armed robbery); or the crime was particularly vile and horrible, involving torture, depravity or aggravated battery. After his conviction for rape and armed robbery, Coker was sentenced to death by a jury that found the first two aggravating factors applied. When Georgia's highest court affirmed the sentence on automatic appeal, Coker petitioned the Supreme Court to declare the death penalty for rape unconstitutional

LEGAL ISSUES: In **Gregg v. Georgia** the Supreme Court upheld the constitutionality of capital punishment laws that provided for a consideration of aggravating and mitigating circumstances prior to sentencing. The question in *Coker v. Georgia* was not whether Georgia's statutes were procedurally flawed but whether death was an appropriate punishment for rape. Coker's counsel noted that the rape had not involved the loss of life and contended the sentence was disproportionate to the crime committed. Such an excessively harsh penalty violated the Eighth Amendment's ban on cruel and unusual punishment.

State attorneys argued the case was beyond the reach of proper judicial review. The Court should not substitute its policy judgment for that of the state legislature. Rape was not a minor crime, and it was the considered reasoning of Georgia's elected representatives that there were times the offense merited the ultimate sanction.

DECISION: The Supreme Court ruled in favor of Coker on June 29, 1977. The Court followed its normal practice in determining the constitutionality of a given punishment. A punishment was cruel and unusual under the Eighth Amendment if it was incompatible with "evolving standards of decency." Measured against contemporary American sensibilities, a sentence of death was wholly disproportionate to the offense of raping an adult woman. The Court cited the fact that Georgia was the only state still to authorize the death sentence for rape. The 7–2 majority also underscored the difference between murder and crimes such as rape where the defendant, whatever the aggravating circumstances, had not taken the victim's life.

IMPACT: *Coker* was the first time the Supreme Court specifically limited the authority of either federal or state government to impose the death penalty for a specific type of crime. In a summary opinion released at the same time, *Eberheart v. Georgia*, the Court also overturned the death penalty for kidnapping when homicide was not involved. The two decisions served to suggest the Court was drawing a clear link between death as a punishment and crimes that involved a loss of life. This apparent linkage raised serious doubts about the constitutionality of capital punishment for other crimes, such as treason, espionage and airplane hijacking, which might not result in immediate death. The Court has yet to rule on these questions.

LOCKETT V. OHIO (1978)

BACKGROUND: Sandra Lockett drove the getaway car in a pawnshop robbery during which the owner was killed. Ohio laws required the death sentence for a conviction of aggravated murder, unless the sentencing authority determined at least one of the following three mitigating circumstances existed: The victim induced or facilitated the crime; the defendant was under duress, coercion or strong provocation; or the crime resulted from the defendant's mental deficiency short of actual legal insanity. Lockett was found guilty of committing murder during the course of another major felony. At the penalty phase of her trial, the judge determined that none of the mitigating factors applied and imposed the death penalty. After the state courts turned down her appeals, Lockett successfully petitioned the Supreme Court to review the constitutionality of Ohio's sentencing procedures.

LEGAL ISSUES: The applicable Ohio statute attempted to conform to the requirement for individualized sentencing determinations mandated by the Supreme Court in **Woodson v. North Carolina.** The state contended that its procedures allowed for a balanced weighing of aggravating and mitigating elements prior to sentencing. Defense lawyers stressed that Ohio's limited list of mitigating factors actually denied their client a fair hearing by preventing her from offering a wide range of pertinent information on her own behalf. For example, the court had not learned of Lockett's youth, her history of drug addiction or her lack of serious previous criminal activity. As a consequence, her rights to due process and an individualized sentence had not been guaranteed.

DECISION: The Supreme Court overturned Lockett's death sentence on July 3, 1978. The Court held that the Ohio statute in question unconstitutionally limited the presentation of mitigating evidence in violation of the Eighth and Fourteenth Amendments. In a related ruling, the justices left standing lower court orders that struck down comparable laws in New York and Pennsylvania.

In the principal opinion for the majority, Chief Justice Warren E. Burger stated that a death penalty statute could not preclude a sentencing authority from considering "as a mitigating factor, any aspect of the defendant's character or record and any of the circumstances of the offense that the defendant proffers as a basis for a sentence less than death." In keeping with the Court's traditional emphasis on the unique nature of capital cases, Burger observed the death sentence differed profoundly from other penalties in its irreversibility. The nonavailability of corrective remedies once the sentence was carried out underscored the need for individualized treatment in the imposition of the death penalty.

IMPACT: The immediate effect of *Lockett v. Ohio* was to invalidate the death sentences of approximately 100 inmates on Ohio's death row. The decision cast serious doubts as to the validity of capital punishment laws in two dozen other states. State legislatures subsequently moved to align their statutes with the principle established in *Lockett.*

In later rulings, the Supreme Court continued to insist on the broadest possible consideration of mitigating factors prior to sentencing. In *Eddings v. Oklahoma* (1982), the Court nullified a death sentence on the grounds the sentencing judge had refused to consider the defendant's history of emotional disturbance and turbulent family background. Exclusion of testimony that the defendant would adjust well to prison life was cause for reversing the death sentence in *Skipper v. South Carolina* (1986). In 1988 the Court found, in *Mills v. Maryland*, that a jury did not have to unanimously agree a mitigating circumstance existed before considering it in sentencing.

GODFREY V. GEORGIA (1980)

BACKGROUND: In **Gregg v. Georgia** the Supreme Court found that a provision of the Georgia code that allowed a person convicted of murder to be sentenced to death if the offense was "outrageously or wantonly vile, horrible or inhuman in that it involved torture, depravity of mind, or an aggravated battery to the victim" was not unconstitutional. Robert Godfrey was subsequently found guilty of two counts of murder and a single count of aggravated assault. The defendant, experiencing marital difficulties, had shot his wife and mother-in-law, killing both instantly. He also struck and injured his fleeing daughter with the barrel of a shotgun. At the sentencing phase of the trial, the jury relied on the provision in question in imposing the death penalty for each murder. The sentence was upheld by Georgia's highest court. The Supreme Court then agreed to consider Godfrey's charge that the definition of the aggravating circumstance for which he had received the death penalty was unconstitutionally vague.

LEGAL ISSUES: Godfrey v. Georgia presented the Supreme Court with two interrelated questions. The first was whether the Georgia law had been correctly applied in Godfrey's case. The Court could rule that the evidence did not support the jury's finding of the aggravating circumstance without overturning the provision on which it was based. The Court could also hold that the language in the statute was so broad and imprecise, or unconstitutionally vague, that it violated a defendant's right to clear sentencing standards.

DECISION: On May 19, 1980, the Supreme Court left standing the Georgia law but set aside Godfrey's death sentence imposed under the statute. In a plurality opinion announcing the judgment of the 6–3 majority, Justice Potter Stewart emphasized that a state which authorized capital punishment had a constitutional responsibility to design and apply its laws so as to avoid arbitrary and capricious infliction of the death penalty. In previous decisions, the Georgia Supreme Court had constrained use of the provision under which Godfrey was sentenced to instances evidencing serious physical abuse of the victim before death. The statute, however, had not been similarly limited in the case at hand. The Court concluded that there was "no principled way to distinguish this case, in which the death penalty was imposed, from the many cases in which it was not" and as such the sentence was improperly derived.

IMPACT: *Godfrey* marked the first time the Supreme court directly addressed the constitutionality of a given aggravating circumstance. Although the Court did not overturn the provision in question, *Godfrey* made clear the Court was exercising particular care to insure the administration of capital punishment did not revert to the kinds of standardless death sentence determinations ruled unconstitutional in **Furman v. Georgia.** The Court established a very different yardstick for aggravating circumstances than it had for mitigating circumstances in **Lockett v. Ohio.** The two decisions indicated that constitutional safeguards for a defendant facing a possible death sentence required the widest possible consideration of mitigating factors and a very precisely drawn and applied set of aggravating conditions.

ENMUND V. FLORIDA (1982)

BACKGROUND: Under Florida law, a killing committed during another major crime was a "felony murder" for which all the participants in the other crime were legally responsible. Earl Enmund was convicted of the murder of two persons during the course of a robbery at their farm house. The Supreme Court of Florida upheld his death sentence, although the trial record revealed that Enmund's involvement in the crime was limited to waiting outside in a car for his two accomplices at the time the killings occurred. The state's highest court ruled this was sufficient to establish Enmund as a principal in the first-degree murder. Enmund's appeal that the Eighth Amendment barred capital punishment in those instances where the defendant did not intend to take life was accepted for review by the Supreme Court.

LEGAL ISSUES: The question was not whether Enmund should have been convicted of a felony murder but whether he should receive the same sentence as those who were directly involved in the killing. Enmund maintained his punishment was disproportionate to his peripheral role in the crime. Florida's counsel noted that the law had long recognized the joint responsibility borne by all the accomplices to a given crime. Enmund actively took part in a felony that resulted in murder and then assisted the actual killers to escape.

DECISION: By a 5–4 margin, the Supreme Court on July 2, 1982, reversed Enmund's death sentence. Writing for the majority, Justice Byron White stated that death was an excessive and disproportionate punishment for a defendant who aided and abetted in the commission of a felony which resulted in murder but who neither killed, attempted to kill nor intended to kill the victim. Enmund's sentence was impermissibly cruel and unusual under the Eighth Amendment.

IMPACT: On its face, *Enmund v. Florida* seemed to establish a major new precedent that only those who were directly responsible for a homicide could receive the death sentence for the crime. Although the language of the decision was somewhat ambiguous, *Enmund* was widely viewed as prohibiting the execution of felons who neither actively participated in murder committed by their accomplices nor intended that the offense occur. Still, the Court's exact meaning in its use of the legal concept of intent was unclear.

The Supreme Court returned to the issue of intent in 1987. In *Tison v. Arizona* the Court held that an accomplice to felony murder was legally responsible for the crime if the person demonstrated a "reckless disregard for human life implicit in knowingly engaging in criminal activity known to carry a grave risk of death." Participation in such activity represented a "highly culpable mental state" which could be taken into account in capital sentencing judgments. Based on the fact 26 states authorized capital sentences for accomplices to felony murders, many saw the decision as leading to an expanded use of the death penalty.

BAREFOOT V. ESTELLE (1983)

BACKGROUND: In 1978 Thomas A. Barefoot was convicted of the murder of a police officer in Texas. At a separate sentencing hearing, the jury decided that the death penalty should be imposed. The Texas Court of Criminal Appeals rejected Barefoot's contention that the state's use of psychiatric testimony to predict the future dangerousness of capital defendants was unconstitutional. Successive appeals to the U.S. Supreme Court, again to the Texas Court of Criminal Appeals and then to a federal district court for the western part of Texas were likewise denied. Although the district court ruled against Barefoot's claim, it granted him a certificate of probable cause to appeal its judgment to the Fifth Circuit Court of Appeals. This appeal was filed in November 1982.

Texas authorities meanwhile set a new execution date of January 25, 1983. Another request for review and motion for stay of execution were subsequently turned down by the Texas Court of Criminal Appeals. In early January 1983, Barefoot petitioned the Fifth Circuit Court of Appeals for a stay of execution pending its consideration of his appeal of the district court ruling. The court of appeals heard arguments on this motion and, in turn, issued an order denying the stay.

On January 24, 1983, the Supreme Court agreed to consider Barefoot's contention that the court of appeals had erred in not granting a stay of execution while the appeal of the lower court's ruling was still pending. The Supreme Court's action halted his execution less than 11 hours before the scheduled time.

LEGAL ISSUES: *Barefoot v. Estelle* specifically addressed the narrow procedural question of the circuit court's actions. In a broader sense, the case illustrated the serious problems the mounting number of appeals in capital cases posed to the fair and timely administration of justice. The federal court system was struggling to distinguish substantive from frivolous appeals and to respond correctly to last-minute requests for stays of execution. The Supreme Court had to consider how best to balance the rights of defendants, the need for particular care in capital cases and the necessity of workable appeals procedures.

DECISION: On July 6, 1983, the Supreme Court ruled that the court of appeals had acted properly in its refusal to grant Barefoot a stay of execution even though the death row inmate's constitutional challenge to his sentence was technically still pending. In his majority opinion, Justice Byron R. White noted that the federal law governing the right to appeal prevented a prisoner from presenting his case to a federal appeals court unless the federal district court issued a certificate of probable cause. Once the certificate was granted, the appeals court was "obligated to decide the merits of the appeal." The appeals court was also required to issue a stay of execution if necessary to provide sufficient time to properly dispose of the appeal.

The majority found that the court of appeals had clearly considered the merits of Barefoot's appeal as part of its decision to deny his request for a stay of execution. The expedited process used by the appeals court, condensing the motions for appeal and stay of execution into one proceeding, was an acceptable handling of the case. Although the court of appeals had not specifically affirmed the fact it had ruled on Barefoot's appeal in its opinion, to conclude that the defendant had not had a full hearing "would be an unwarranted exaltation of form over substance."

The Supreme Court used *Barefoot v. Estelle* as a vehicle for issuing guidelines to the lower federal courts on the handling of appeals in death penalty cases. The subordinate courts were authorized to enact local rules which would implement these guidelines. In a general sense, the Court observed that appeals in the federal court system were only appropriate when a federal question was involved. Federal courts were not "forums in which to relitigate state trials." Similarly, repetitive appeals were not meant to function as a mechanism by which a defendant could delay an execution indefinitely. The appeals process was not a "legal entitlement" that a defendant had a right to pursue regardless of the substance of the issue in question.

The Court tightened the standards for separating meritorious from frivolous appeals. The different nature of the death penalty was a relevant consideration in deciding whether or not to grant an appeal, but the severity of the sanction did not justify automatic approval of an appeal in every case. A lower court should only allow an appeal to go forward if the petitioner had made a "substantial showing of the denial of a federal right" where the issues involved were at least "debatable among jurists of reason." When a court determined that these conditions were met, then the petitioner was entitled to a full hearing on the merits of the appeal. Circuit courts were encouraged to adopt and make known rules which would speed the appeals process. Expedited procedures were particularly appropriate in instances of second and successive appeals.

IMPACT: *Barefoot* was intended at least in part to relieve the burden on the Supreme Court of last-minute appeals in capital cases. The guidelines established by the Court, however, did not succeed in appreciably reducing either these appeals or the volume of death-penalty-related legal actions in general. In subsequent years a number of justices, most notably William H. Rehnquist and Lewis F. Powell Jr., have expressed their concern over the impact the growing number of appeals in death penalty cases was having on the entire criminal justice system. On several occasions, Justice Powell suggested publicly that if the issue could not be resolved, then the death penalty itself should be abandoned as unworkable.

In 1988, Chief Justice Rehniquest appointed then-retired Justice Powell to head a commission charged with finding ways to expedite the handling of capital appeals. The panel submitted its proposal for strict new limits on multiple appeals by death row inmates in 1989. Its recommendations have been incorporated into deliberations in the Senate over possible federal legislation in this area.

Underlying the debate over death-penalty appeals is the more basic struggle between proponents and opponents of capital punishment. Lawyers for death row inmates have a professional responsibility to pursue every possible avenue on the behalf of their clients. At the same time, many abolitionist groups believe that the generation of time-consuming and costly litigation will eventually lead the public to conclude that capital punishment is not worth the trouble its imposition causes.

PULLEY V. HARRIS (1984)

BACKGROUND: Robert A. Harris was convicted in a California court of killing two teenage boys to use their car for a bank robbery. He was sentenced to death. California's capital punishment statute did not require that a state appellate court conduct a "proportionality review" to insure that a given sentence was in line with other sentences imposed in the state for similar crimes. The California Supreme Court rejected Harris' claim that lack of this special review rendered the state's death penalty law invalid under the Constitution. Harris then shifted his appeal to the federal court system. The court of appeals subsequently held that the proportionality review was constitutionally required and directed the California Supreme Court to undertake such an analysis within 120 days. Otherwise, the appeals court would reverse Harris' sentence. State officials contested the decision to the U.S. Supreme Court.

LEGAL ISSUES: Harris' lawyers cited the Supreme Court's ruling in **Furman v. Georgia** that an arbitrary and capricious administration of the death penalty constituted cruel and unusual punishment under the Eighth Amendment. Without a comparative review of sentences, it was impossible to determine whether capital punishment was being imposed in an evenhanded and rational, or constitutional, manner. They argued that the Court's decisions in 1976 reinstating the death penalty had implicitly placed proportionality review on the level of a constitutional requirement. California officials maintained there were already sufficient safeguards in the state's procedures in capital cases to insure the death penalty was consistently and fairly applied.

DECISION: The Supreme Court sided with California. In a ruling announced January 23, 1984, the Court found that a state could carry out a death sentence without first conducting a proportionality review. The majority decision, written by Justice Byron R. White, stated that such a review was not required either by the Court's own death penalty precedents or by the Constitution's ban on cruel and unusual punishment.

Justice White observed that "any capital sentence may occasionally produce aberrational outcomes" but such inconsistencies were substantively different from the "major systemic defects" that led the Court to invalidate all existing death penalty laws in **Furman**. It was possible for a state to design a law which adequately protected against arbitrary executions without recourse to proportionality review. The fact the Court in 1976 had upheld Florida and Georgia statutes that included such review did not mean the procedure was indispensable. At the same time, the Court had found the Texas law, which did not contain proportionality review, was also constitutional.

IMPACT: Pulley v. Harris had little direct effect on the pace of executions in California, where most death row inmates were far from exhausting their appeals. The decision had a more immediate impact in Texas, the only state other than California without proportionality review to also have a sizeable death row population. The proportionality question was the only substantive basis of appeal remaining for a number of prisoners there.

In his opinion, Justice White was careful to distinguish between insuring a sentence was proportionate to the crime committed and the concept of proportionality review. He made it clear that the Court in *Pulley* was not retreating from the precedent established in cases such as **Coker v. Georgia** (where the death penalty was ruled an excessive punishment for rape) that capital punishment was only appropriate when it fit the crime.

FORD V. WAINWRIGHT (1986)

BACKGROUND: In 1974 Alvin B. Ford killed a Florida police officer while robbing a restaurant. He was convicted of murder and sentenced to death the same year. There was no suggestion of mental incompetence at the time of the offense, during his trail or at his sentencing hearing. After an extended period on Florida's death row, Ford began to show signs of serious mental disorder. His attorneys argued that he had gone insane and consequently should not be executed. At their request, the governor of Florida, following the procedures in state law for determining the competency of a condemned inmate, appointed a panel of three psychiatrists who interviewed Ford for approximately 30 minutes. When the panel reported, as required by state law, that the accused understood why he was to die, the governor signed a death warrant for his execution. After a series of unsuccessful appeals in state and lower federal courts, Ford's attorneys prevailed upon the Supreme Court to hear their claim that Florida's procedure for assessing the mental competency of convicted prisoners did not meet minimum due process standards.

LEGAL ISSUES: Ford's counsel argued that a 30-minute interview was insufficient to determine their client's sanity. State procedures, however, had stopped the attorneys from introducing additional information about his psychiatric condition. They contended that the fact Ford had not received an impartial hearing where all relevant evidence of his mental state could be considered was a violation of his due process rights under the Fourteenth Amendment. In a broader sense, *Ford v. Wainwright* raised the question of whether it was appropriate to inflict the death penalty on a person who was insane. Even if Ford were found to be mentally incompetent, there was no clear legal precedent which would preclude his execution.

DECISION: On June 26, 1986, the Supreme Court blocked Ford's execution, at least until Florida implemented new procedures to evaluate his sanity. These procedures had to meet basic standards of due process. At a minimum, this meant designation of an impartial board or officer to consider all available evidence to include psychiatric presentations or legal arguments made on behalf of the prisoner.

The Court went on to rule that the Eighth Amendment prohibited the execution of death row inmates who had become so insane they no longer understood they were going to be put to death or the reason why. In his majority opinion, Justice Thurgood Marshall wrote: "For centuries no jurisdiction has countenanced the execution of the insane, yet this Court has never decided whether the Constitution forbids the practice. Today we keep faith with our common-law heritage in holding that it does." Marshall concluded that the basic meaning of a punishment was negated if a person no longer comprehended its purpose. Execution of the insane was closer to "mindless vengeance" than it was to retribution.

IMPACT: *Ford*'s real significance was in the procedural safeguards it extended to prisoners who possibly suffered mental difficulties. Prior to the ruling, many states had essentially cursory procedures for testing for insanity. Interestingly, the Court also held that if a death row inmate who had been judged mentally incompetent was subsequently cured of the condition, then a state was free to go forward with the execution. Opponents of capital punishment pointed out the irony that an inmate who went insane had to remain insane to stay alive.

The decision was also important symbolically. The Court's statement that the Constitution did not allow the execution of the insane had no direct legal relevance because no state permitted such a proceeding. However, *Ford* represented a continued narrowing by the Court of those circumstances under which a person could be put to death.

MCCLESKEY V. KEMP (1987)

BACKGROUND: In October 1978 Warren McCleskey, a black man, was convicted of killing a white Atlanta police officer during an armed robbery. At the penalty phase of his trial, the jury of eleven whites and one black sentenced him to die in Georgia's electric chair. After Mc-

Cleskey lost two rounds of appeals in state and federal courts, the NAACP Legal Defense and Education Fund (LDF) took over his case.

LDF attorneys filed a new appeal in Federal District Court challenging the constitutionality of Georgia's death penalty law on the grounds that it was administered in a racially discriminatory manner. In support of this claim, they cited a study conducted by Professor David C. Baldus of the University of Iowa. The Baldus study was a detailed and sophisticated statistical analysis of over 2,000 murder cases in Georgia in the 1970s. The research indicated that black defendants were substantially more likely to receive the death sentence than white defendants. The disparity was even greater when the study compared the rate at which the death penalty was applied for black defendants who killed white victims as against white defendants who killed black victims. After the appeal was denied by both the district court and a circuit court of appeals, the Supreme Court agreed to hear the case.

LEGAL ISSUES: Since the early 1960s, the NAACP LDF had been engaged in defending black persons accused of capital crimes. At first, this activity was an outgrowth of the organizations's involvement in the civil rights movement. Most of the court cases took place in the South. However, by the mid-1960s the LDF had committed to a nationwide campaign to abolish capital punishment.

Many LDF lawyers had concluded from personal experiences that the death penalty was imposed in a discriminatory manner. In 1965 the organization initiated an exhaustive study of racial discrimination in the use of the death penalty for rape. The study revealed that blacks frequently were sentenced to death for raping a white women while whites who raped black women almost invariably were not. This statistical information was incorporated into a number of LDF challenges to capital punishment in the late 1960s and early 1970s. Although the Supreme Court did not specifically refer to racial bias in its 1972 decision striking down the nation's death penalty statutes, many of the opinions in **Furman v. Georgia** mentioned racial minorities as disproportionately affected by the capricious and arbitrary way capital punishment was administered.

When the Supreme court reinstated the death penalty in 1976, patterns of racial discrimination in capital sentencing again became an issue. LDF's legal argument on behalf of McCleskey had two parts. First, the fact that black defendants convicted of murder were treated differently than white defendants convicted of murder was a violation of the equal protection clause of the Fourteenth Amendment. This clause requires that the laws be applied equally and uniformly to all. There cannot be one system of justice for whites and another for blacks. The LDF also maintained that the Baldus study demonstrated that Georgia's death penalty was not being imposed in an evenhanded manner. Although the law had been ruled constitutional by the Court in 1976, the actual practice of capital punishment in Georgia still singled out blacks for the harshest penalties. The LDF argued the new death penalty statutes in Georgia were being applied in a way that did not meet the requirements the Court had established in **Furman** for fair and objective standards to guide capital sentencing decisions. McCleskey's counsel concluded this use of the death penalty was unconstitutional under the Eighth Amendment's ban on cruel and unusual punishment.

DECISION: A closely divided Supreme Court on April 22, 1987, ruled against McCleskey. The 5–4 majority accepted the validity of the Baldus study but held that it was not enough to prove actual discrimination against the individual defendant in the case at hand. Writing for the majority, Justice Lewis F. Powell Jr. allowed that the discretion provided to prosecutors and juries in the U.S. criminal justice system would inevitably lead to occasional abuses and disparities. For a defendant to show unconstitutional racial bias in a given death sentence, though, it was necessary to "prove that the decision makers in his case acted with discriminatory purpose." This proof required evidence specific to the case. A generalized study documenting "a discrepancy that appears to correlate with race" was insufficient.

The Court rejected the basic argument that statistics revealing a seeming disparity in sentencing were grounds for overturning Georgia's death penalty statute under the Fourteenth Amendment's equal protection provisions. The statistical evidence was not clear and convincing enough to warrant a finding of racial discrimination affecting the entire Georgia capital sentencing process. Similarly, the Baldus study by itself was not proof that the state's capital punishment system was arbitrary and capricious in application and that McCleskey's death sentence consequently was excessive in violation of the Eighth Amendment.

In previous decisions, the Court had approved the use of statistics in demonstrating instances of discrimination in areas such as employment. The majority found that drawing an inference of prejudice in a specific trial from broad statistics was substantively different from inferring discrimination in a wide range of employment practices.

Justice Powell characterized the claim that Georgia juries were more prone to sentence a black man to death as an attack on the fundamental role discretion played in the criminal justice system. He contended that the discretion afforded to a jury was, in fact, a criminal defendant's core "protection of life and liberty against race or color prejudice." To the extent racism still infected the criminal justice system, the answer was to surround the process by which guilt and punishment were determined with procedural safeguards.

In an unusual step, the Court revealed several associated concerns that had guided its finding. McCleskey's claim, taken to its logical conclusion, meant that not only death sentences but potentially all criminal penalties were impermissibly tainted by racism. Similarly, the methodology used in the Baldus study could be employed to allege patterns of discrimination involving other minority groups, gender or any other arbitrary variable such as physical attractiveness. Absent the most compelling evidence, the Court was reluctant to reach a conclusion in the *McCleskey* case which might undermine the basic workings of the criminal justice system.

IMPACT: *McCleskey v. Kemp* is considered the most important Supreme Court decision on capital punishment since the death penalty was restored in 1976. The ruling removed what abolitionists had called their last sweeping challenge to the constitutionality of the death penalty itself. Numerous court challenges to capital punishment statutes remained but none applicable to more than a fraction of the death row population. The immediate effect of *McCleskey* for the approximately 1,900 prisoners on death row was unclear. Although it was expected that the pace of executions would eventually quicken, the majority of the death row inmates had not yet exhausted their appeals on other issues.

Many opponents of capital punishment bitterly criticized the decision. They accused the Court of distorting established legal principles to avoid overturning numerous death sentences and creating disarray in the judicial system. Civil rights leaders also condemned the ruling. Legal experts pointed out that the Court had made it extremely difficult, if not impossible, to prove racial discrimination in the use of the death penalty. While it was possible to accumulate statistics evidencing a pattern of bias across a wide number of cases, it was an entirely different proposition to establish discriminatory intent in actions of a particular prosecutor, judge or jury.

BOOTH V. MARYLAND (1987)

BACKGROUND: A 1983 Maryland law provided for the use of "victim impact statements" in death sentencing hearings. John Booth was subsequently convicted of two counts of first-degree murder. Together with an accomplice, he had bound, gagged and stabbed to death an elderly couple in their Baltimore home during a robbery. At the sentencing phase of his trial, the prosecutor introduced a victim impact statement that described the personal characteristics of the victims and the emotional impact of their murders upon their family.

The state trial court refused to exclude the victim impact statement, rejecting the defendant's claim that its use in a capital case violated the Eighth Amendment. Based at least in part on the statement, the jury sentenced Booth to death. The Maryland Court of Appeals upheld the sentence, and Booth successfully petitioned the Supreme Court for review.

LEGAL ISSUES: Booth contended the victim impact statement was irrelevant to an appropriate consideration of the circumstances of his crime. Because of its inherently inflammatory nature, the statement had unduly influenced the jury in its deliberations. As a consequence, emotion rather than objective standards had guided the imposition of the death sentence in his case. This kind of subjective and capricious capital sentencing process was unconstitutional under the Eighth Amendment's ban on cruel and unusual punishment. Maryland officials maintained that a jury was entitled to consider any evidence which had a bearing on the sentencing decision. The victim impact statement served to inform the jury, as sentencing authority, of the full extent of harm caused by the crime.

DECISION: On June 11, 1987, the Supreme Court invalidated the Maryland law in question. The Court found that the introduction of a victim impact statement at the sentencing phase of a capital trial was unconstitutional.

A capital sentencing decision, Justice Lewis F. Powell Jr. wrote in the majority opinion, should center on the "blameworthiness" of the defendant. The victim impact statement created an unacceptable risk that a jury might impose the death penalty in an arbitrary and capricious manner in violation of the Eighth Amendment. A statement containing descriptions of the family's grief and suffering had the potential to divert a jury from its proper focus on the moral culpability of the defendant. Decisions on the death penalty had to be "based on reason rather than caprice or emotion." Many of the factors in a victim impact statement were irrelevant to the question of blameworthiness because they were unknown to the killer at the time of the crime.

Justice Powell pointed out that victim impact statements could lead to a double standard of justice. "We are troubled by the implication that defendants whose victims were assets to their community are more deserving of punishment than those whose victims are perceived to be less worthy."

In dissent, Justice Antonin Scalia emphasized the growing concern for victims' rights. He noted this concern stemmed from the feeling many citizens had that the criminal justice system increasingly failed to balance mitigating factors on behalf of a defendant against the harm that person caused to innocent members of society. He disputed the idea that blameworthiness was the only relevant consideration in death sentencing, observing that criminal codes routinely attached "more severe penalties to crimes based on the consequences to victims."

IMPACT: Justice Scalia's dissent was echoed by groups advocating the rights of crime victims. These organizations, which had become increasingly active in recent years, denounced *Booth v. Maryland* as a setback to legitimate efforts to furnish victims a more important role in the criminal justice process. At the time of the *Booth* ruling, 36 states and the federal government provided for the inclusion of victim impact statements in a variety of criminal proceedings. *Booth* made it clear that laws permitting the use of these statements at capital trials were unconstitutional. Many legal experts, noting the Supreme Court's historical tendency to treat the death penalty as different not only in degree but also in kind from other sanctions, believed it unlikely that subsequent decisions would extend the ban on victim impact statements to noncapital cases.

THOMPSON V. OKLAHOMA (1988)

BACKGROUND: William Wayne Thompson was 15 when he participated in the murder of his brother-in-law in January 1983. The prosecutor obtained an order allowing Thompson to be tried as an adult under the provisions of an Oklahoma statute which permitted such a proceeding if the court found the circumstances of the crime warranted the action and there were no reasonable prospects for rehabilitation of the defendant in the juvenile system. The young man was convicted of first-degree murder and sentenced to death. After the Oklahoma Court of Appeals rejected his contention that the execution of a minor constituted cruel and unusual punishment in violation of the Eighth Amendment, Thompson successfully petitioned the Supreme Court for review.

LEGAL ISSUES: The question before the Supreme Court was whether it was appropriate to execute a defendant for a capital offense committed while the person was a juvenile. The issue was not the age of the defendant at the time the execution would be carried out. Thompson was 21 when the Court considered his case. Rather, the challenge to the Court was to determine whether a person at age 15 could be held fully accountable for criminal actions. American jurisprudence had gradually evolved to the belief that minors were not responsible in the same way as adults for their behavior. However, there was no clear precedent for deciding at what age a juvenile could, or should, be treated as an adult.

DECISION: The Supreme Court on June 29, 1988, held that the execution under Oklahoma law of a defendant who was 15 at the time of the capital offense was unconstitutional. The five justices in the majority were unable to agree on a common opinion. In a plurality opinion, Justice John Paul Stevens stated the view of four of the five members of the majority that the execution of any person who committed a capital crime under age 16 offended contemporary standards of decency. It was excessive under the Eighth Amendment to punish with death a young person who was not yet "capable of acting with the degree of culpability" that would justify the ultimate penalty.

Justice Sandra Day O'Connor became the decisive or swing vote in the decision. Her opinion consequently expressed the basic consensus of the Court. She stopped short of declaring that all executions of defendants under 16 were unconstitutional. There was no conclusive evidence that the sentiment of society in general was against all such executions. However, she ruled that states could not sentence to death persons aged 15 or younger under capital punishment statutes which specified no minimum age standard for when the crime was committed.

IMPACT: Thompson v. Oklahoma effectively ended the execution of persons who committed capital offenses below the age of 16. No state had a capital punishment law that expressly allowed the execution of minors at this age, and none was considered likely to enact such a measure. The *Thompson* case had attracted international attention. Many opponents of capital punishment and others felt that the Supreme Court had not gone far enough in its decision. They argued that 18 should be the minimum age at which a person involved in a capital crime should be liable for the death penalty. In 1989 the Court declined to raise the minimum age when it upheld the death sentences of two defendants who committed their offenses at ages 16 and 17.

PENRY V. LYNAUGH (1989)

BACKGROUND: In late 1979 Johnny Paul Penry was arrested for the rape and murder of a Texas woman. At a competency hearing before his trial, a clinical psychologist testified that Penry was mentally retarded. He was evaluated as having the mental age of six-and-one-half. His social maturity, or ability to function in the world, was described as that of a nine- or ten-year-old child. The jury at the hearing found Penry competent to stand trial.

At the guilt-innocence phase of his trial, Penry's lawyers presented an insanity defense. The defendant was said to suffer from an organic brain disorder that resulted in an inability to learn and a lack of self-control. At the time of his offense, he did not grasp the difference between right and wrong and could not conform his behavior to the law. The prosecution countered with expert testimony that Penry was legally sane but had an antisocial personality. The jury rejected the insanity defense and convicted Penry of capital murder. During the penalty phase of his trial, he was sentenced to death.

The Texas Court of Criminal Appeals rejected the contention that Penry's sentence violated the Eighth Amendment. Although it denied a similar petition, a federal court of appeals noted that Penry's claim raised important issues. The Supreme Court subsequently decided to review the case.

LEGAL ISSUES: Penry's counsel argued first that Texas' capital punishment law was worded in such a way that it did not allow the jury to properly take into account the mental retardation of their client as a mitigating factor. The sentencing jury was instructed to include the evidence introduced at the trial in its deliberations. However, the aggravating circumstances presented to the jury were defined in a way that the fact of Penry's limited mental ability was made essentially irrelevant. At a more fundamental level, defense lawyers contended that the Eighth Amendment ban on cruel and unusual punishment prohibited the execution of the mentally retarded. Penry was not fully responsible, or culpable, for his actions and should not be punished as if he were.

DECISION: The Supreme Court agreed with Penry's lawyers on their procedural issue. On June 26, 1989, the Court reversed Penry's death sentence and instructed Texas officials to revise their sentencing procedures to insure that full consideration was given to a defendant's mitigating evidence of mental retardation. The Court again stressed the point it first had made in **Lockett v. Ohio** that a state's capital sentencing process had to provide for inclusion of any mitigating factor relevant to a defendant's background, character and crime.

By a 5–4 vote, the Court declined to state that the Eighth Amendment categorically barred the execution of the mentally retarded. Writing for the majority, Justice Sandra Day O'Connor observed the broad consensus against holding the severely retarded culpable for their actions. Retarded persons, though, were individuals whose abilities varied greatly. There was no basis to conclude that mentally impaired persons invariably lacked the capacity to act with the degree of responsibility which would justify use of the death penalty. Instead, the courts must make an individualized determination as to whether the death sentence is appropriate in each instance where retardation is a possible factor.

IMPACT: The decision in *Penry v. Lynaugh* has raised a number of difficult questions. Criminal justice experts estimate that roughly 10% of the death row population nationwide is at least mildly retarded. However, many of the inmates have never been formally evaluated for mental ability, and the number is at best an approximation. It is unclear what impact *Penry* will have on their legal status.

In large part, this uncertainty is due to the problems involved in determining mental retardation and its effect on criminal behavior. There is no single way to define retardation. In her opinion, Justice O'Connor noted that the concept of "mental age" was too imprecise to serve as a hard and fast rule for deciding whether to hold retarded persons accountable for their actions. In the aftermath of *Penry*, state criminal justice systems are struggling to find workable answers to the question of how retardation affects a person's ability to distinguish right from wrong, to act accordingly and even to participate in a criminal proceeding.

CHAPTER 4

BIOGRAPHICAL LISTING

This chapter contains brief biographical sketches on a cross-section of significant figures in the history of capital punishment in the United States. Each entry provides the years of birth and, when applicable, death, identifies the relationship of the individual to the issue of capital punishment and describes the person's pertinent involvement and impact.

Anthony G. Amsterdam (1935–)   A prominent law professor and constitutional expert, Amsterdam directed the NAACP Legal Defense and Education Fund's campaign to have the death penalty declared unconstitutional. He is widely considered the leading figure in the legal struggle over capital punishment. Amsterdam has argued numerous capital cases before the Supreme Court.

Cesare Beccaria (1738–1794)   An Italian jurist, Beccaria was the first modern writer to urge complete abolition of the death penalty. His book *Essay on Crimes and Punishment*, published in 1764, is considered the single most influential work on criminal justice reform. Beccaria argued that the certainty of punishment was more effective as a deterrent than the severity and that penalties should be proportionate to the crime. His ideas strongly influenced early American abolitionists.

Hugo Adam Bedau (1926–)   Chairman of the philosophy department at Tufts University since 1966, Bedau has been a leading opponent of capital punishment for the past 30 years. His anthology *The Death Penalty in America*, first published in 1964 and revised periodically since, is considered the authoritative work on the subject.

Marvin H. Bovee (1827–1888)   As a state senator, Bovee led the successful fight to repeal the death penalty in Wisconsin in 1853. He subsequently dedicated himself over the next 30 years to ending capital punishment nationwide. At a time when the country was absorbed by the issues of the Civil War, his efforts generated little support. Nonetheless, his perseverance kept the question of capital punishment an object of public debate.

William J. Brennan Jr. (1906–) Nominated by President Eisenhower, Brennan joined the Supreme Court as an associate justice in 1956. In numerous opinions, he argued the death penalty constitutes cruel and unusual punishment under the Constitution and should be prohibited.

Edmund G. Brown (1905–) As Governor of California (1959–1967), Brown opposed the continuance of capital punishment in the state. He sought without success to have the death penalty repealed. Brown subsequently headed the National Commission on Reform of Federal Criminal Laws which issued a report in 1971 critical of capital punishment.

Theodore R. Bundy (1946–1989) The subject of numerous books and a television miniseries, "The Deliberate Stranger," the case of Ted Bundy fascinated and horrified America. An intelligent and attractive young man, he was also one of the most infamous serial killers in the nation's history. Sentenced to death in Florida in 1980 for the murder of a 12-year-old girl, Bundy was executed on January 24, 1989, after many appeals and delays. In his final days he reportedly confessed to killing at least 20 young women in five states. Bundy was frequently cited by advocates of capital punishment as an example of the kind of criminal who merited the death penalty.

Warren E. Burger (1907–) Chief Justice of the Supreme Court from 1969 to 1986, Burger presided over several landmark judicial rulings on capital punishment. He was in the minority when the Court declared the nation's death penalty laws unconstitutional in 1972. Four years later, Burger was part of the majority which authorized a resumption of executions.

George H. W. Bush (1924–) Considered a moderate Republican earlier in his political career, Bush moved toward the conservative wing of his party during his tenure as vice-president in the Reagan administration. In the 1988 presidential campaign, he stressed his support for the death penalty in contrast to Democratic candidate Dukakis' opposition to the measure. As president, Bush has continued to call for wider use of capital punishment.

Albert Camus (1913–1960) A French intellectual and author who won the Nobel Prize for Literature. Camus wrote a powerful critique of the death penalty in 1957. His essay "Reflections on the Guillotine" contributed to the growing debate over capital punishment in the United States in the late 1950s. Camus' ideas and the response they provoked became part of an ultimately successful effort to repeal the death penalty in France.

Truman Capote (1924–1984)   Capote was the best known writer of his generation to oppose capital punishment. His controversial 1968 TV documentary "Death Row, USA," strongly criticized the practice.

Caryl Chessman (1921–1960)   In trouble with the law since his youth, Chessman was convicted in 1948 of kidnapping with bodily injury, a crime he insisted he did not commit, and was sentenced to death. While on death row in California, Chessman discovered a natural talent for writing and authored three books against capital punishment which won him an international audience. He became "the world's most famous prisoner," and his case provoked the largest public outcry against the death penalty since the Sacco and Vanzetti trial 30 years earlier. After 12 years of legal maneuvering, Chessman was executed on May 2, 1960.

William Ramsey Clark (1927–   )   As attorney general in the Johnson administration, Clark was the first and only head of the Justice Department to call for an end to the death penalty. In testimony before Congress, he urged elimination of the federal death sentence. Since leaving office, Clark has remained a prominent and active opponent of capital punishment.

Mario M. Cuomo (1932–   )   Governor of New York since 1983, Cuomo has earned a national reputation for his forceful and outspoken opposition to capital punishment. He has successfully resisted efforts to reimpose the death penalty in his state, vetoing reinstatement measures each year in office.

Newton M. Curtis (1835–1910)   Elected to the U.S. House of Representatives from New York in 1890, Curtis was the first member of Congress to introduce legislation that would terminate the federal death penalty. Although Congress did not approve his abolitionist proposals, in 1897 it enacted his bill to greatly reduce the number of federal capital offenses.

Clarence S. Darrow (1857–1938)   A renowned criminal lawyer, Darrow was an ardent opponent of the death penalty. In a famous trial in 1924, he persuaded the judge to sentence Nathan Leopold and Richard Loeb, young men convicted of kidnapping and murder, to life imprisonment rather than death. The verdict infused new energy into the abolitionist movement nationwide. The following year he helped found the American League to Abolish Capital Punishment. Darrow continued to attack capital punishment in various lectures and in his autobiography in 1935.

Michael S. Dukakis (1933–)   Governor of Massachusetts from 1975–1979 and again since 1983, Dukakis was the Democratic Party's nominee for president in 1988. His opponent, Vice-President George Bush, sought to make their differences over capital punishment a major issue in the campaign. Political analysts believe Dukakis' candidacy was seriously weakened by his opposition to the death penalty.

Herbert B. Ehrmann (1891–1970)   Ehrmann was deeply affected by his experience as a defense attorney in the Sacco and Vanzetti case. Together with his wife Sara R. Ehrmann, he became active in the movement to abolish capital punishment. He published two books critical of the Sacco-Vanzetti verdict as well as articles on the death penalty and the criminal justice system.

Gary M. Gilmore (1941?–1977)   Gilmore was the first person put to death following the Supreme Court decision in 1976 reinstating the death penalty. His case attracted worldwide attention and eventually became the subject of a Pulitzer Prize-winning book, *The Executioner's Song*, by Norman Mailer. Gilmore refused to contest his pending death sentence and twice attempted to commit suicide when appeals filed by various legal groups opposed to capital punishment threatened to block his execution. He was shot by a Utah firing squad on January 17, 1977.

Horace Greeley (1812–1872)   In 1841 Greeley founded the *New York Tribune*. He used the influential newspaper as a nationwide platform to campaign for a number of reform causes to include the abolition of capital punishment. A frequent lecturer across the country, Greeley provided many rural Americans their first exposure to arguments against the death penalty.

Jack Greenberg (1924–)   As director of the NAACP Legal Defense and Education Fund (1961 to 1984), Greenberg coordinated the legal campaign against capital punishment which resulted in the Supreme Court striking down the nation's death penalty laws in 1972. He participated in several of the most important cases argued before the Court. Following the reinstatement of capital punishment in 1976, Greenberg maintained his organization's leading role in the legal fight against the death penalty.

Arthur Koestler (1905–1983)   A renowned Hungarian-born author who became a British subject, Koestler was deeply involved in the successful campaign to abolish the death penalty in his adopted country. His 1955 book *Reflections on Hanging*, a critical study of the death penalty in Great Britain and an indictment of the practice in general, is considered among the classic works on the subject. Published in the United States in 1957, the book has had a major impact on abolitionist activity.

Lewis E. Lawes (1883–1947)   In his 20 years as warden of Sing Sing prison in New York, Lawes took part in hundreds of electrocutions. His first-hand experience with criminals and his study of death sentence statistics led him to conclude capital punishment was misguided and wrong. A founder and later chairman of the American League to Abolish Capital Punishment, he presented his views in six books and numerous articles and speeches.

Edward Livingston (1764–1836)   Livingston's long career in the law and politics culminated in his service as secretary of state under President Andrew Jackson. As a member of the Louisiana Assembly in the early 1820s, he introduced several new arguments against capital punishment: the risk of executing the innocent, the ineffectiveness of the death penalty as a deterrent and the problems the sanction posed in the administration of justice. Livingston's writings had a major impact across the nation and in Europe. Considered by many the preeminent American abolitionist, he raised issues that continue to shape the terms of the debate over capital punishment today.

Thurgood Marshall (1908–   )   Director of the NAACP's Legal Defense and Education Fund from 1940 until 1961, Marshall was nominated by President Johnson and confirmed as an associate justice of the Supreme Court in 1967. While on the Court, he has consistently voted against capital punishment. Marshall has frequently stated his belief the death penalty is unconstitutional in all circumstances.

Edwin Meese III (1931–   )   As an assistant to then-Governor of California Ronald Reagan, Meese helped coordinate the successful referendum drive to restore the death penalty in the state. Counselor to the president and attorney general in the Reagan administration, he was an outspoken advocate of capital punishment.

John L. O'Sullivan (1813–1895)   A champion of American expansionism (he coined the term "Manifest Destiny"), O'Sullivan advocated repeal of the death penalty. He believed that capital punishment was incompatible with the "democratic genius" of the United States. O'Sullivan's 1841 report to the New York Assembly, written while he was a member, became one of the most influential abolitionist appeals of the time.

Lewis F. Powell Jr. (1907–   )   Powell was nominated to the Supreme Court by President Nixon and took his seat as an associate justice in 1972. Considered the swing vote on many issues during his years on the Court, he cast the decisive ballot in many important capital punishment decisions. He retired in 1987. Since the mid-1980s, Powell has suggested that if a solution could not be found to the protracted appeals process in capital cases, then the death penalty should be abandoned as unworkable.

Robert Rantoul Jr. (1805–1852)   The leading American opponent of capital punishment in the 1830s and 1840s, Rantoul served as president of the Massachusetts Society for the Abolition of Capital Punishment and assisted in reform efforts nationwide. In his writings, he strongly contested the inherent right of society to inflict the death penalty.

Ronald W. Reagan (1911–   )   Reagan first came to the forefront of the capital punishment debate as governor of California from 1967–1975. When the California Supreme Court ruled the state's death penalty unconstitutional in 1972, he initiated a successful campaign for passage of a referendum amending the constitution to restore capital punishment. As president, Reagan spoke out frequently in defense of the death penalty. He vigorously supported enactment by the Congress of legislation in 1988 which made drug-related murders a federal capital offense.

William H. Rehnquist (1924–   )   Confirmed as an associate justice during the Nixon presidency, Rehnquist became chief justice of the Supreme Court in 1986. Throughout his tenure on the Court, he has maintained the issue of capital punishment should be decided in the legislative branch of government. More recently, he has criticized the lengthy appeals process involved in capital cases. As chief justice, Rehnquist has attempted to find ways to reduce the volume of these legal actions.

Benjamin Rush (1745–1813)   A signer of the Declaration of Independence as well as a leading physician in his native Pennsylvania, Rush was the first prominent American to publicly oppose capital punishment. In 1787 he published the first of several essays calling for the complete abolition of the death penalty. Rush is credited with building support for the elimination of many death penalty statutes in the early 19th century.

Sacco & Vanzetti   Nicola Sacco (1891–1927), a shoemaker, and Bartolomeo Vanzetti (1888–1927), a fish peddler, were Italian-born anarchists who became the central figures in one of the most controversial trials of the century. Maintaining their innocence to the end, the two men were executed on August 23, 1927, for the 1920 murder of a shoe factory paymaster and guard in South Braintree, Massachusetts. Their supporters claimed that guilt had been established on inconclusive evidence and that the two men were convicted at least in part for their radical political beliefs. Defense attorneys filed numerous unsuccessful motions and appeals in state and federal court in what was the first instance of a now-common protracted legal struggle over a death sentence.

Henry Schwarzschild (1925–)   Schwarzschild has served as the director of the Capital Punishment Project of the American Civil Liberties Union since 1976. He was the founder and first executive director of the National Coalition to Abolish the Death Penalty.

Thorsten Sellin (1896–)   Affiliated with the University of Pennsylvania throughout his professional life, Sellin was one of the most important American criminologists of the century. He based his opposition to the death penalty on a detailed study of the subject. He wrote numerous scholarly books and articles. Sellin's expertise led to frequent invitations to testify before legislative hearings on capital punishment.

John A. Spenkelink (1948?–1979)   Spenkelink was the second person executed after the Supreme Court reinstated the death penalty in 1976. Unlike Gary Gilmore, he fought his death sentence to the last moment. For this reason, many viewed his case as signaling a full resumption of executions in America. Numerous abolitionist individuals and groups joined in efforts to halt his execution. Spenkelink was electrocuted on May 25, 1979.

Ernest van den Haag (1914–)   A leading conservative intellectual who has written extensively on capital punishment since the late 1960s, van den Haag is widely viewed as the most influential advocate of the death penalty today. He has consistently maintained the sanction is morally justified for certain crimes and that it does, in fact, serve as a deterrent.

Bartolomeo Vanzetti   See Sacco & Vanzetti.

PART II

GUIDE TO
FURTHER RESEARCH

CHAPTER 5

INFORMATION ON CAPITAL PUNISHMENT

There is no shortage of information on capital punishment. Sources include an extensive body of books and articles and a considerable range of nonprint and audiovisual (AV) materials. Many of the organizations involved in the issue maintain brochures, pamphlets and other educational resources. This chapter is a brief primer on research into the death penalty. After describing the principal reference tools used in finding information on capital punishment, it then profiles some of the primary works on the subject.

A standard, medium-sized municipal or school library will contain most of the information on capital punishment normally sought by students and others interested in the topic. Several basic library reference resources are an indispensable aid to identifying and locating materials on the death penalty.

CARD CATALOGS

The card catalog remains a key reference tool. It is a central inventory of a library's holdings, from books and periodicals to AV materials and microfilms. The catalog contains individual bibliographic citations on all items in the library. Rather than consolidate all holdings in a single catalog, some libraries maintain separate ones for AV materials, non-circulating reference works, government documents and special collections.

Most libraries utilize the traditional manual card catalog. A growing number of facilities are converting to automated systems. The advent of automated catalogs has marked a parallel trend toward interlibrary networks. Computers allow libraries to cross-reference holdings more readily. With this capability, public and school facilities are joining in cooperative lending systems. A library that is part of such a network now has access to vastly enlarged resources.

AUTOMATED SYSTEMS

Automated, or computer-based, information systems and services have emerged as major research tools. On-line and CD ROM systems offer quick access to numerous databases encompassing a broad range of subjects. On-line means the library, as a subscriber, is tapped into a regional, national or international database network over a phone line. CD ROM is a system of information storage on laser disks for use with microcomputers.

Most of these databases furnish bibliographic citations and abstracts of articles, documents, books and reports. Some provide the full text of articles. Political, legislative and judicial developments continually change the status of the death penalty in American society. Computer-based systems are particularly helpful because they are updated frequently and therefore capture the most current resources.

Several automated databases and information systems are valuable guides to the expansive book and periodical literature on capital punishment. *InfoTrac*, which indexes mainstream and generally accessible periodical sources, is easy to use and widely available. It provides bibliographic records from more than 900 business, technical and general interest magazines and newspapers. *InfoTrac* covers the current year plus the 3 preceding years. *WILSONLINE* provides the full range of printed H. W. Wilson Co. indexes. Users have access to *Reader's Guide to Periodical Literature*, *Book Review Digest*, *Social Science Index* and *Humanities Index*. These and the other indexes available on *WILSONLINE* identify some of the most recent capital punishment sources.

INDEXES

Indexes are an integral part of a library's reference complement. These guides compile citations on books, magazine literature, newspaper articles, scholarly tracts, government publications, film strips, audio recordings and historical materials. There is significant overlap of the book- or pamphlet-form indexes and the automated information systems. Some guides appear both in the traditional printed form and in automation. Other indexes are converting from print to computer-based systems.

Book Review Index is a guide to book reviews published in over 300 magazines and newspapers. This bimonthly publication furnishes just the citation to the reviews. The monthly *Book Review Digest* provides citations to reviews of current English-language fiction and nonfiction. In addition, the *Digest* prints excerpts from the reviews, which are drawn from some 90 selected periodicals and journals. A good source for annotated citations to reference books is Sheehy's *Guide to Reference Books*.

Major city daily newspapers can be excellent sources on many aspects of capital punishment. The *New York Times* gives full coverage to major legal, political, social and cultural developments. The *New York Times Index* is an invaluable research tool for anyone interested in contemporary death penalty issues. It concisely summarizes all articles and gives citations to the dates, pages and columns on which they appeared. Back issues of the *New York Times* and some other major dailies are recorded on microfilm. The *Newspaper Index* is a monthly publication that indexes major newspapers such as the *Chicago Tribune, Los Angeles Times, Denver Post, Detroit News* and *San Francisco Chronicle*.

The periodical literature on capital punishment is vast. Two sources stand out as useful in finding articles in mainstream publications. *Reader's Guide to Periodical Literature* indexes more than 200 general-interest periodicals published in the United States; *Magazine Index* compiles citations to the approximately 370 popular magazines and professional journals. Other indexes track the periodical literature on subject areas in the social sciences and liberal arts. *Social Science Index, Humanities Index* and *Education Index* cite articles from publications devoted to these disciplines.

The *Encyclopedia of Associations* is standard to any basic library reference collection. A guide to national and international organizations, it provides short explanatory abstracts on each entry. The *Encyclopedia of Associations: Regional, State and Local Organizations* is a seven-volume, geographically-organized guide to more than 50,000 nonprofit organizations on the state, city and local levels. Both of these indexes also are available on-line.

GOVERNMENT DOCUMENTS

The federal and state governments issue a variety of information on capital punishment. These materials are made available to the public through the depository library system. A depository member library—possibly a college facility or a municipal library—receives government publications and maintains a government documents collection. The *Monthly Catalog of United States Government Publications* has bibliographic entries for virtually all documents published by federal agencies, including books, reports, studies and serials. The *Monthly Catalog* also is on CD ROM. This version is called *GPO Silverplatter*.

The *Index to U.S. Government Periodicals* covers periodicals of the federal government. *Congressional Information Service Index* (CIS), a directory to the publications of the U.S. Congress, is an excellent source. It is the primary tool for locating documents issued by the various committees of both houses of Congress: hearings, committee prints, reports, treaties and public laws. This source is issued in two parts. One volume is the index. The other volume contains abstracts on the cited publications.

The methods for cataloging public documents vary. Generally, libraries will maintain a separate catalog for federal and state government sources. Certain government documents may also be housed in the reference or general book collections, in which event they most likely are listed in the main card catalog.

The *Congressional Quarterly Almanac* is considered the preeminent readily accessible source on the federal government. It provides a thorough overview of political and legislative developments and reviews the major activities of Congress, the White House and the Supreme Court.

LEGAL RESEARCH

The law and the courts have played a key role in the evolution of capital punishment in the past quarter century. Familiarity with a few basic legal research tools will benefit anyone who is interested in following legal developments. Morris L. Cohen's *How to Find the Law* is a helpful guide for newcomers to legal research. It discusses basic techniques and describes the main references encountered in researching court decisions and legislative history. *The Guide to American Law: Everyone's Legal Encyclopedia*, a comprehensive source written for the layperson, covers all aspects of the American legal system and includes helpful articles on landmark court cases.

Decisions of the United States Supreme Court (The Lawyer's Cooperative Publishing Company, volumes since 1965) is an excellent guide for the legal novice. Cases ruled on by the nation's high court are reviewed and summarized in the series. Yearly volumes coincide with completed terms of the court. The *New York Times* also is good on major Supreme Court rulings. Normally, the *Times* will have extensive background coverage and analysis, along with excerpts from the majority decision.

Several indexes can also prove helpful. The *Index to Legal Periodicals* includes a subject and author index, a separate table of cases and a book review index. *Criminal Justice Abstracts* and *Criminal Justice Periodicals Index* make reference to books, articles, government publications and other legal materials.

Computerized research can accelerate dramatically the process of locating legal resources. But these on-line services are expensive and legal nonprofessionals invariably have problems gaining access to them. The two leading services are *LEXIS* (Meade Data) and *WESTLAW* (West Publishing Company). Both are full-text databases containing federal and state case law, statutes and administrative regulations.

Capital punishment is a complex and controversial topic. Following is a discussion of some basic sources which cover the major aspects and issues involved. Publication information can be found in Chapter 6.

The basic source book on capital punishment in the United States is Hugo Adam Bedau's *The Death Penalty in America*. The work is an anthology of writings by leading authorities on all aspects of the death penalty. Bedau's several introductory chapters provide background information and a general overview of the issue. Earlier editions published in 1964 and 1967 still remain useful.

Bedau is among the foremost experts on capital punishment. He has written extensively on the subject and any of his works is an excellent source. His *Death is Different: Studies in the Morality, Law, and Politics of Capital Punishment* is a comprehensive examination of the subject.

Several other general texts provide an overview of capital punishment. A broad discussion is found in *The Penalty of Death* by Thorsten Sellin. *Capital Punishment in the United States: A Consideration of the Evidence* by Sarah T. Dike is a thorough examination of the entire subject. It includes an analysis of the major issues involved in the use of the death penalty. *Legal Homicide: Death as Punishment in America, 1864–1982* by William J. Bowers contains extensive data on executions over the past century.

Three earlier anthologies that continue to provide valuable information and perspectives are: *Capital Punishment*, edited by Thorsten Sellin; *Capital Punishment*, edited by James A. McCafferty; and *Capital Punishment in the United States*, edited by Hugo Adam Bedau and Chester M. Pierce.

The results of a recent study on capital punishment in America conducted by the human rights organization Amnesty International can be found in *United States of America: The Death Penalty*. The group, which maintains a national office in New York City, also is a source of information on capital punishment around the world. Its address and telephone number are included in Chapter 7.

Many of the general works have sections on the historical background of capital punishment. *When Men Play God: The Fallacy of Capital Punishment* by Eugene B. Block opens with a discussion of the death penalty in early times. The introductory essay in *Voices Against Death*, edited by Philip E. Mackey, traces the 200-year history of the abolitionist movement in the United States. In *Cruel and Unusual: The Supreme Court and Capital Punishment*, Michael Meltsner recounts the legal campaign mounted against the death penalty in the 1960s and early 1970s.

Voices Against Death also contains excerpts from the writings and statements of leading abolitionists in American history. Among those included are Walt Whitman, Horace Greeley and Clarence Darrow. A similar compendium of contemporary abolitionist statements is *A Punishment in Search of Crime: Americans Speak Out Against the Death Penalty*, edited by Ian Gray and Moira Stanley.

The debate over capital punishment is well-documented in the general sources cited above. Several specific studies also are worth noting. *Capital Punishment: The Inevitability of Caprice and Mistake*, 2d edition, by Charles L. Black Jr., is considered one of the most important and effective critiques of the death penalty in recent years. Black focuses on the impossibility of ever insuring capital punishment is administered in an evenhanded and foolproof way.

Other critics have concentrated on the apparent racial discrimination in the imposition of the death penalty. Both *Death and Discrimination: Racial Disparities in Capital Sentencing* by Samuel R. Gross and Robert Mauro and *Equal Justice and the Death Penalty: A Legal and Empirical Analysis* by David C. Baldus, George C. Woodworth and Charles A. Pulaski Jr. make the case that use of the death penalty is flawed by racial bias.

For Capital Punishment: Crime and the Morality of the Death Penalty by Walter Berns is widely viewed as a forceful statement of the arguments for retaining the sanction. Another frequently cited source is Ernest van den Haag's *Punishing Criminals: Concerning a Very Old and Painful Question*. Van den Haag generally is acknowledged as the preeminent scholarly advocate of the pro death penalty position.

The issue of capital punishment is tied integrally to the law. Each of the general works already mentioned addresses the various legal aspects of the subject. The major law journals, such as *Columbia Law Review*, *Harvard Law Review*, *Stanford Law Review* and *Yale Law Journal*, frequently publish articles, analyses and synopses of major court cases. Several publications of the American Bar Association, *American Bar Foundation Research Journal* and *American Criminal Law Review*, are likewise a source of information on recent legal developments concerning the death penalty.

Several journals in the field of criminology often publish pieces on capital punishment. *Crime and Delinquency* and the *Journal of Criminal Law and Criminology* have dedicated entire issues to the legal and sociological ramifications of the sanction. Other serials that explore the relationship of the death penalty to the criminal justice system include *Criminology* and *Criminal Justice and Behavior*. The November 1986 issue of the United Nations' *Crime Prevention and Criminal Justice Newsletter* provides an international overview of capital punishment.

A number of renowned authors have turned to the question of the death penalty. Norman Mailer's *The Executioner's Song*, which won the Pulitzer Prize, is a fictionalized account of the life and death of Gary Gilmore. Truman Capote based his now-classic work *In Cold Blood* on his research into the actual murder of a Kansas family and the execution of two men for the crime. In "Reflections on the Guillotine," an essay in *Resistance, Rebellion and Death*, Albert Camus pondered and finally rejected the death penalty. Arthur Koestler likewise condemned capital punishment in a famous treatise, *Relections on Hanging*.

Released in the summer of 1988, the film *The Thin Blue Line* is an examination of the conviction and sentencing to death of a possibly innocent man. The documentary, by Errol Morris, raises many of the difficult questions inherent to capital punishment. Now available on video cassette, it can be located in the audiovisual collections of many libraries. Other readily accessible film studies of capital punishment include the prize-winning *The Death Penalty* and *Death Row and the Death Penalty*.

Several organizations are prominently involved in death penalty education and information activities. Both the Capital Punishment Project of the ACLU and the National Coalition to Abolish the Death Penalty (NCADP) make available numerous brochures, pamphlets and other resource materials on capital punishment. The National Execution Alert Network, located with the NCADP, tracks and monitors pending executions across the nation. The NAACP Legal Defense Fund maintains comprehensive information and statistics on the death row population and executions. (See Chapter 7 for the addresses and the telephone numbers of these organizations.)

Each year the Bureau of Justice Statistics publishes a report, *National Prisoner Statistics—Capital Punishment*, on the use of the sanction in the United States. Information on the volume and rate of capital crimes is reported annually by the Federal Bureau of Investigation in its *Uniform Crime Reports*. Also part of the Department of Justice, the National Institute of Justice operates a National Criminal Justice Reference Service. The service includes an information clearinghouse. Reference specialists are available to respond to a wide range of queries and requests for information on criminal justice issues.

CHAPTER 6

ANNOTATED BIBLIOGRAPHY

This chapter is an annotated bibliography of capital punishment sources. It includes materials drawn from a broad spectrum of print and other media. Separate listings are provided for bibliographies, books, encyclopedias, periodicals, articles, government documents, brochures and pamphlets and audiovisual materials. Each item is identified by a standard library citation. A brief annotation then describes the resource's contents and scope.

There is a large volume of information on capital punishment. Two basic rules have guided the inclusion of materials in this bibliography. First, emphasis is on sources which are available in a medium-sized public or school library. Second, items have been selected for their usefulness to students and others doing general research on the death penalty. Readers desiring further specialized information should consult either the listing of bibliographies in this chapter or the discussion of reference sources in Chapter 5.

BIBLIOGRAPHIES

Abel, Ernest L. *Homicide: A Bibliography*. Westport, CT: Greenwood Press, 1987.

Extensive scientific references dealing with homicide through 1984.

Annotated Bibliography

Bedau, Hugo Adam. A survey of the debate on capital punishment in Canada, England, and the United States, 1948–1958. *Prison Journal* 38 (1958): 35–45.

Examines laws and debates during the specific time period and has an extensive bibliography including 119 entries on the death penalty between 1948 and 1958.

Beyleveld, Deryck. *A Bibliography of General Deterrence Research.* Westmead, England: Saxon House, 1980.

Covers English-language deterrence research published between 1946 and 1978.

Cook, Earleen H. *Death Penalty Since Witherspoon and Furman.* Monticello, IL: Vance Bibliographies, 1979.

An unannotated bibliography to articles and books, 1968–1979.

Dikijian, Armine. Capital punishment: a selected bibliography, 1940–1968. *Crime and Delinquency* 15 (1969): 162–164.

A list of 20 articles and 38 books published in that time period.

Lyons, Douglas B. Capital punishment: a selected bibliography. *Criminal Law Bulletin* 8 (1972): 783–802.

Categorized but not annotated, the bibliography concentrates on materials published after 1968.

Meyer, Herman H. B. *Select List of References on Capital Punishment.* Washington, DC: U.S. Government Printing Office, 1912.

Lists 282 items published before 1912.

Miller, Alan V. *Capital Punishment as a Deterrent: A Bibliography.* Monticello, IL: Vance Bibliographies, 1980.

Recent works on deterrence and capital punishment; a 10-page list.

Radelet, Michael L., and Margaret Vandiver. *Capital Punishment in America: An Annotated Bibliography.* New York: Garland Publishing, 1988.

An annotated listing of more than 950 books and articles on capital punishment. Includes citations to relevant congressional publications and brief synopses of major Supreme Court decisions.

Triche, Charles W. *The Capital Punishment Dilemma, 1950–1977, A Subject Bibliography.* Troy, NY: Whitston, 1979.

Not annotated, this 278-page work contains a sizable number of newspaper article citations.

BOOKS
GENERAL

Amnesty International. *The Death Penalty.* London: Amnesty International Publications, 1979.

A comprehensive source of international data on the death penalty, including its history and current status by country. Amnesty International advocates the abolition of capital punishment.

Amnesty International. *United States of America: The Death Penalty.* London: Amnesty International Publications, 1987.

Comprehensive resource on the death penalty in the United States resulting from a study conducted by the human rights group.

Archer, Dane, and Rosemary Gartner. *Violence and Crime in Cross-National Perspective.* New Haven, CT: Yale University Press, 1984.

Provides information on major crimes for 100 countries, exploring such trends as an increase or decrease in homicide rates if the death penalty is abolished.

Atholl, Justin. *Shadow of the Gallows.* London: John Long, 1954.

A history of capital punishment in England.

Barfield, Velma. *Woman on Death Row.* Nashville: Oliver-Nelson, 1985.

An autobiographical account of a conviction for quadruple murder and subsequent religious conversion before the author's execution in 1984.

Bedau, Hugo Adam. *Death is Different: Studies in the Morality, Law and Politics of Capital Punishment.* Boston: Northeastern University Press, 1987.

A collection of the author's essays, revised for this edition.

————, ed. *The Death Penalty in America.* 3d ed. New York: Oxford University Press, 1982.

A leading, comprehensive examination of the issue.

Bedau, Hugo Adam, and Chester M. Pierce, eds. *Capital Punishment in the United States.* New York: AMS Press, 1976.

A collection of essays on the subject, published for the American Orthopsychiatric Association.

Beeman, Lamar, ed. *Selected Articles on Capital Punishment.* New York: H. W. Wilson, 1925.

Although dated, this compendium includes extensive information about the status of the death penalty at the time.

Block, Eugene B. *When Men Play God: The Fallacy of Capital Punishment.* San Francisco: Cragmont Publishers, 1983.

A general overview of the abolitionist movement in several contexts, including historical and international.

Bowers, William J. *Executions in America.* Lexington, MA: Lexington Books, 1974.

Reviews the history of capital punishment in America, focusing on the issue of racial bias.

Bowers, William J., Glenn L. Pierce and John F. McDevitt. *Legal Homicide: Death as Punishment in America, 1864–1892.* Boston: Northeastern University Press, 1984.

An important source providing extensive information on executions. Portions of this work were previously published in *Executions in America.*

Brasfield, Philip, with Jeffrey M. Elliot. *Deathman Pass Me By: Two Years on Death Row.* San Bernardino, CA: Borgo Books, 1983.

Account of the author's two years as an inmate in death row in Texas.

Bye, Raymond T. *Capital Punishment in the United States.* Philadelphia: The Committee of Philanthropic Labor of Philadelphia Yearly Meeting of Friends, 1919.

An early exploration of the history of capital punishment, its deterrence value and error factor.

Capote, Truman. *In Cold Blood: The True Account of a Multiple Murder and Its Consequences.* New York: Random House, 1965.

An extensive account of a 1959 multiple murder in Kansas.

Chessman, Caryl. *Cell 2455, Death Row.* Englewood Cliffs, NJ: Prentice-Hall, 1954.

The first of three works by a California inmate executed in 1960, describing life on death row.

———. *The Face of Justice.* Englewood Cliffs, NJ: Prentice-Hall, 1957.

The third and final book of the celebrated death row author.

———. *Trial by Ordeal.* Englewood Cliffs, NJ: Prentice-Hall, 1955.

Describes Chessman's ongoing legal battles and stays of execution and the emotional toll death row takes on prisoners, their families and legal counsel.

Cohen, Bernard L. *Law Without Order: Capital Punishment and the Liberals.* New Rochelle, NY: Arlington House, 1970.
Maintains that capital punishment is the cornerstone of any credible law enforcement system.

Cooper, David D. *The Lesson of the Scaffold: The Public Execution Controversy in Victorian England.* Athens, OH: Ohio University Press, 1974.
Discusses social attitudes surrounding efforts to abolish public executions in Victorian England.

Dance, Daryl Cumber. *Long Gone: The Mecklenburg Six and the Theme of Escape in Black Folklore.* Knoxville, TN: University of Tennessee Press, 1987.
In the context of themes in black folklore, describes the escape and recapture of six condemned men in Virginia in 1984 and the subsequent execution of two of them.

Davis, Christopher. *Waiting for It.* New York: Harper and Row, 1980.
A biography of Troy Gregg. In 1976 the Supreme Court denied his death sentence appeal, upholding Georgia's death penalty law.

Dike, Sarah T. *Capital Punishment in the United States: A Consideration of the Evidence.* Hackensack, NJ: National Council on Crime and Delinquency, 1982.
An overview of contemporary debates about the issue.

DiSalle, Michael V. *The Power of Life or Death.* New York: Random House, 1965.
A former Ohio governor recounts his experiences with the death-penalty and clemency during his gubernatorial tenure and his own strong opposition to capital punishment.

Draper, Thomas, ed. *Capital Punishment.* New York: H. W. Wilson, 1985.
An anthology of articles, largely popular, examining capital punishment from different perspectives.

Duffy, Clinton T., with A. Hirshberg. *88 Men and 2 Women.* New York: Doubleday, 1962.
A San Quentin warden's account of 90 executions, with strong arguments for the abolition of the death penalty.

Annotated Bibliography

Ehrmann, Herbert B. *The Case That Will Not Die: Commonwealth Vs. Sacco and Vanzetti.* Boston: Little, Brown, 1969.

The account of an attorney for the defense in this controversial case from the 1920s in which two immigrant anarchists were executed.

Elliot, Robert G. *Agent of Death: The Memoirs of an Executioner.* New York: Dutton, 1940.

An executioner in several states during the first decades of the twentieth century recounts his experiences and his opposition to the death penalty.

Ellsworth, Phoebe C., and Lee Ross. *Public Opinion and Capital Punishment: A Close Examination of the Views of Abolitionists and Retentionists.* New Haven, CT: Yale University Press, 1980.

Results of a survey on public attitudes and beliefs about capital punishment.

Eshelman, Byron, with Frank Riley. *Death Row Chaplain.* Englewood Cliffs, NJ: Prentice-Hall, 1962.

A former chaplain at San Quentin recounts his experiences and criticizes the death penalty.

Fisher, Jim. *The Lindbergh Case.* New Brunswick: Rutgers University Press, 1987.

From the perspective of New Jersey's state police, an account of the 1936 execution of Bruno Richard Hauptmann for the kidnapping of the Lindbergh child; the police view is that Hauptmann in fact committed the crime.

Frankfurter, Marion Denman, and Gardner Jackson, eds. *The Letters of Sacco and Vanzetti.* New York: Octagon Books, 1971.

A collection of the letters and court speeches of two prisoners executed in Massachusetts in 1927. The case provoked widespread controversy.

Gowers, Sir Ernest. *A Life for a Life? The Problem of Capital Punishment.* London: Chatto and Windus, 1956.

A discussion of capital punishment issues in England by the chairman of the 1953 Royal Commission on Capital Punishment. Sir Ernest came to be an ardent abolitionist.

Gray, Ian, and Moira Stanley, eds. *A Punishment in Search of a Crime: Americans Speak Out Against the Death Penalty.* New York: Avon Books, 1989.

Contemporary writings and statements against capital punishment.

Horwitz, Elinor Lander. *Capital Punishment, U.S.A.* Philadelphia: Lippincott, 1973.

A general introduction to the topic; provides historical background and descriptions of notable cases.

Huie, William Bradford. *Ruby McCollum: Woman in the Suwanee Jail.* New York: Signet Books, 1957.

An account of the case of Ruby McCollum, who received the death sentence in 1952 in Florida but was transferred to an asylum instead of being executed.

Isenberg, Irwin, ed. *The Death Penalty.* New York: H. W. Wilson, 1977.

An anthology of articles on capital punishment from the popular press.

Jackson, Bruce, and Diane Christian. *Death Row.* Boston: Beacon Press, 1980.

Interviews with 26 inmates on death row in Texas.

Jayewardene, C. H. S. *The Penalty of Death: The Canadian Experience.* Lexington, MA: D. C. Heath, 1977.

Considers Canada's moratorium on and subsequent abolition of the death penalty.

Johnson, Robert. *Condemned to Die: Life Under Sentence of Death.* New York: Elsevier, 1981.

Examines the effect of the death sentence on death row inmates and their families.

Jones, Ann. *Women Who Kill.* New York: Holt, Rinehart and Winston, 1980.

Studies women and homicide from several viewpoints, focusing on notable cases of female murderers.

Joyce, James Avery. *Capital Punishment: A World View.* New York: Thomas Nelson, 1961.

General background on the international status of the death penalty.

Kennedy, Ludovic. *The Airman and the Carpenter: The Lindbergh Kidnapping and the Framing of Richard Hauptmann.* New York: Viking, 1985.

The 1932 Lindbergh kidnapping case; presents the theory that Hauptmann's execution in 1936 was a mistake.

———. *Ten Rillington Place*. New York: Simon and Schuster, 1961.

Discusses an English case in 1949 in which one man was executed for a murder committed by another.

Koestler, Arthur. *Dialogue with Death*. New York: Macmillan, 1966.

An account of Koestler's capture, incarceration and death sentence during the Spanish Civil War.

———. *Reflections on Hanging*. New York: Macmillan, 1957.

Classic exposition in opposition to capital punishment.

Koestler, Arthur, and C. J. Rolph. *Hanged by the Neck: An Exposure of Capital Punishment in England*. London: Penguin, 1961.

An expansion of Koestler's *Reflections on Hanging*.

Kunstler, William M. *Beyond a Reasonable Doubt?: The Original Trial of Caryl Chessman*. New York: William Morrow, 1961.

An account of the case of Caryl Chessman, executed in 1960. Chessman became renowned for several books he wrote while on death row.

Laurence, John. *The History of Capital Punishment*. Secaucus, NJ: Citadel Press, 1960.

The work, first published in 1932 with a preface by Clarence Darrow, outlines the historical development of capital punishment.

Lawes, Lewis. *Man's Judgment of Death: An Analysis of Capital Punishment Based on Facts, Not Sentiment*. New York: Putnam, 1924.

A Sing Sing warden's opposition to capital punishment. Lawes became a leading abolitionist of his time.

Leslie, Jack. *Decathlon of Death*. Mill Valley, CA: Tarquin Books, 1979.

Discusses three California cases leading to executions in 1955.

Lester, David. *The Death Penalty: Issues and Answers*. Springfield, IL: Charles C. Thomas, 1987.

A concise introduction to the topic.

Levin, Jack, and James Alan Fox. *Mass Murder: America's Growing Menace*. New York: Plenum, 1985.

Examines recent mass murder cases, reviews their characteristics and discusses several theories.

Levine, Stephen, ed. *Death Row*. San Francisco: Glide Publications, 1972.

Essays, the majority of which are written by death row inmates.

Levy, Barbara. *Legacy of Death*. Englewood Cliffs, NJ: Prentice-Hall, 1973.
History of the Sanson family, the official executioners of France for seven generations.

Loeb, Robert H. *Crime and Capital Punishment*. 2d ed. New York: Franklin Watts, 1986.
A basic introduction.

Mackey, Philip English. *Voices Against Death: American Opposition to Capital Punishment, 1787–1975*. New York: Burt Franklin, 1976.
A collection of 26 statements by leading abolitionists throughout the nation's history.

Magee, Doug. *Slow Coming Dark: Interviews on Death Row*. New York: Pilgrim Press, 1980.
Focuses on the lives of death row inmates before and after their death sentences.

Magee, Doug. *What Murder Leaves Behind: The Victim's Family*. New York: Dodd, Mead, 1983.
Accounts of the impact of homicide on victims' families.

Mailer, Norman. *The Executioner's Song*. Boston: Little, Brown, 1979.
A fictionalized account of the last months of convicted murderer Gary Gilmore, the first person executed following the reinstatement of capital punishment in 1976.

McCafferty, James A., ed. *Capital Punishment*. Chicago: Aldine-Atherton, 1972.
Essays on both sides of the question.

McClellan, Grant S., ed. *Capital Punishment*. New York: H. W. Wilson, 1961.
Articles from the popular press, both supporting and opposing capital punishment.

McGehee, Edward G., and William H. Hildebrand, eds. *The Death Penalty: A Literary and Historical Approach*. Boston: D. C. Heath, 1964.
Fifty opinions on capital punishment, covering several centuries.

McGovern, James R. *Anatomy of a Lynching: The Killing of Claude Neal*. Baton Rouge, LA: Louisiana State University Press, 1982.
The story of a 1934 lynching in Florida.

Meador, Roy. *Capital Revenge: 54 Votes Against Life.* Philadelphia: Dorrance and Co., 1975.

Essays directed specifically to the 54 U.S. Senators who voted in 1974 to reinstate the death penalty.

Miller, Arthur S., and Jeffrey Brown. *Death by Installments: The Ordeal of Willie Francis.* Westport, CT: Greenwood Press, 1988.

Study of the case of Willie Francis, who was executed in Louisiana in 1947 after a previous attempt to put him to death in the electric chair had failed.

Miller, Gene. *Invitation to a Lynching.* Garden City, NY: Doubleday, 1975.

An account of two men twice sentenced to death in Florida who received pardons in 1975.

Otterbein, Keith F. *The Ultimate Coercive Sanction.* New Haven, CT: Human Relations Area Files Press, 1986.

Studies the death penalty from an anthropological viewpoint; examination of 53 primitive societies suggests that capital punishment is universal.

Pearson, Bruce L., ed. *The Death Penalty in South Carolina: Outlook for the 1980's.* Columbia, SC: ACLU Press, 1981.

Examines the death penalty in general, then focuses on its administration in South Carolina in particular.

Pierrepoint, Albert. *Executioner: Pierrepoint.* Sevenoaks, Kent, England: Hodder and Stoughton, 1974.

The autobiography of a British executioner whose father and uncle had preceded him in the trade; the author now opposes capital punishment.

Reid, Don, with John Gurwell. *Eyewitness.* Houston: Cordovan Press, 1973.

A journalist's eyewitness account of nearly 200 executions in Texas.

Schwed, Roger E. *Abolition and Capital Punishment: The United States' Judicial, Political, and Moral Barometer.* New York: AMS Press, 1983.

A concise historical overview.

Scott, George Ryley. *The History of Capital Punishment.* London: Torchstream Books, 1950.

A classic discussion of capital punishment.

Sellin, Thorsten, ed. *Capital Punishment*. New York: Harper and Row, 1967.

A collection of influential essays on the death penalty.

———. *The Penalty of Death*. Beverly Hills, CA: Sage, 1980.

General background on the subject.

Smead, Howard. *Blood Justice: The Lynching of Mack Charles Parker*. New York: Oxford University Press, 1986.

Recounts a 1959 lynching in Mississippi.

Smith, Edgar. *Brief Against Death*. New York: Knopf, 1968.

An autobiographical account of trial for murder, conviction and years on death row.

Spierenburg, Pieter. *The Spectacle of Suffering: Executions and the Evolution of Repression: From a Preindustrial Metropolis to the European Experience*. New York: Cambridge University Press, 1984.

Explores the evolution of capital punishment debates.

Stevens, Leonard A. *Death Penalty: The Case of Life Vs. Death in the United States*. New York: Coward, McCann and Geoghegan, 1978.

Describes the events leading up to the landmark Supreme Court ruling in *Furman v. Georgia*.

Strauss, Frances. *Where Did the Justice Go?: The Story of the Giles-Johnson Case*. Boston: Gambit, Inc., 1970.

The wrongful capital sentencing of three men in a Maryland case in 1961.

Syzumski, Bonnie, ed. *Death Penalty: Opposing Viewpoints*. St. Paul, MN: Greenhaven Press, 1986.

Overview of both sides of the death penalty debate, including discussion of the sanction's morality and its success as a deterrent.

Teeters, Negley K. *Hang by the Neck: The Legal Use of Scaffold and Noose, Gibbet, Stake, and Firing Squad from Colonial Times to the Present*. Springfield, IL: Charles C. Thomas, 1967.

An excellent history of executions in the United States.

van den Haag, Ernest. *Punishing Criminals: Concerning a Very Old and Painful Question*. New York: Basic Books, 1975.

General discussion of the concept of punishment and the appropriateness of the death penalty.

van den Haag, Ernest, and John P. Conrad. *The Death Penalty: A Debate.* New York: Plenum, 1983.

A lay introduction to the major issues.

White, Walter Francis. *Rope and Faggot: A Biography of Judge Lynch.* New York: Knopf, 1929.

Classic study of lynching.

White, Welsh S. *The Death Penalty in the Eighties: An Examination of the Modern System of Capital Punishment.* Ann Arbor, MI: University of Michigan Press, 1987.

Examines the modern capital punishment system, focusing on recent Supreme Court rulings.

Wilson, James Q. *Thinking About Crime.* New York: Basic Books, 1983.

Argues that criminal behavior is rational and can be deterred.

Woffinden, Bob. *Miscarriages of Justice.* London: Hodder and Stoughton, 1987.

Discusses several cases of mistaken conviction in the British Isles after World War II.

Woodward, Bob, and Scott Armstrong. *The Brethren: Inside the Supreme Court.* New York: Simon and Schuster, 1979.

Looks at the workings of the Supreme Court 1969–1975, including background on the *Furman* ruling.

Zimmerman, Isidore. *Punishment Without Crime.* New York: Manor Books, 1973.

Autobiography of a man erroneously convicted and sentenced to death.

Zimring, Franklin E., and Gordon Hawkins. *Capital Punishment and the American Agenda.* New York: Cambridge University Press, 1986.

Examines capital punishment in the United States in the 1980s.

ETHICAL

Arendt, Hannah. *Eichmann in Jerusalem: A Report on the Banality of Evil.* New York: Viking Press, 1963.

Describes the trial and execution of Adolph Eichmann in Israel for crimes he committed as a Nazi official.

Beccaria, Cesare. *On Crimes and Punishments*. Translated by Henry Paolucci. New York: Macmillan, 1963.

An eighteenth-century abolitionist essay, arguing that certainty rather than severity of punishment is the more effective deterrent.

Berns, Walter. *For Capital Punishment: Crime and the Morality of the Death Penalty*. New York: Basic Books, 1979.

Advocates the continuance of capital punishment, based on the concept of justice as retribution.

Black, Charles L., Jr. *Capital Punishment: The Inevitability of Caprice and Mistake*. 2d ed. New York: W. W. Norton, 1981.

Strong advocacy for abolition on the grounds of unavoidable discrimination and imprecision in the administration of the death penalty.

Bockle, Franz, and Jacques Pohiers, eds. *The Death Penalty and Torture*. New York: The Seabury Press, 1979.

Essays on the death penalty and torture, from a range of religious viewpoints.

Carrington, Frank G. *Neither Cruel Nor Unusual*. New Rochelle, NY: Arlington House, 1978.

Defends the death penalty, refuting abolitionist reasoning step by step.

Devine, Philip E. *The Ethics of Homicide*. Ithaca, NY: Cornell University Press, 1978.

Considers the moral issues of homicide and possible exceptions. Discusses homicide in the context of abortion, capital punishment, war, suicide and euthanasia.

Endres, Michael E. *The Morality of Capital Punishment: Equal Justice Under Law?* Mystic, CT: Twenty-Third Publications, 1985.

Moral and legal opposition to capital punishment due to the sanction's unfair application and lack of valid usefulness.

Erdahl, Lowell O. *Pro-Life/Pro-Peace: Life-Affirming Alternatives to Abortion, War, Mercy Killing, and the Death Penalty*. Minneapolis, MN: Augsburg Publishing House, 1986.

A Lutheran bishop's call for a consistent, Christian and pro-life stance on a number of issues.

Glover, Jonathan. *Causing Death and Saving Lives*. New York: Penguin, 1977.

Considers various moral approaches to such life-or-death issues as suicide, euthanasia, capital punishment and abortion.

Gorecki, Jan. *Capital Punishment: Criminal Law and Social Evolution.* New York: Columbia University Press, 1983.

Argues that state use of violence declines as a society evolves.

Hibbert, Christopher. *The Roots of Evil.* Boston: Little, Brown, 1963.

Discusses the historical evolution of punishment and attitudes towards criminals. A chapter on capital punishment, with a British focus, argues for abolition of the death penalty.

Hook, Donald D., and Lothar Kahn. *Death in the Balance: The Debate Over Capital Punishment.* Lexington, MA: Lexington Books, 1989.

Explores the moral complexities of the issue, focusing on recent cases in which the death penalty was implemented or requested.

Ingram, T. Robert, ed. *Essays on the Death Penalty.* Houston: St. Thomas Press, 1963.

Essays on capital punishment from several Christian viewpoints.

Jacoby, Susan. *Wild Justice: The Evolution of Revenge.* New York: Harper and Row, 1983.

Discusses the meaning of justice and the corollary issue of revenge. Finds that revenge is legitimate but capital punishment is excessive and damaging to societal morality.

McManners, John. *Death and the Enlightenment: Changing Attitudes to Death Among Christians and Unbelievers in Eighteenth-Century France.* New York: Oxford University Press, 1981.

Includes information on public executions and changing attitudes towards death.

Moberly, Walter. *The Ethics of Punishment.* London: Faber and Faber, 1968.

An in-depth examination of penal theory, including a section on the morality of capital punishment.

Nathanson, Stephen. *An Eye for an Eye? The Morality of Punishing by Death.* Totowa, NJ: Rowman and Littlefield, 1987.

An evaluation and rejection of arguments supporting capital punishment.

Phillipson, Coleman. *Three Criminal Law Reformers: Beccaria, Bentham, Romilly*. Montclair, NJ: Patterson Smith, 1970.

Examines the backgrounds, thought, and achievements of Beccaria, Bentham and Romilly.

Playfair, Giles, and Derrick Singleton. *The Offenders: The Case Against Legal Vengeance*. New York: Simon and Schuster, 1957.

Presents six capital cases as examples of the ineffectiveness of legal vengeance.

Sorrell, Tom. *Moral Theory and Capital Punishment*. New York: Basil Blackwell, 1988.

Discusses the various moral and philosophical theories current in capital punishment debates.

LEGAL

Andenaes, Johannes. *Punishment and Deterrence*. Ann Arbor, MI: University of Michigan Press, 1974.

A collection of essays on methods of deterrence and their effectiveness.

Annual Chief Justice Earl Warren Conference on Advocacy in the United States. *The Death Penalty: Final Report*. Washington, DC: The Roscoe Pound-American Trial Lawyers Foundation, 1980.

A collection of three papers advocating the abolition of the death penalty.

Avrich, Paul. *The Haymarket Tragedy*. Princeton, NJ: Princeton University Press, 1984.

History of the 1886 Haymarket Riot in Chicago and the legal fate of eight anarchists convicted of murder; four were executed, one committed suicide, and three were pardoned.

Baldus, David C., George G. Woodworth and Charles A. Pulaski, Jr. *Equal Justice and the Death Penalty: A Legal and Empirical Analysis*. Boston: Northeastern University Press, 1990.

A comprehensive examination of racial discrimination and the death sentence.

Bedau, Hugo Adam. *The Courts, the Constitution, and Capital Punishment*. Lexington, MA: Lexington Books, 1977.

A collection of the author's essays.

Berger, Raoul. *Death Penalties: The Supreme Court's Obstacle Course.* Cambridge, MA: Harvard University Press, 1982.

Discusses limitations on Supreme Court authority; traces the history of the Eighth Amendment.

Berkson, Larry Charles. *The Concept of Cruel and Unusual Punishment.* Lexington, MA: D. C. Heath, 1975.

A review of the Eighth Amendment's origins and its importance in the concept of punishment.

Carter, Dan T. *Scottsboro: A Tragedy of the American South.* Baton Rouge, LA: Louisiana State University Press, 1969.

An account of an Alabama case in which nine black men were wrongfully convicted of raping two white women.

Cederblom, J. B., and William L. Blizek, eds. *Justice and Punishment.* Cambridge, MA: Ballinger, 1977.

Essays originally presented at a University of Nebraska-Omaha symposium on "Criminal Justice and Punishment." Focuses on the issue of retribution.

Chandler, David B. *Capital Punishment in Canada: A Sociological Study of Repressive Law.* Toronto: McClelland and Stewart, 1976.

Describes the status of the issue in Canada, emphasizing the impact of legislative debates in 1967 and 1973.

Cortner, Richard C. *A Scottsboro Case in Mississippi: The Supreme Court and Brown v. Mississippi.* Jackson, MS: University Press of Mississippi, 1986.

Describes a case in Mississippi in which three black men were accused in the murder of a white man. The Supreme Court ruled that confessions gained by torture were not a sound basis for conviction.

Darrow, Clarence. *Attorney for the Damned.* Edited by Arthur Weinberg. New York: Simon and Schuster, 1957.

A collection of the defense lawyer's speeches and addresses.

Fogelson, Robert M., advisory ed. *Capital Punishment: Nineteenth Century Arguments.* New York: Arno Press, 1974.

Arguments in the Massachusetts Legislature during the 19th century on capital punishment.

Frankfurter, Felix. *Of Law and Men*. New York: Harcourt, 1956.

Papers by the late Supreme Court Justice, including an essay opposing capital punishment.

Gibbs, Jack P. *Crime, Punishment and Deterrence*. New York: Elsevier, 1975.

Discusses theories of deterrence and presents research findings.

Gross, Samuel R., and Robert Mauro. *Death and Discrimination: Racial Disparities in Capital Sentencing*. Boston: Northeastern University Press, 1989.

Traces the history of racial differences in sentencing for capital crimes.

Haas, Kenneth C., and James A. Inciardi, eds. *Challenging Capital Punishment: Legal and Social Science Approaches*. Newbury Park, CA: Sage, 1988.

A collection of essays.

Hammer, Richard. *Between Life and Death*. New York: Macmillan, 1969.

An account of the trial, incarceration and appeal of John Brady, leading to the 1963 Supreme Court ruling *Brady v. Maryland*.

Lassers, Willard J. *Scapegoat Justice: Lloyd Miller and the Failure of the American Legal System*. Bloomington, IN: Indiana University Press, 1973.

An account of the case of Lloyd Miller, who received the death sentence for a 1955 murder but was exonerated.

Loh, Wallace D. *Social Research in the Judicial Process: Cases, Readings, and Text*. New York: Russell Sage Foundation, 1984.

A collection of legal studies. Chapter 5 covers capital punishment.

Mackey, Philip English. *Hanging in the Balance: The Anti-Capital Punishment Movement in New York State, 1776–1861*. New York: Garland Books, 1982.

Recounts the history of New York State's death penalty law, from the American Revolution to the Civil War.

Meltsner, Michael. *Cruel and Unusual: The Supreme Court and Capital Punishment*. New York: Random House, 1973.

Recounts the legal campaign against capital punishment leading to the *Furman* decision.

Nakell, Barry, and Kenneth A. Hardy. *The Arbitrariness of the Death Penalty*. Philadelphia: Temple University Press, 1987.

Explores the effect of the victim's race on the disposition of homicide cases.

New York State Defenders Association. *Capital Losses: The Price of the Death Penalty for New York State.* Albany, NY: New York State Defenders Association, 1982.

A cost analysis of the reinstatement of the death penalty in New York State. The sum would exceed the cost of life imprisonment by several times.

Pannick, David. *Judicial Review of the Death Penalty.* White Plains, NY: Sheridan, 1982.

A comparison of judicial review of death sentences in a number of countries.

Prettyman, Barrett, Jr. *Death and the Supreme Court.* New York: Harcourt, Brace and World, 1961.

Examines six U.S. Supreme Court capital punishment cases.

Ramcharan, B. G., ed. *The Right to Life in International Law.* Dordrecht, MA: Martinus Nijhoff, 1985.

Surveys international human rights law, including capital punishment.

Raper, Arthur F. *The Tragedy of Lynching.* Chapel Hill, NC: University of North Carolina Press, 1933.

A study of the causes, supposed and actual, of more than 3,000 lynchings that took place between 1889 and 1930. Prepared for the Southern Commission for the Study of Lynching.

Sheleff, Leon Shaskolsky. *Ultimate Penalties: Capital Punishment, Life Imprisonment, Physical Torture.* Columbus, OH: Ohio State University Press, 1987.

Considers justifiable penalties for heinous crimes.

Shin, Kilman. *Death Penalty and Crime: Empirical Studies.* Fairfax, VA: George Mason University Press, 1978.

Discusses the impact that capital punishment has on crime rates in America and worldwide.

Silberman, Charles E. *Criminal Violence, Criminal Justice.* New York: Random House, 1978.

A general examination of the problem of crime in America.

119

Streib, Victor. *Death Penalty for Juveniles.* Bloomington, IN: Indiana University Press, 1987.

Considered an authoritative work on the issue.

Tuttle, Elizabeth Orman. *The Crusade Against Capital Punishment in Great Britain.* London: Stevens and Sons, 1961.

The decline of capital punishment in Great Britain over 150 years.

White, Welsh S. *Life in the Balance: Procedural Safeguards in Capital Cases.* Ann Arbor, MI: University of Michigan Press, 1984.

A collection of essays.

Wolfe, Burton H. *Pileup on Death Row.* New York: Doubleday, 1973.

Relates the events which led to the Supreme Court's *Furman* ruling.

Zimring, Franklin E., and Gordon Hawkins. *Deterrence: The Legal Threat in Crime Control.* Chicago: University of Chicago Press, 1973.

Discusses the current status of deterrence research and possible avenues for future inquiry.

ENCYCLOPEDIAS

Allen, Francis A. "Capital Punishment." In *International Encyclopedia of the Social Sciences.* Vol. 2, 290–294. New York: Macmillan, 1968.

Overview of capital punishment's history, the 18th century abolition movement, trends in the United States and worldwide and the sanction's effectiveness.

Bedau, Hugo Adam. "Capital Punishment." In *Academic American Encyclopedia.* Vol. 4, 123–124. Danbury, CT: Grolier, 1988.

Synopsis of the topic and its current status.

———. "Capital Punishment." In *Encyclopedia of Crime and Justice.* Vol. 1, 133–143. New York: Free Press, 1983.

Overview of the topic: its history and trends.

———. "Capital Punishment." In *The Guide to American Law.* Vol. 2, 221–226. St. Louis, MO: West Publishing, 1983.

Overview of the death penalty in America and the constitutional issues involved.

Borock, Donald M. "Capital Punishment." In *Dictionary of American History*. Vol. 1, 449–450. New York: Charles Scribner's Sons, 1972.

Very brief overview with information on the 1972 Supreme Court ruling in *Furman v. Georgia*.

Caldwell, Robert G. "Capital Punishment." In *Encyclopedia Americana*. Vol. 5, 596–599. Danbury, CT: Grolier, 1987.

Brief summary of the history of capital punishment from ancient times. Reviews the effect of the Enlightenment on the treatment of criminals and discusses issues surrounding capital punishment today.

Campion, D. R. "Capital Punishment." In *The New Catholic Encyclopedia*. Vol. 3, 79–81. Palatine, IL: Jack Heraty and Assoc., 1981.

Covers ancient history of capital punishment, Catholic recognition of the practice and the Church's role in the debate.

Rabinowitz, Louis I. "Capital Punishment." In *Encyclopedia Judaica*. Vol. 5, 142–146. New York: Macmillan, 1972.

Discusses capital punishment from the point of view of the Bible and Talmudic Law and practice.

Scott, Austin W., Jr. "Criminal Law and Procedures." In *Collier's Encyclopedia*. Vol. 7, 447–467. New York: Macmillan, 1976.

Discusses capital punishment within a thorough overview of the criminal justice system.

Weisberg, Robert. "Capital Punishment." In *Encyclopedia of the American Constitution*. Vol. 1, 201–206. New York: Macmillan, 1986.

A detailed review of the Supreme Court's constitutional regulation of the death penalty, followed by brief articles on capital punishment cases of 1972 and 1976.

Zimring, Franklin E. "Capital Punishment." In *The World Book Encyclopedia*. Vol. 3, 193. Chicago: World Book, 1990.

The current status of the death penalty in the United States.

PERIODICALS

Information and articles on capital punishment frequently appear in the following periodicals.

American Bar Foundation Research Journal. Chicago: American Bar Association (quarterly).

American Criminal Law Review. Chicago: American Bar Association (quarterly).

American Journal of Criminal Law. Austin, TX: University of Texas (3 per year).

American Lawyer. New York: American Lawyer (10 per year).

Annual Survey of American Law. New York: Annual Survey Office (annually).

Behavioral Sciences and the Law. New York: John Wiley and Son, Inc. (quarterly).

Columbia Law Review. New York: Columbia University School of Law (monthly).

Crime and Delinquency. Hackensack, NJ: National Council on Crime and Delinquency (quarterly).

Crime Prevention and Criminal Justice Newsletter. Vienna, Austria: United Nations (irregular).

Crime and Social Justice. Berkeley, CA: Crime and Social Justice (semiannually).

Criminal Justice Abstracts. Monsey, NY: Willow Tree Press (quarterly).

Criminal Justice and Behavior. Newbury Park, CA: SAGE Publications (quarterly).

Criminal Justice Ethics. New York: Institute of Criminal Justice Ethics (semiannually).

Criminal Justice Review. Atlanta, GA: Georgia State University (semiannually).

Criminal Law Bulletin. Boston, MA: Warren Gorham and Lamont (bimonthly).

Criminology. Columbus, OH: American Society of Criminology (quarterly).

Ethics. Chicago: University of Chicago Press (quarterly).

Harvard Law Review. Cambridge, MA: Harvard Law Review Association (quarterly).

Human Rights. Chicago: American Bar Association (quarterly).

International Journal of the Sociology of Law. London: Academic Press, Inc. (quarterly).

Journal of Contemporary Law. Salt Lake City, UT: University of Utah, College of Law (annually).

Journal of Criminal Justice. Elmsford, NY: Pergamon Press (bimonthly).

Journal of Criminal Law and Criminology. Chicago: Northwestern University School of Law (quarterly).

Journal of Juvenile Law. Laverne, CA: Laverne College Law Center (semi-annually).

Journal of Research in Crime and Delinquency. Newbury Park, CA: SAGE Publications (quarterly).

Justice Quarterly. Omaha, NE: University of Nebraska (quarterly).

Law and Human Behavior. New York: Plenum Press (quarterly).

Social Science Quarterly. Austin, TX: University of Texas Press (quarterly).

Stanford Law Review. Stanford, CA: Stanford Law School (bimonthly).

University of Chicago Law Review. Chicago: University of Chicago Law School (quarterly).

Woodrow Wilson Journal of Law. Atlanta, GA: Woodrow Wilson Journal of Law (irregularly).

Yale Law Journal. New Haven, CT: Yale Law Journal (8 per year).

ARTICLES

GENERAL

Anderson, G. M. The death penalty in the United States: the present situation. *America* 147 (November 20, 1982): 306–309.

Assesses the current status of capital punishment in America.

Archer, Dane, Rosemary Gartner and Marc Beittel. Homicide and the death penalty: a cross-national test of a deterrence hypothesis. *Journal of Criminal Law and Criminology* 74 (1983): 991–1013.

Using data from 14 countries, the authors determined that homicide rates may decrease after the death penalty is abolished.

Austen, Ian, and Frank Klimko. An everyday death. *Maclean's* 100 (March 16, 1987). 16ff.

Discusses one particular execution.

Bailey, William C. Murder and capital punishment in the nation's capital. *Justice Quarterly* 1 (1984): 211–233.

Examines the correlation between the homicide rate and the possibility of execution in Washington, D.C. between 1890 and 1970. The homicide rate increased slightly after executions.

Barnett, Arnold. Crime and capital punishment: some recent studies. *Journal of Criminal Justice* 6 (1978): 291–303.

Surveys the deterrence research of Isaac Ehrlich and that of his critics. Suggests possibilities for future research in this area.

Barrett, Cindy. When death was a spectator sport. *Maclean's* 100 (March 16, 1987): 18.

A look at public executions in Canada.

Bartels, Robert. Capital punishment: the unexamined issue of special deterrence. *Iowa Law Review* 68 (1983): 601–607.

An entirely satirical paper, arguing that those who are executed are thereby deterred from committing murder again.

Bedau, Hugo Adam. Challenging the death penalty. *Harvard Civil Rights— Civil Liberties Law Review* 9 (1974): 626–643.

Reviews Michael Meltsner's *Cruel and Unusual*. Examines the effects of the *Furman* ruling.

———. The death penalty in America: review and forecast. *Federal Probation* 35 (1971): 32–43.

A review of the history and status, to date, of capital punishment in the United States.

———. Justice in punishment and assumption of risks: some comments in response to van den Haag. *Wayne Law Review* 33 (1987): 1423–1433.

Criticizes an essay by Ernest van den Haag on deterrence and retribution as justifications of punishment. A response by van den Haag follows.

————. The 1964 death penalty referendum in Oregon: some notes from a participant-observer. *Crime and Delinquency* 26 (1980): 528–536.

Relates the defeat of the Oregon death penalty in 1964 by a wide voter margin.

————. Problems of capital punishment. *Current History* 71 (July 1976): 14–18ff.

Surveys the history of the movement to abolish the death penalty, focusing on action during the 1960s. Provides the status of the death penalty from 1846 to 1972 by state.

————. Social science research in the aftermath of *Furman v. Georgia:* creating new knowledge about capital punishment in the United States. In Marc Reidel and Duncan Chappell, eds., *Issues in Criminal Justice: Planning and Evaluation.* 75–86. New York: Praeger, 1976.

Advocates increased social science research on capital punishment.

Beichman, Arnold. The first electrocution. *Commentary* 35 (1963): 410–419.

The history of the first electrocution in 1890. Discusses the dispute between George Westinghouse and Thomas Edison. Edison argued the person electrocuted would feel no pain.

The bench and the chair. *National Review* 39 (May 22, 1987): 15.

Discusses a Supreme Court ruling on racial bias in capital sentencing.

Black, Charles L., Jr. Governors' dilemma. *The New Republic* 180 (April 25, 1979): 12–13.

In the face of growing numbers of inmates on death row, state governors are faced with the choice of execution or commutation of sentence.

Bohm, Robert. American death penalty attitudes: a critical examination of recent evidence. *Criminal Justice and Behavior* 4 (1987): 380–396.

Considers the factors which most frequently lead people to support the death penalty.

Bruning, Fred. Why did Randall Adams almost die? *Maclean's* 102 (March 27, 1989): 9.

Examines a recent capital punishment case.

Buckley, William F., Jr. Execute Ronald Monroe? *National Review* 41 (September 15, 1989): 63.

Analyzes evidence suggesting that Monroe may be innocent.

Campbell, Ruth. Sentence of death by burning for women. *Journal of Legal History* 5 (1984): 44–59.

Discusses the history of burning women at the stake, a method of execution used in England until 1790. The method was used only for women who were found guilty of petty treason, such as murdering their husbands.

Carroll, Ginny, and Aric Press. Only two weeks to live: As an execution nears, troubling questions are raised about a murder case. *Newsweek* 114 (August 21, 1989): 62ff.

Discusses the Louisiana case of Ronald Monroe.

Cheatwood, Derral. Capital punishment and corrections: Is there an impending crisis? *Crime and Delinquency* 31 (1985): 461–479.

Discusses possible solutions to the growing number of inmates on death row.

Chop chop. *The Economist* 313 (October 21, 1989): 29ff.

Discusses the death penalty in America.

Clark, Ramsey. Rush to death: Spenkelink's last appeal. *The Nation* 229 (October 27, 1979): 385, 400–404.

Describes the appeals made in the last 48 hours before John Spenkelink was executed in Florida in 1979.

Cohen, Daniel A. In defense of the gallows: justifications of capital punishment in New England execution sermons, 1674–1825. *American Quarterly* 40 (June 1988): 147ff.

A historical look at justification of the death penalty.

Cohodas, Nadine. Senate supports death penalty for "drug kingpins" who kill. *Congressional Quarterly Weekly Report* 46 (June 11, 1988): 1598.

Proposed federal death sentences for major drug-related offenses.

Davis, David Brion. The movement to abolish capital punishment in America, 1787–1861. *American Historical Review* 63 (1957): 23–46.

An account of the movement to abolish capital punishment between the Revolution and the Civil War.

Death penalty: cruel and even more unusual punishment. *The Economist* 303 (May 2, 1987): 24–25.

Discusses the current status of the issue.

Deparle, Jason. Executions aren't news. *Washington Monthly* 18 (February 1986): 12–21.

The author argues against the death penalty, following discussions with murder victims' families and death row inmates and witnessing an execution.

———. Louisiana diarist: killing folks. *The New Republic* 190 (January 30, 1984): 43.

An account of the electrocution and funeral of a Louisiana death row inmate in 1983.

Devine, Edward, Marc Feldman, Lisa Giles-Klein, Cheryl A. Ingram, and Robert F. Williams. Special project: The constitutionality of the death penalty in New Jersey. *Rutgers Law Journal* 15 (1984): 261–397.

Examines the death penalty's history in New Jersey. Raises the question of whether or not the present statute violates the state constitution.

Dieter, Richard C. The death penalty dinosaur: capital punishment heads for extinction. *Commonweal* 115 (January 15, 1988): 11ff.

Growing support for the abolition of capital punishment.

Dorius, Earl F. Personal recollections of the Gary Gilmore case. *Woodrow Wilson Journal of Law* 3 (1981): 49–129.

Diary account by a Utah Assistant Attorney General who was one of the state attorneys in the case that culminated in the execution of Gary Gilmore in 1977.

Drinan, Robert F. Pressure in New York for death penalty. *The Christian Century* 106 (June 7, 1989): 582–583.

The current status of the issue in New York.

Dugger, Ronnie. The numbers on death row prove that blacks who kill whites receive the harshest judgment. *Life* 11 (Spring 1988): 88–92.

A look at racial bias in death sentencing.

Edelson, Sharon. The ACLU's teen problem. *Savvy*, September 1989, 19ff.

The American Civil Liberties Union has contradictory stances on abortion and capital punishment.

Erskine, Hazel. The polls: capital punishment. *Public Opinion Quarterly* 34 (1970): 290–307.

A summary of major opinion polls starting in 1936 and showing a sharp drop in support for the issue.

Fotheringham, Allan. Between life and death row. *Maclean's* 100 (April 13, 1987): 52.

Another chapter in the capital punishment debate.

Four for the chair. *Time* 129 (June 29, 1987): 19.

The execution of four inmates in Louisiana following a Supreme Court denial of an objection.

Friedman, Robert. Death row. *Esquire* 93 (April 1980): 84–92.

Interviews with 18 inmates on Florida's death row.

Gelman, David. The Bundy carnival: A thirst for revenge provokes a raucous send-off. *Newsweek* 113 (February 6, 1989): 66.

Public reaction to the execution of mass murderer Ted Bundy.

Gest, Ted. Open door to the execution chamber? *U.S. News & World Report* 102 (May 4, 1987): 25.

Examines a recent Supreme Court ruling on racial bias in the use of the death penalty.

Gettinger, Stephen H. Robert A. Sullivan. *Rolling Stone*, February 2, 1984, 60.

Eulogy for Robert Sullivan, executed November 30, 1983, in Florida.

Goldberg, Steven. So what if the death penalty deters? *National Review* 41 (June 30, 1989): 42–43.

Another look at deterrence.

Grupp, Stanley. Some historical aspects of the pardon in England. *The American Journal of Legal History* 7 (1963): 51–62.

Provides historical background on the power of pardon in England before the 18th century.

Hanging. *Maclean's* 97 (October 8, 1984): 48–54ff.

A special section on the issue, with editorial comment.

Hitchens, Christopher. Minority report. *The Nation* 245 (August 29, 1987): 150.

A view of death row in Mississippi.

Hughes, Graham. License to kill. *New York Review of Books* 26 (June 28, 1979): 22–25.

Reviews Berns' *For Capital Punishment*, arguing that capital punishment is never justified.

Johnson, Guy B. The Negro and crime. *The Annals of the American Academy of Political and Social Science* 217 (1941): 93–104.

Studies the racial demographics of homicide convicts and victims in parts of the South in the 1930s. Concludes there is a correlation between race, criminal occurrences and the response of the judicial system.

Johnson, Robert. "This man has expired": witness to an execution. *Commonweal* 116 (January 13, 1989): 9ff.

Account of an execution.

Jolly, Robert W., Jr., and Deward Sagarin. The first eight after *Furman:* who was executed with the return of the death penalty? *Crime and Delinquency* 30 (1984): 610–623.

Examines newspaper accounts of the first eight executions after the death penalty was reinstated in the United States in 1976.

Kaplan, David A. Breaking the death barrier. *Newsweek* 115 (February 19, 1990): 72–73.

The first California execution in 23 years is scheduled for the spring of 1990.

———. Death rides a judicial roller coaster: an inmate's fate. *Newsweek* 115 (January 22, 1990): 55.

The case of Warren McCleskey.

Kaufman, E. Capital punishment: an international perspective. *Humanist* 43 (November/December 1983): 19–21ff.

Discusses the issue in an international context.

Kay, Marvin L. Michael, and Loren Lee Cary. "The planters suffer little or nothing": North Carolina compensations for executed slaves, 1748–1772. *Science and Society* 40 (1976) 288–306.

Except in New England, the American colonies compensated slave owners for slaves who were executed. The compensation was more than the cost of the replacement.

King, W. M. The end of an era: Denver's last legal public execution, July 27, 1886. *Journal of Negro History* 68 (1983): 37–53.

The execution of Andrew Green became the catalyst that pushed Colorado governor Job Cooper to sign legislation ending public hangings.

Kleinman, M. A. R. Dead wrong: capital punishment for murders by drug dealers. *The New Republic* 199 (September 26, 1988): 14ff.

Argues that executing drug traffickers would have virtually no effect on the drug trade.

Kramer, Michael. Cuomo, the last holdout. *Time* 135 (April 2, 1990): 20.

New York Governor Mario Cuomo firmly opposes capital punishment.

Kroll, Michael. Pro-life parents: Their children were murdered. Still, they oppose the death penalty. *Mother Jones* 15 (February-March 1990): 13.

A strong pro-life ethic may outweigh personal tragedy.

Lacayo, Richard. The politics of life and death: As California prepares to use the gas chamber for the first time in 23 years, candidates call for more executions. *Time* 135 (April 2, 1990): 18ff.

The status of capital punishment in California.

Lehman, Susan. A matter of engineering: capital punishment as a technical problem. *The Atlantic* 265 (February 1990): 26ff.

Examines the technical aspects of electrocution.

Lempert, Richard O. The effect of executions on homicides: a new look in an old light. *Crime and Delinquency* 29 (1983) 88–115.

A state-by-state comparison of execution and homicide rates finds no evidence of deterrence.

Levoy, Gregg. The $2 million execution. *Omni* 9 (January 1987): 30.

Explores the costs of capital punishment.

Lowenstein, L. F. Licence to kill: Is there a case for the death penalty? *Contemporary Review* 252 (January 1988): 32–36.

This study concludes that capital punishment may be the only means of providing the victim's relatives with a sense of retribution.

Meehan, M. The death penalty in the United States: ten reasons to oppose it. *America* 147 (November 20, 1982): 310–312.

Arguments for the abolition of the death penalty.

Meltsner, Michael, and M. E. Wolfgang. Symposium on current death penalty issues. *Journal of Criminal Law and Criminology* 74 (Fall 1983): 659–1114.

Examines the current status of the issues surrounding the death penalty.

Metzenbaum, H. M. Mistakes and the death penalty. *Harper's* 269 (July 1984): 18ff.

Discusses several dozen cases in which people were condemned, and in some cases executed, for crimes they did not commit.

Mishan, E. J. The lingering debate on capital punishment. *Encounter* 80 (March 1988): 61–75.

An essay on the ongoing issue.

Murder most foul. *The Progressive* 53 (May 1989): 10.

An editorial.

Murton, Tom. Treatment of condemned prisoners. *Crime and Delinquency* 15 (1969): 94–111.

Discusses Arkansas' successful integration of death row inmates with the general prison population.

National Council on Crime and Delinquency. Policy statement on capital punishment. *Crime and Delinquency* 10 (1964): 105–109.

Advocates the abolition of the death penalty.

Nesbitt, Charlotte A. Managing death row. *Corrections Today* 48 (July 1986): 90–94ff.

Describes an American Correctional Association project to determine how death row inmates are managed.

Newton, E., and J. Nelson. The death penalty. *Black Enterprise* 13 (May 1983): 52–55ff.

An overview of the issue.

No execution. *The Christian Century* 104 (February 4, 1987): 104–105.

The case of death row inmate Mark Hoffman.

O'Sullivan, John. O'Sullivan's first law. *National Review* 41 (October 27, 1989): 14.

Critique of Amnesty International's abolitionist stance.

Pallone, N. J. Advocacy scholarship on the death penalty. *Society* 26 (November/December 1988): 84–87.

Reviews research advocating capital punishment.

Phillips, David P. The deterrent effect of capital punishment: new evidence on an old controversy. *American Journal of Sociology* 86 (1980): 139–148.

Explores the effects of 22 notorious executions in London between 1858 and 1921; finds a temporary deterrence, lasting about two weeks, after each execution.

Press, Aric. Gridlock on death row: the U.S. Supreme Court rejects a key challenge to capital punishment. *Newsweek* 109 (May 4, 1987): 60ff.

The Supreme Court rules on possible racial discrimination in cases of death sentencing.

Race, death, and justice. *The Progressive* 51 (June 1987): 8ff.

The Supreme Court rules on a possible connection between racial bias and the death penalty.

Radelet, Michael L., Margaret Vandiver and Felix Berardo. Families, prisons, and men with death sentences: the human impact of structured uncertainty. *Journal of Family Issues* 4 (1983): 593–612.

Discusses the psychological impact of the death sentence on death row inmates and their families.

Radolf, Andrew. Executions. *Editor and Publisher* 122 (April 22, 1989): 21ff.

Discusses the experience of journalists who have witnessed executions.

Relin, D. O. Crime and the constitution. *Scholastic Update* 120 (December 4, 1987): 10–11.

Update on the death penalty.

Right ruling, wrong reason. *The Economist* 312 (July 15, 1989): 25ff.

Discusses the ethics of extraditing an alleged murderer to a country that has the death penalty.

Roberts, Steven V., and Ted Gest. A growing cry: "Give them death": legal changes will speed the pace of executions. *U.S. News & World Report* 108 (March 26, 1990): 24–25.

Changes in the legal system will affect the handling of executions.

Rosenbaum, Ron. Too young to die? *The New York Times Magazine* 138 (March 12, 1989): 32–35ff.

Examines the case of Heath Wilkins, a death row inmate awaiting the Supreme Court ruling on age limitations on the death penalty.

Satlow, Barry. Witness at an execution. *Juris Doctor* 2 (November 1971): 13.

Recounts the 1963 electrocution of Ralph Hudson in New Jersey.

Sawyer, Darwin O. Public attitudes toward life and death. *Public Opinion Quarterly* 46 (1982): 521–533.

Explores the consistency of public attitudes on life and death issues such as capital punishment, abortion, suicide and euthanasia.

Schedler, G. Capital punishment and its deterrent effect. *Social Theory and Practice* 4 (1976): 47–56.

Suggests that deterrence may be irrelevant in capital punishment debates.

Sellin, Thorsten. Two myths in the history of capital punishment. *Journal of Criminal Law, Criminology, and Police Science* 50 (1959): 114–117.

Examines the inflated statistics of death sentences in earlier eras.

Setting ahead the clock on death row. *U.S. News & World Report* 108 (March 19, 1990): 14ff.

Discusses the drawn-out process of death sentence implementation.

Sherrill, Robert. Death row on trial. *The New York Times Magazine* 133 (November 13, 1983): 80–83ff.

The present status of capital punishment, focusing on the situation in Florida.

Sloan, Clifford. Death row clerk. *The New Republic* 196 (February 16, 1987): 18–21.

A former clerk for a Supreme Court Justice describes last minute appeals before executions. Feels that those receiving the death sentence either were not wealthy or were inadequately represented.

Smith, A. LaMont, and Robert M. Carter. Count down for death. *Crime and Delinquency* 15 (1969): 77–93.

A detailed chronicle of the life of an inmate in California during the week before his execution.

Smykla, John Ortiz. The human impact of capital punishment: interviews with families of persons on death row. *Journal of Criminal Justice* 15 (1987): 331–347.

Explores the impact of capital punishment on those who work with or are related to death row inmates.

Spence, K. Crime and punishment. *National Review* 35 (September 16, 1983): 18ff.

Argues that society must accept the duty of exacting retribution until or unless research proves that capital punishment is not a deterrent.

Stack, S. Publicized executions and homicide, 1950–1980. *American Sociological Review* 52 (1987): 532–540.

Finds that publicized executions were associated with a decrease in homicides.

Stout, David G. The lawyers of death row: long hours and low pay in the battle against capital punishment. *The New York Times Magazine* 137 (February 14, 1988): 46ff.

Examines the lives and jobs of death row lawyers.

Styron, William. The death-in-life of Benjamin Reid. *Esquire* 57 (February 1962): 114ff. The aftermath of Benjamin Reid. *Esquire* 57 (November 1962): 79–81ff.

A pair of articles describing the Connecticut case of a death row inmate who eventually received clemency.

Sullivan, Robert A. Waiting to die: a prisoner's diary from Florida's death row. *Rolling Stone*, March 6, 1980, 48–49ff.

A diary account of experiences on death row. Sullivan was executed four years later.

Time, Editors of. Overview: killing the killers. *Opposing Viewpoints SOURCES: Criminal Justice*. Vol. 1, 223–229. St. Paul, MN: Greenhaven Press, 1983.

An overview of the merits and costs of capital punishment.

van den Haag, Ernest. Can any legal punishment of the guilty be unjust to them? *Wayne Law Review* 33 (1987): 1413–1421.

Holds that retribution and deterrence justify punishment.

————. Death and deterrence. *National Review* 38 (March 14, 1986): 44ff.

New evidence to support the author's claim that the death penalty acts as a deterrent to murder.

————. Refuting Reiman and Nathanson. *Philosophy and Public Affairs* 14 (1985): 165–176.

A response to articles by Jeffrey H. Reiman and Stephen Nathanson, both of whom oppose the death penalty.

Waldo, Gordon P. The death penalty and deterrence: a review of recent research. In Israel Barak-Glantz and Ronald Huff, eds. *The Mad, The Bad, and The Different*. 169–178. Lexington, MA: Lexington Books, 1981.

Concise assessment of Isaac Ehrlich's work and that of his supporters and opponents.

War, Mark, and Mark Stafford. Public goals of punishment and support for the death penalty. *Journal of Research in Crime and Delinquency* 21 (1984): 95–111.

A survey of Seattle residents found that the major goals of punishment were viewed as incapacitation and retribution. Retribution was supported most by older or less educated respondents.

Whitaker, Charles. Should teenagers be executed? *Ebony* 43 (March 1988): 118ff.

An 18-year-old woman on death row as the result of a homicide conviction.

Wicker, Tom. Cuomo and Feinstein. *The New York Times* 139 (March 19, 1990): A17.

Mario Cuomo of New York and Dianne Feinstein of California present differing views on abortion and capital punishment.

Wilkes, John. Murder in mind. *Psychology Today* 21 (June 1987): 27–32.

Profiles homicide expert Dale Archer. Argues that when a nation inflicts violence on humans, via war or capital punishment, it incites people to increased violence.

Zaller, Robert. The debate on capital punishment during the English Revolution. *American Journal of Legal History* 31 (1987): 126–144.

Discusses the debate over capital punishment reform during the 17th century.

Zeisel, Hans. Race bias in the administration of the death penalty: the Florida experience. *Harvard Law Review* 95 (1981): 456–468.

Evidence that the race of the victim affected sentencing in capital cases in Florida.

ETHICAL

Amsterdam, Anthony G. Capital punishment. In H. A. Bedau, ed., *The Death Penalty in America*. 346–58. New York: Oxford University Press, 1982.

A concise and forceful call for abolition of the death penalty.

————. The case against the death penalty. *Juris Doctor* 2 (November 1971): 11–12.

Finds the death penalty to be violent and irrational.

————. The Supreme Court and capital punishment. *Human Rights* 14 (Winter 1987): 14–17ff.

A critique of the Supreme Court's review of, or refusal to review, execution appeals.

Andenaes, Johannes. The morality of deterrence. *University of Chicago Law Review* 37 (1970): 649–664.

A justification of punishment as a deterrent, illustrated with Norwegian case studies.

Anders, James. Should juvenile murderers be sentenced to death? Punish the guilty. *American Bar Association Journal* 72 (June 1, 1986): 32–33.

A debate with Richard Brody. Anders believes that death sentences should not have a minimum age limitation.

Barzun, Jacques. In favor of capital punishment. *Crime and Delinquency* 15 (1969): 21–28.

A critique of arguments for abolishing the death penalty. The author stresses the value of human life.

Bedau, Hugo Adam. Bentham's utilitarian critique of the death penalty. *Journal of Criminal Law and Criminology* 74 (1983): 1033–1066.

Examines the work of Jeremy Bentham (1748–1832) and his opposition to the death penalty.

————. Capital punishment. In Tom Regan, ed., *Matters of Life and Death.* 147–182. New York: Random House, 1980.

Argues for the abolition of the death penalty, based on the premise of the sanctity of human life.

————. A condemned man's last wish: organ donation and a "meaningful" death. *Hastings Center Report* 9 (February 1979): 16–17.

In commentaries on a case that raised the question of whether a condemned man might choose the method by which he dies so that his organs can be donated, Bedau takes a negative stance while Michael Zeik supports the concept.

————. The death penalty: social policy and social justice. *Arizona State Law Journal* (1977): 767–802.

Discusses constitutional, philosophical and ethical bases for capital punishment.

————. Retribution and the theory of punishment. *The Journal of Philosophy* 75 (1978): 601–620.

Considers the idea of retribution, its possible definitions, scope, role and limitations.

————. Thinking of the death penalty as cruel and unusual punishment. *University of California-Davis Law Review* 18 (1985): 873–925.

Explores ways in which punishment can be determined to be too severe.

Beristain, Antonio. Capital punishment and Catholicism. *International Journal of Criminology and Penology* 5 (1977): 321–333.

Considers the contemporary Catholic view on capital punishment. Concludes that the death penalty should be abolished.

Bernardin, Joseph Cardinal. The consistent ethic after "Webster": opportunities and dangers. *Commonweal* 117 (April 20, 1990): 242ff.

Following the Supreme Court's change in stance on abortion law, a Roman Catholic leader examines the need for a consistent pro-life ethic covering issues such as abortion and capital punishment.

Berns, Walter. Defending the death penalty. *Crime and Delinquency* 26 (1980): 503–511.

Defends capital punishment as a means of retribution and a promotion of respect for life.

————. Executions are moral retribution. *Opposing Viewpoints SOURCES: Criminal Justice.* Vol. 1, 245–246. St. Paul, MN: Greenhaven Press, 1983.

Sees the death penalty as the enactment of righteous societal anger in response to heinous crime.

Black, Charles L., Jr. The crisis in capital punishment. *Maryland Law Review* 31 (1971): 289–311.

A classic statement opposing the death penalty.

Block, Richard A. "Death, thou shalt die": Reform Judaism and capital punishment. *Journal of Reform Judaism* 30 (Spring 1983): 1–10.

A survey of Jewish doctrine opposing capital punishment.

Boyd, George N. Capital punishment: deserved and wrong. *The Christian Century* 105 (February 17, 1988): 162–165.

Examines several aspects of the morality of capital punishment.

Brown, Edmund G., and Dick Adler. Private mercy: as debate over the death penalty opens again, a former state governor reflects on the 36 people he let die. *Common Cause Magazine* 15 (July–August 1989): 28ff.

A former governor reassesses his stance on capital punishment.

Bruck, David. The death penalty is unjust. *Opposing Viewpoints SOURCES: Criminal Justice*. Vol. 1, 1984 supplement, 85–91. St. Paul, MN: Greenhaven Press, 1984.

Views the application of the death penalty in specific instances as non-objective.

Camus, Albert. Reflections on the guillotine. In Albert Camus, *Resistance, Rebellion and Death*. 173–234. New York: Knopf, 1966.

A classic abolitionist essay, opposing capital punishment for moral and philosophical reasons.

Chapman, Frank. The death penalty, U.S.A.: racist and class violence. *Political Affairs* 66 (July 1987): 17–19.

Discusses class and racial bias in death penalty sentencing from a Marxist viewpoint.

Clark, Ramsey. The death penalty and reverence for life. In Ramsey Clark, *Crime in America*. 308–315. New York: Simon and Schuster, 1970.

A former U.S. Attorney General discusses his opposition to the death penalty.

Conduct unbecoming: civilised societies do not need the death penalty. *The Economist* 311 (May 6, 1989): 10–11.

Assesses the need for capital punishment in an advanced society.

Dake, Norman F. Who deserves to live? Who deserves to die? Reflections on capital punishment. *Currents in Theology and Mission* 10 (April 1983): 67–77.

The chaplain of the St. Louis County jail argues against capital punishment from an ecumenical Christian viewpoint.

Annotated Bibliography

Davis, Michael. Death, deterrence, and the method of common sense. *Social Theory and Practice* 7 (1981): 145–177.

Examining deterrence from a philosophical viewpoint, determines that, by common sense, the most effective deterrent is death.

———. Is the death penalty irrevocable? *Social Theory and Practice* 10 (1984): 143–156.

Argues that the risk of mistaken execution is not a strong abolitionist argument, since time mistakenly served cannot be given back.

DeVries, Brian and Lawrence J. Walker. Moral reasoning and attitudes toward capital punishment. *Developmental Psychology* 22 (1986): 509–513.

Using Kohlberg's moral development theory, finds that university students at higher stages of moral development do in fact oppose capital punishment.

Ellsworth, Phoebe C., and Lee Ross. Public opinion and capital punishment: a close examination of the views of abolitionists and retentionists. *Crime and Delinquency* 29 (1983): 116–169.

Surveys basis for beliefs about capital punishment. Found that most opinions were grounded more in general values than specific information and thought.

Erez, Edna. Thou shalt not execute: Hebrew law perspective on capital punishment. *Criminology* 19 (1981): 25–43.

Examines the Hebraic historical and legal context for capital punishment.

Finckenauer, J. O. Public support for the death penalty: retribution as just desserts or retribution as revenge? *Justice Quarterly* 5 (1988): 81–100.

Reviews literature demonstrating that public support for capital punishment is largely a matter of wanting revenge.

Fortas, Abe. The case against capital punishment. *The New York Times Magazine* 127 (January 23, 1977): 8–9ff.

A former U.S. Supreme Court associate justice speaks out against the death penalty, soon after the execution of Gary Gilmore.

Friedlander, Robert A. The death penalty deters murder. 89–93. *Opposing Viewpoints SOURCES: Criminal Justice.* 1988 annual, 89–93. San Diego, CA: Greenhaven Press, 1988.

If one potential murderer is deterred by the concept of capital punishment, then the system is justifiable.

Gardner, Martin R. Mormonism and capital punishment: a doctrinal perspective, past and present. *Dialogue: A Journal of Mormon Thought* 12 (1979): 9–26.

Explores the historical context for Mormon support of the death penalty. Little evidence of doctrinal basis for that support appears.

Goldberg, Steven. On capital punishment. *Ethics* 85 (1974): 67–74.

Finds that both supporters and opposers of capital punishment use the theory of deterrence to support their viewpoints.

Gould, Donald. Dispensers of death. *New Scientist* 123 (August 5, 1989): 63.

Examines the ethical aspects of the death penalty.

Harvey, O. J. Belief systems and attitudes toward the death penalty and other punishments. *Journal of Personality* 54 (December 1986): 659–675.

Explores the values and attitudes from which opinions of punishment stem.

Hertzberg, Hendrik. Burning question. *The New Republic* 200 (February 20, 1989): 4ff.

Reflects on the retributive aspect of capital punishment.

Ihm, Stephen L. Executing insane prisoners is unconstitutional. *Opposing Viewpoints SOURCES: Criminal Justice.* 1988 annual, 111–114. San Diego, CA: Greenhaven Press, 1988.

Supports the Supreme Court decision that the execution of an insane death row prisoner is cruel and unusual punishment.

Jeffko, Walter G. Capital punishment in a democracy. *America* 135 (December 11, 1976): 413–414.

Argues that advocates of capital punishment carry responsibility for proving the necessity for continuing it.

Johnson, Perry M. Society should not impose the death penalty. *Opposing Viewpoints SOURCES: Criminal Justice.* Vol. 1, 241–242. St. Paul, MN: Greenhaven Press, 1983.

Argues that capital punishment cheapens the value of life.

Joyce, Jim. Christianity rejects the death penalty. *Opposing Viewpoints SOURCES: Criminal Justice.* 1988 annual, 121–122. San Diego, CA: Greenhaven Press, 1988.

Opposition to the death penalty as expressed by Catholic bishops in the United States who say the Gospels advocate mercy for sinners.

Kelly, Matthew J., and George Schedler. Capital punishment and rehabilitation. *Philosophical Studies* 34 (1978): 329–331.

The hypothetical proposal that the condemned also could have their humanity destroyed if they were "tinkered with" medically rather than killed outright is no justification for capital punishment.

Koch, Edward I. How capital punishment affirms life—death and justice. *The New Republic* 192 (April 15, 1985): 12–15.

The mayor of New York City makes the case that murderers should be killed because life is valuable.

Kohlberg, Lawrence, and Donald Elfenbein. Capital punishment, moral development, and the Constitution. In Lawrence Kohlberg, *Essays on Moral Development.* Vol. 1, 243–293. New York: Harper and Row, 1981.

An updated revision of the authors' earlier paper.

———. The development of moral judgments concerning capital punishment. *American Journal of Orthopsychiatry* 45 (1975): 614–640.

The results of a 20-year study of American males' development of moral judgment. At the most mature stages, the men rejected the concept of capital punishment.

Lempert, Richard O. Desert and deterrence: an assessment of the moral bases of the case for capital punishment. *Michigan Law Review* 79 (1981): 1177–1231.

Assesses retribution and deterrence as moral justifications.

Long, Thomas A. Capital punishments: "cruel and unusual"? *Ethics* 83 (1973): 214–223.

Examines "cruel" and "unusual" as ideas. Advocates the abolition of capital punishment on the grounds that it is both.

Margolis, Joseph. Capital punishment. *Journal of Behavioral Economics* 6 (1977): 269–278.

Discusses the philosophy of deterrence. Argues that the issue should not be a primary focus in discussions of capital punishment.

———. Punishment. *Social Theory and Practice* 2 (1973): 347–363.

Explores the philosophical goals of punishment. Assesses the death penalty's success.

Mead, Margaret. A life for a life: what that means today. *Redbook*, June 1978, 56–60.

The anthropologist's opposition to capital punishment.

Meehan, Mary. Arguments against the death penalty. *Opposing Viewpoints SOURCES: Criminal Justice.* Vol. 1, 235–238. St. Paul, MN: Greenhaven Press, 1983.

Outlines basic arguments against the death penalty, pointing out that we know enough to say that some crimes deserve strong punishment but not enough to determine when a criminal should die.

Minor, W. W. Reflections on the killing of criminals. *Journal of Criminal Law and Criminology* 76 (Fall 1985): 764–772.

An essay.

Morris, Norval, and Gordon Hawkins. The death penalty and abortion. In Norval Morris and Gordon Hawkins, *Letter to the President on Crime Control.* 79–86. Chicago: University of Chicago Press, 1977.

Advocates the abolition of capital punishment, finding it irrelevant to crime control in today's society.

NAACP Legal Defense Fund. The death penalty discriminates against blacks. *Opposing Viewpoints SOURCES: Criminal Justice.* 1988 annual, 99–102. San Diego, CA: Greenhaven Press, 1988.

Murderers are more likely to be sentenced to death if the victim is white or if the murderer is black.

Rehyansky, Joseph A. The death penalty is just. *Opposing Viewpoints SOURCES: Criminal Justice.* Vol. 1, 1984 supplement, 79–84. St. Paul, MN: Greenhaven Press, 1984.

Suggests that the death penalty is a just response in some situations and that its infrequent use stems from "moral squeamishness."

Reiman, Jeffrey H. Justice, civilization, and the death penalty: answering van den Haag. *Philosophy and Public Affairs* 14 (1985): 115–148.

Advocates the abolition of the death penalty, disagreeing with Ernest van den Haag.

Reiman, Jeffrey H., and Sue Headlee. Marxism and criminal justice policy. *Crime and Delinquency* 27 (1981): 24–47.

Discusses criminal justice policy in a Marxist context.

Roome, Frank B. Society must impose the death penalty. *Opposing View-points SOURCES: Criminal Justice.* Vol. 1, 239–240. St. Paul, MN: Greenhaven Press, 1983.

Advocates capital punishment as retribution for "monstrous" crimes.

Satre, Thomas W. The irrationality of capital punishment. *Southwestern Journal of Philosophy* 6 (Summer 1975): 75–87.

A philosophical theory of punishment supporting the abolition of the death penalty. It focuses on the concept that error is unavoidable.

Schwarzschild, Henry. A social and moral atrocity. *ABA Journal* 71 (April 1985): 38–42.

A debate about capital punishment with Ernest van den Haag.

Shelley, Marshall. The death penalty: two sides of a growing issue. *Christianity Today* 28 (March 2, 1984): 14–17.

Discusses opposing viewpoints held by Christians.

Shultz, Robinette R. Executing insane prisoners is constitutional. *Oppos-ing Viewpoints SOURCES: Criminal Justice.* 1988 annual, 115–119. San Diego, CA: Greenhaven Press, 1988.

Opposes the Supreme Court decision that executing an insane death row inmate is cruel and unusual punishment. Argues that the ruling adds a loophole that will lessen the deterrent impact of the death pen-alty.

Tabak, Ronald, with Vicki Quade. The death penalty is unjust. *Opposing Viewpoints SOURCES: Criminal Justice.* 1988 annual, 85–88. San Diego, CA: Greenhaven Press, 1988.

The judicial system imposes the death sentence too randomly for it to be effective. Capital punishment should be discontinued.

Turnbull, Colin. Death by decree. *Natural History* 87 (1978): 51–66.

Discusses the inhumanity of the death penalty from an anthropological viewpoint.

van den Haag, Ernest. Arguments for the death penalty. *Opposing View-points SOURCES: Criminal Justice.* Vol. 1, 231–234. St. Paul, MN: Greenhaven Press, 1983.

Points out the flaws in arguments against the death penalty.

Van Ness, Daniel W. Is the death penal constitutional? *Christianity Today* 31 (July 10, 1987): 26.

From a Christian viewpoint examines the constitutionality of the death penalty.

————. Punishable by death: Constitutional questions about the death penalty may be largely resolved, but the moral issues persist. *Christianity Today* 31 (July 10, 1987): 24ff.

Examines the ethical aspects of capital punishment from a Christian perspective.

Vanauken, Sheldon. Christianity supports the death penalty. *Opposing Viewpoints SOURCES: Criminal Justice.* 1988 annual, 123–126. San Diego, CA: Greenhaven Press, 1988.

While it is not moral to take an innocent life, the convicted murderer is not innocent. The death penalty encourages the murderer to repent.

Vincent, Paul. Capital punishment is immoral. *Opposing Viewpoints SOURCES: Criminal Justice.* Vol. 1, 243–244. St. Paul. MN: Greenhaven Press, 1983.

Offers the viewpoint that capital punishment is a kind of murder.

Ward, Cynthia V. The death penalty is just. *Opposing Viewpoints SOURCES: Criminal Justice.* 1988 annual, 81–83. San Diego, CA: Greenhaven Press, 1988.

In cases of certain heinous crimes, the death penalty is an appropriate response.

White, Welsh S. The death penalty may promote murder. *Opposing Viewpoints SOURCES: Criminal Justice.* 1988 annual, 95–98. San Diego, CA: Greenhaven Press, 1988.

The death penalty may be an incentive to those who kill because they themselves want to be put to death.

Wilbanks, William. Discrimination in death penalty cases has not been proven. *Opposing Viewpoints SOURCES: Criminal Justice.* 1988 annual, 103–109. San Diego, CA: Greenhaven Press, 1988.

The death sentence is imposed on blacks more than on whites, but there are other variables to be considered besides the possibility of racism.

Young, Robert. What is so wrong with killing people? *Philosophy* 54 (1979): 515–528.

A philosophical essay about the morality of killing people.

Annotated Bibliography

LEGAL

Allen, Charlotte Low. Ending abuse of death penalty appeals. *The Wall Street Journal*, May 14, 1990, A16.

Commentary on abuse of the system.

An attack on its life. *The Economist* 302 (February 28, 1987): 30.

Amnesty International intends to persuade the United States to abolish the death penalty.

Andenaes, Johannes. General prevention revisited: research and policy implications. *Journal of Criminal Law and Criminology* 66 (1975): 338–365.

A pioneer in deterrence research provides a survey of the field.

Arkin, Steven D. Discrimination and arbitrariness in capital punishment: an analysis of post-*Furman* murder cases in Dade County, Florida, 1973–1976. *Stanford Law Review* 33 (1980): 75–101.

A study of 350 homicide cases in Miami provided no clear evidence of a correlation between racial discrimination and the death sentence.

Bailey, William C. Capital punishment and lethal assaults against police. *Criminology* 19 (1982): 608–625.

An analysis of state data nationwide, 1961–1971, seeking a link between the rate of murders of police and presence of the death sentence. Found that sociodemographic factors had greater effect on the rate of lethal assaults of police.

———. Imprisonment v. the death penalty as a deterrent to murder. *Law and Human Behavior* 1 (1977): 239–260.

Examines execution and homicide rates and sentence severity in 1920 and 1960; finds no evidence that either executions or severe sentences affect homicide rates.

———. Murder and the death penalty. *Journal of Criminal Law and Criminology* 65 (1974): 416–423.

A comparison of the rates in 40 states of first- and second-degree murder. In comparing states with and without the death penalty, no evidence was found to support deterrence as a hypothesis.

———. Rape and the death penalty: a neglected area for deterrence research. In H. A. Bedau and C. M. Pierce, eds., *Capital Punishment in the United States*. 336–358. New York: AMS Press, 1976.

145

Considers the death penalty as a deterrent for rape; finds that the rate of rape is higher in states that have the death penalty.

Bailey, William C., and Ruth D. Peterson. Murder and capital punishment: a monthly time-series analysis of execution publicity. *American Sociological Review* 54 (Oct 89): 722ff.

Further research finds that publicized executions do act as a deterrent.

————. Police killings and capital punishment: the post-*Furman* period. *Criminology* 25 (1987): 1–25.

Explores the relationship between capital punishment and police murders between 1973 and 1984. Found no support for the argument that the death penalty affects the rate of police murders.

Baldus, David C., Charles A. Pulaski, Jr., and George Woodworth. Comparative review of death sentences: an empirical study of the Georgia experience. *Journal of Criminal Law and Criminology* 74 (1983): 661–753.

Reports on a study of sentencing patterns in Georgia, attempting to identify possibly excessive sentences.

Balske, Dennis N. New strategies for the defense of capital cases. *Akron Law Review* 13 (1979): 331–361.

Discusses ideas for the improvement of defense attorney skills in capital cases.

Barry, Rupert V. *Furman* to *Gregg:* the judicial and legislative history. *Howard Law Journal* 22 (1979): 53–117.

Examines the development of opposition to capital punishment in America, including the changing status of the death penalty through the 1970s.

Bedau, Hugo Adam. Capital punishment in Oregon, 1903–1964. *Oregon Law Review* 45 (1965): 1–39.

A history of the death penalty in Oregon in the 20th century.

————. The death penalty in the United States: imposed law and the role of moral elites. In Sandra B. Burman and Barbara E. Harrell-Bond, eds., *The Imposition of the Law*. 45–68. New York: Academic Press, 1979.

A review of the movement toward abolishing the death penalty.

————. Deterrence and the death penalty: a reconsideration. *Journal of Criminal Law, Criminology and Police Science* 61 (1970): 539–548.

A response to a paper by Ernest van den Haag; Bedau does not feel that the unproven possibility of deterrence can justify the death penalty.

————. Felony murder rape and the mandatory death penalty: a study in discretionary justice. *Suffolk University Law Review* 10 (1976): 493–520.

Comments on Massachusetts' mandatory death sentence for homicides in cases of rape or attempted rape. In fact, no executions have resulted from the "mandatory" sentence.

————. *Gregg v. Georgia* and the new death penalty. *Criminal Justice Ethics* 4 (1985): 3–17.

Examines Supreme Court decisions on capital punishment, focusing on *Gregg* and the issues raised in that case.

————. The Nixon administration and the deterrent effect of the death penalty. *University of Pittsburgh Law Review* 34 (1973): 557–566.

A consideration of Nixon administration comments in support of the deterrent effect of the death penalty. Shows that the statements were founded on the speakers' personal beliefs rather than empirical data.

————. The politics of death. *Trial* 8 (March-April 1972): 44–46.

Discusses recent Supreme Court decisions relating to the death penalty.

————. Rough justice: the limits of novel defenses. *Hastings Center Report* 8 (Dec 1978): 8–11.

Examines recent, unusual defenses in murder trials.

————. Witness to a persecution: the death penalty and the Dawson Five. *Black Law Journal* 8 (1983): 7–28.

An account of the 1977 trial of five black men accused of the murder of a white woman in Georgia and the author's participation in the case.

Bedau, Hugo Adam, and Michael L. Radelet. Miscarriages of justice in potentially capital cases. *Stanford Law Review* 40 (1987): 21–179.

Discusses 350 cases in the 20th century in America of people receiving the death sentence for rape or homicide convictions who later were proved innocent.

Begley, Sharon. The slow pace of death row: a system no one likes. *Newsweek* 111 (February 8, 1988): 64.

Extensive stays on death row are evidence of a legal system in need of reform.

Bersoff, Donald M. Social science data and the Supreme Court: *Lockhart* as a case in point. *American Psychologist* 42 (1987): 52–58.

Discusses the social science research used in *Lockhart v. McCree*. The case is used to show how judicial behavior can be influenced by studies.

Biskupic, Joan. Justices weigh age minimum for capital punishment. *Congressional Quarterly Weekly Report* 47 (April 1, 1989): 697ff.

The Supreme Court explores a possible minimum age limit for execution.

Bonner, Raymond A. Death penalty. *Annual Survey of American Law*, 1984, 483–513.

Discusses the recent elimination of procedural safeguards curbing executions and the questionable reliability of psychiatric testimony. Focuses on *Zant v. Stephens* and *Barefoot v. Estelle*.

Bowers, William J. The pervasiveness of arbitrariness and discrimination under post-*Furman* capital statutes. *Journal of Criminal Law and Criminology* 74 (1983): 1067–1100.

Considers the effects of arbitrariness and discrimination on sentencing and decisions in Georgia and Florida.

Bowers, William J., and Glenn L. Pierce. Arbitrariness and discrimination under post-*Furman* capital statutes. *Crime and Delinquency* 26 (1980): 563–635.

Considers patterns in death sentencing in four states. Found that the race of the defendant and the victim affect sentencing. Geographic variations within states also correlate to sentencing.

———. Deterrence or brutalization: what is the effect of executions? *Crime and Delinquency* 26 (1980): 453–484.

Examines homicide rates in New York from 1907 to 1963, finding that in the month following an execution, the homicide rate rose slightly. Discusses data in broader context of brutalizing effect of capital punishment.

———. The illusion of deterrence in Isaac Ehrlich's research on capital punishment. *Yale Law Journal* 85 (1975): 187–208.

Criticizes Ehrlich's deterrence research for unreliability.

Brennan, William J., Jr. Constitutional adjudication and the death penalty: a view from the Court. *Harvard Law Review* 100 (1986): 313–331.

Discusses experiences handling capital punishment cases over 30 years on the bench. (The author is an Associate Justice on the Supreme Court.)

———. Interpreting the Constitution. *Social Policy* 18 (Summer 1987): 24ff.

Discusses the constitutionality of the death penalty.

Broderick, Daniel J. Insanity of the condemned. *Yale Law Journal* 88 (1979): 533–564.

Discusses the historical background for not executing the insane. Acknowledges the inadequacy of sanity assessment methods.

Brodie, D. P. The imposition of the death penalty on juvenile offenders: how should society respond? *Journal of Juvenile Law* 10 (1986): 117–124.

A review of case law which concludes that executing juvenile offenders is not a viable solution to the problem of juvenile crime. Society should seek ways to treat the causes of the problem rather than react to the results.

Brody, Richard J. Should juvenile murderers be sentenced to death? Don't kill children. *American Bar Association Journal* 72 (June 1, 1986): 32–33.

Debating with James Anders, Brody holds that there should be restrictions against executing minors.

Bruck, David. The death penalty: an exchange. *The New Republic* 192 (May 20, 1985): 20–21.

Responds to Mayor Koch's position that capital punishment emphasizes the sanctity of life.

———. Decisions of death. *The New Republic* 189 (December 12, 1983): 18–25.

A death row defense lawyer discusses the arbitariness and racial bias of sentencing.

———. On death row in Pretoria Central. *The New Republic* 197 (July 13 and 20, 1987): 18–25.

Discusses the status of the death penalty in South Africa, finding some similarities to that of the United States.

Burris, Scott. Death and a rational justice: a conversation on the capital jurisprudence of Justice John Paul Stevens. *Yale Law Journal* 96 (1987): 521–546.

An imaginary discussion of capital punishment among Justices Stevens, Marshall, Brennan and Berger, drawing on the opinions of each but emphasizing Justice Stevens'.

Callans, Patrick J. Assembling a jury willing to impose the death penalty: a new disregard for a capital defendant's rights. *Journal of Criminal Law and Criminology* 76 (1985): 1027–1050.

Focuses on jury selection in *Wainwright v. Witt.*

Cover, James Peery, and Paul D. Thistle. Time series, homicide, and the deterrent effect of capital punishment. *Southern Economic Journal* 54 (January 1988): 615ff.

Discusses deterrence theory.

Cowan, Claudia L., William C. Thompson and Phoebe C. Ellsworth. The effects of death qualification on jurors' predisposition to convict and on the quality of deliberation. *Law and Human Behavior* 8 (1984): 53–79.

A tape of a murder trial simulation was viewed by 288 subjects. Those who supported the death penalty, and therefore qualified for capital juries, were more likely to vote to convict the defendant.

Culver, John H. The states and capital punishment: executions from 1977–1984. *Justice Quarterly* 2 (1985): 567–578.

Describes the demographics of 32 executions in the United States between 1977 and 1984.

Curran, William J. Psychiatric evaluations and mitigating circumstances in capital punishment sentencing. *New England Journal of Medicine* 307 (December 2, 1982): 1431–1432.

Examines the Supreme Court's ruling in *Eddings v. Oklahoma,* which held that the defendant's psychiatric record must be taken into account in trial court sentencing.

Davis, Peggy C. The death penalty and the current state of the law. *Criminal Law Bulletin* 14 (1978): 7–17.

Recent Supreme Court rulings on the death penalty; part of a symposium on capital punishment in the United States.

Death delayed. *The Economist* 315 (April 7, 1990): 37.

Execution delayed in the case of Robert Alton Harris.

Annotated Bibliography

Deparle, Jason. The juice ain't no use: Why the death penalty won't work in D.C. *Washington Monthly* 21 (May 1989): 32–33.

The death penalty will not act as a deterrent in the nation's high-crime capital.

Dolinko, David. Foreward: how to criticize the death penalty. *Journal of Criminal Law and Criminology* 77 (1986): 546–601.

Reviews major procedural arguments against the death penalty.

Donovan, Beth. Congress could focus the debate: death penalty is re-emerging as a presidential-level issue. *Congressional Quarterly Weekly Report* 46 (June 18, 1988): 1657–1658.

Calls for refocusing of the death penalty debate.

Ehrlich, Isaac. Capital punishment and deterrence: some further thoughts and additional evidence. *Journal of Political Economy* 85 (1977): 741–788.

Further support for the theory of deterrence through correlation of murders and executions in America in 1940 and 1950.

———. Deterrence: evidence and inference. *Yale Law Journal* 85 (1975): 209–227.

Response to criticisms of his research by others, including Bowers and Pierce.

———. The deterrent effect of capital punishment: a question of life and death. *American Economic Review* 65 (1975): 397–417.

A controversial study of homicides in America from 1933 to 1967 which concluded that every execution reduced the probable number of murders by eight.

Ehrmann, Sara R. For whom the chair waits. *Federal Probation* 26 (1962): 14–25.

Exposes the risks of mistaken execution. Argues that influence plays a role in commutation of a sentence, and that homicide convicts are successful parolees.

Ellsworth, Phoebe C. Juries on trial. *Psychology Today* 19 (July 1985): 44–46.

An overview of recent research which found that death penalty supporters were more likely to vote for conviction than opponents of capital punishment.

Capital Punishment

Excerpts from decision on death-case appeals. *The New York Times* 139 (April 25, 1990): A10.

Transcript of Supreme Court decision prohibiting court hearings of appeals brought on behalf of death row inmates who themselves had chosen not to appeal their sentences.

Forst, Brian E. Capital punishment and deterrence: conflicting evidence? *Journal of Criminal Law and Criminology* 74 (1983): 927–942.

Examines deterrence research and criticism from several angles. Finds no evidence that the death penalty is more of a deterrent than long prison terms.

Gallup, George. The death penalty. *Gallup Reports* 244 and 245 (January/February 1986): 10–16.

Findings from national polls on death penalty support, with demographic breakdowns.

Gardner, Martin R. Illicit legislative motivation as a sufficient condition for unconstitutionality under the establishment clause: a case for consideration: the Utah firing squad. *Washington University Law Quarterly* (1979): 435–499.

Execution by firing squad in Utah is based on the Mormon belief that bloodshed is necessary in an execution. The author argues for the invalidation of the law, on grounds of illicit religious motivation.

Gaylord, C. L. Capital punishment in ancient United States: a legal-anthropological perspective from 12,000 A.D. *Case and Comment* 82 (January–February, 1977): 3–10.

A look back at today's "primitive" executions from the vantage point of 12,000 A.D.

Gersten, S. N. The constitutionality of executing juvenile offenders: *Thompson v. Oklahoma. Criminal Law Journal* 24 (1988): 91–125.

Reports on a Supreme Court case that questions the "cruel and unusual punishment" of executing a person for a crime committed as a juvenile.

Gibbs, Jack P. The death penalty, retribution, and penal policy. *Journal of Criminal Law and Criminology* 69 (1978): 291–299.

Summarizes the theory of retribution as a justification for the death sentence, drawing attention to the theory's flaws.

————. Deterrence theory and research. In Gary B. Melton, ed., *The Law as a Behavioral Instrument* (Nebraska Symposium on Motivation). 87–130. Lincoln: University of Nebraska Press, 1986.

Discusses the theory of deterrence, its various types and the status of research in the field.

Gillers, Stephen. Deciding who dies. *University of Pennsylvania Law Review* 129 (1980): 1–124.

Reviews the problems inherent in capital punishment laws that do not involve mandatory sentencing.

Goldberg, Arthur J. Death penalty and the Supreme Court. *Arizona Law Review* 15 (1973): 355–368.

Discusses the 10 Supreme Court rulings involving the Eighth Amendment prior to the *Furman* ruling. Former Justice Goldberg holds the opinion that the death penalty violates the Eighth Amendment.

————. The death penalty for rape. *Hastings Constitutional Law Quarterly* 5 (1978): 1–13.

An account of Eighth Amendment rulings through the Supreme Court's *Coker* decision; urges the Court to reverse its ruling on *Gregg*.

Goldberg, Arthur J., and Alan M. Dershowitz. Declaring the death penalty unconstitutional. *Harvard Law Review* 83 (1970): 1773–1819.

Reviews Supreme Court cases involving the Eighth Amendment; holds that capital punishment is unconstitutional.

Gottlieb, Gerald H. Testing the death penalty. *Southern California Law Review* 34 (Spring 1961): 268–281.

Now-famous article that first proposed the idea of a constitutional attack on capital punishment.

Granuci, Anthony F. "Nor cruel and unusual punishments inflicted": the original meaning. *California Law Review* 57 (1969): 839–865.

Explores the thoughts of the framers of the American Bill of Rights on cruel and unusual punishment. Traces the historical background in English law. Holds that the Americans misinterpreted the English precedent.

Greenberg, Jack. Against the American system of capital punishment. *Harvard Law Review* 99 (1986): 1670–1680.

Criticizes present systems of sentencing for failing to isolate the worst, and only the worst, offender for the death penalty.

———. Capital punishment as a system. *Yale Law Journal* 91 (1982): 908–936.

Examines the system of appellate court review, and frequent reversal, of death sentences. Argues for special care in death sentencing but finds that the appellate reversal system negates capital punishment's intended effects.

Greenberg, Jack and Jack Himmelstein. Varieties of attack on the death penalty. *Crime and Delinquency* 15 (1969): 112–120.

Discusses the activities of the NAACP Legal Defense and Education Fund in opposing capital punishment.

Greenhouse, Linda. Appeal rejected in death sentence: justices rule that outsider lacks the legal standing needed to bring case. *The New York Times* 139 (April 25, 1990): A10.

Supreme Court ruling on death sentence appeals.

Greenwald, Helene B. Capital punishment for minors: an Eighth Amendment analysis. *Journal of Criminal Law and Criminology* 74 (1983): 1471–1517.

Examines whether or not capital punishment for minors should be considered a violation of the Eighth Amendment; concludes it should.

———. Minors and the death penalty: decision and avoidance. *Journal of Criminal Law and Criminology* 73 (Winter 1982): 1525–1552.

Discusses the tendency to avoid settling the issue of the execution of minors.

Gross, Samuel R., and Robert Mauro. Patterns of death: an analysis of racial disparities in capital sentencing and homicide victimization. *Stanford Law Review* 37 (1984): 27–153.

Analyzes death sentencing trends in eight states.

Haney, Craig. Epilogue: evolving standards and the capital jury. *Law and Human Behavior* 8 (1984): 153–158.

Considers necessary revision of the death qualification process and social scientists' part in bringing about change in legal standards.

———. Examining death qualification: further analysis of the process effect. *Law and Human Behavior* 8 (1984): 133–151.

Examines the process of death qualification, finding that it may bias jurors towards a guilty verdict.

————. Juries and the death penalty: readdressing the *Witherspoon* question. *Crime and Delinquency* 26 (1980): 512–527.

Examines Supreme Court rulings on jury selection in capital cases.

————. On the selection of capital juries: the biasing effects of the death-qualification process. *Law and Human Behavior* 8 (1984): 121–132.

Studies the process of death qualification and its effect on jurors' likelihood of convicting the defendant.

Human Rights. Why death row needs lawyers. *Human Rights* 14 (Winter 1987): 26–28.

Summary of the focus of the Death Penalty Representation Project of the American Bar Association.

Lawrence, C. Crime and the Constitution. *Scholastic Update* 120 (December 4, 1987): 10–11.

The present status of the issue.

Leavy, Deborah. A matter of life and death: due process protection in capital clemency proceedings. *Yale Law Journal* 90 (1981): 889–911.

Surveys literature on clemency in capital punishment cases.

Lehtinen, Marlene W. The value of life: an argument for the death penalty. *Crime and Delinquency* 23 (1977): 237–252.

An overview of the issue arguing for the continuation of capital punishment.

McDaniels, Ann. The Court: Reagan's legal legacy: a hard line on crime. *Newsweek* 114 (July 10, 1989): 19ff.

The Supreme Court's stance on capital punishment.

Marquart, James W., Sheldon Eckland-Olson and Johnathan R. Sorensen. Gazing into the crystal ball: can jurors accurately predict dangerousness in capital cases? *Law & Society Review* 23 (August 1989): 449–468.

Discusses the validity of dangerousness predictions.

Marshall, Justice Thurgood. Remarks on the death penalty made at the Judicial Conference of the Second Circuit. *Columbia Law Review* 86 (1986): 1–8.

A critique of capital punishment administration arguing that due process is inadequately safeguarded.

Meltsner, Michael. Litigating against the death penalty: the strategy behind *Furman*. *Yale Law Journal* 82 (1973): 1111–1139.

A description of attempts to block executions in Florida and Texas.

———. On death row, the wait continues. In Herman Schwartz, ed., *The Burger Court: Rights and Wrongs of the Supreme Court, 1969–1986*. 169–176. New York: Viking, 1987.

Discusses capital punishment decisions made during Warren Burger's tenure as the Chief Justice of the Supreme Court.

Mikva, Abner J., and John C. Godbold. You don't have to be a bleeding heart: representing death row. *Human Rights* 14 (Winter 1987): 21–25.

Two judges discuss the difficulty of finding attorneys to represent inmates on death row.

Mullin, Courtney. The jury system in death penalty cases: a symbolic gesture. *Law and Contemporary Problems* 43 (1980): 137–154.

Discusses the problem of bias in jury selection for capital cases arguing that social rather than legal factors affect death sentencing.

Murchison, Kenneth M. Toward a perspective on the death penalty cases. *Emory Law Journal* 27 (1978): 469–555.

Discusses the Supreme Court's capital punishment rulings in the context of the abolitionist movement and current Eighth Amendment interpretation.

Partington, Donald H. The incidence of the death penalty for rape in Virginia. *Washington and Lee Law Review* 22 (1965): 43–75.

Traces 53 rape convictions through Virginia courts, of which 41 ended in execution. All 41 were black men. Examines the question of racial prejudice.

Peck, Jon R. The deterrent effect of capital punishment: Ehrlich and his critics. *Yale Law Journal* 85 (1976): 359–367.

Part of the ongoing debate on the validity of the deterrence theory.

Perry, Kent W. Cops: we're losing the war: it's time to change the premise of the corrections system from one of rehabilitation to simple justice. *Newsweek* 113 (March 13, 1989): 6ff.

Evaluates the bases of the criminal justice system.

Peterson, Ruth D., and William C. Bailey. Murder and capital punishment in the evolving context of the post-*Furman* era. *Social Forces* 66 (1988): 774–807.

Considers state murder rates from 1973 to 1984 and their possible correlation with the reinstatement of the death penalty.

Polsby, Daniel D. The death of capital punishment? *Furman v. Georgia.* *Supreme Court Review* (1972): 1–40.

A lengthy consideration of the U.S. Supreme Court's *Furman* ruling and earlier Eighth Amendment cases.

Quade, Vicki. From Wall Street to death row. *Human Rights* 14 (Winter 1987): 18–21ff.

Interviews Ronald Tabak, a Wall Street lawyer performing *pro bono* work for death row inmates.

Radelet, Michael L. Rejecting the jury: the imposition of the death penalty in Florida. *University of California-Davis Law Review* 18 (1985): 1409–1431.

Explores Florida cases since 1972 in which the death penalty was imposed. In 25%, the jury had recommended a life sentence.

————. Sociologists as expert witnesses in capital cases: a case study. In Patrick R. Anderson and L. Thomas Winfree, Jr., eds., *Expert Witnesses: Criminologists in the Courtroom.* 119–134. Albany: State University of New York Press, 1987.

An account of the author's role as an expert witness in several capital cases.

Radelet, Michael L., and Margaret Vandiver. Race and capital punishment: an overview of the issues. *Crime and Social Justice* 25 (1986): 94–113.

Considers historical background and research on the correlation between the races of victims and defendants and the imposition of the death penalty.

Reckless, Walter C. The use of the death penalty: a factual statement. *Crime and Delinquency* 15 (1969): 43–56.

A study of the declining rate of executions and capital crimes. Provides international death penalty status and examines crime rates in the United States.

Reskin, Lauren Rubenstein. Majority of lawyers support capital punishment. *ABA Journal* 71 (April 1985): 44.

The results of a poll of lawyers, 68% of whom support capital punishment.

Rieder, Eric. The right of self-representation in the capital case. *Columbia Law Review* 85 (1985): 130–154.

Discusses the right of self-representation in capital cases. Favors defendants' right to self-representation at trial but advocates counsel for the sentencing and appeals procedures.

Samuelson, Glenn W. Why was capital punishment restored in Delaware? *Journal of Criminal Law and Criminology* 60 (1969): 148–151.

The death penalty was reinstated in Delaware after a three-year hiatus. Homicide rates were not affected by the change.

Sanders, Alain L. Bad news for death row: the court okays the execution of teenage and retarded criminals. *Time* 134 (July 10, 1989): 48–49.

The Supreme Court rules on the execution of juveniles and the mentally incompetent.

Sebba, Leslie. The pardoning power—a world survey. *Journal of Criminal Law and Criminology* 68 (1977): 83–121.

Compares pardoning power provisions in 100 countries.

Should Congress authorize the use of the death penalty for continuing criminal enterprise drug offenders? *Congressional Digest* 65 (November 1986): 280–288.

Eight Congressmen debate the pros and cons of using capital punishment to control drug trafficking in the United States.

Still sweet 16. *Time* 132 (July 11, 1988): 16.

Discusses the Supreme Court decision on the death penalty for offenders who committed crimes before the age of 16.

Stillman, James W. Abolish the death penalty. *Legal Reference Services Quarterly* 4 (1984): 89–95.

Essay opposing the death penalty.

Sutherland, Edwin H. Murder and the death penalty. *Journal of Criminal Law and Criminology* 15 (1925): 522–536.

An early discussion of the deterrence theory; concludes that the death penalty is not a deterrent.

Thornton, Thomas Perry. Terrorism and the death penalty. *America* 135 (December 11, 1976): 410–412.

Argues that the death penalty could incite increased terrorism rather than act as a deterrent.

Annotated Bibliography

Towell, Pat. Death-penalty fight stalls Senate defense bill. *Congressional Quarterly Weekly Report* 46 (May 21, 1988): 1360ff.

Discusses debate over proposed death sentencing for convicted drug lords.

van den Haag, Ernest. The death penalty once more. *University of California-Davis Law Review* 18 (1985): 957–972.

Despite the inconclusiveness of deterrence research, holds that capital punishment is justifiable.

———. The death penalty vindicates the law. *ABA Journal* 71 (April 1985): 38–42.

A debate about capital punishment with Henry Schwarzschild.

———. In defense of the death penalty: a legal-practical-moral analysis. *Criminal Law Bulletin* 14 (1978): 51–68.

Affirms the constitutionality, usefulness and moral justification of the death penalty.

———. On deterrence and the death penalty. *Journal of Criminal Law, Criminology and Police Science* 60 (1969): 141–147.

Supports capital punishment on the theory that the possibility of deterrence is justification enough.

———. A response to Bedau. *Arizona State Law Journal 1977* (1977): 797–802.

Part of an ongoing debate with Hugo Adam Bedau.

———. The ultimate punishment: a defense. *Harvard Law Review* 99 (1986): 1662–1669.

Criticizes abolitionist viewpoints of capital punishment.

Wermeil, Stephen. Court's conservatives don't like delays in death cases, but they're not helping. *The Wall Street Journal*. Mar 12, 1990, B8.

The Supreme Court hears an increasing number of death penalty cases.

Whitford, E. How a family tragedy may lead to a landmark court ruling. *Scholastic Update* 120 (April 8, 1988): 10–12.

The *Thompson* case focuses attention on the issue of sentencing minors to death.

Weisberg, Robert. Deregulating death. *Supreme Court Review* 8 (1983): 305–395.

Reviews recent U.S. Supreme Court capital punishment rulings; assesses the Court's consistency.

Wilson, William. Juvenile offenders and the electric chair: cruel and unusual punishment or firm discipline for the hopelessly delinquent? *University of Florida Law Review* 35 (1983): 344–371.

Considers whether or not a distinction between juveniles and adults should be made in sentencing for heinous crimes.

MEDICAL

Annas, George J. Killing with kindness: why the FDA need not certify drugs used for execution safe and effective. *American Journal of Public Health* 75 (1985): 1096–1099.

The Supreme Court unanimously refused to require FDA approval for drugs used for execution. The author agrees with the decision but feels the real issue is capital punishment, not lethal injections.

Applebaum, Paul S. Competence to be executed: another conundrum for mental health professionals. *Hospital and Community Psychiatry* 37 (1986): 682–684.

Explores the necessity of physician involvement in determining whether an inmate is competent to be executed.

———. Death, the expert witness, and the dangers of going *Barefoot*. *Hospital and Community Psychiatry* 34 (1983): 1003–1004.

A report on psychiatric predictions of dangerousness in death penalty cases in Texas. Focuses on the (Thomas) *Barefoot* case.

———. Psychiatrists' role in the death penalty. *Hospital and Community Psychiatry* 32 (1981): 761–762.

Discusses the effectiveness of psychiatrists in predicting how dangerous a criminal may be. Finds the results of indifferent value.

Bailey, William C. Deterrence and the violent sex offender: imprisonment vs. the death penalty. *Journal of Behavioral Economics* 6 (1977): 107–144.

Explores the effect of the death penalty on rape, using 1951 and 1961 data. A slight deterrent relationship between capital punishment and rape did occur.

Casscells, Ward, and William J. Curran. Doctors, the death penalty, and lethal injection: recent developments. *New England Journal of Medicine* 307 (December 9, 1982): 1532–1533.

A number of medical organizations oppose physicians' participation in administering lethal injections.

Curran, William J. Uncertainty in prognosis of violent conduct: the Supreme Court lays down the law. *New England Journal of Medicine* 310 (June 21, 1984): 1651–1652.

Disagrees with the Supreme Court on allowing psychiatric testimony predicting future violent conduct during capital trial sentencing.

Curran, William J., and Ward Casscells. The ethics of medical participation in capital punishment by intravenous drug injection. *New England Journal of Medicine* 302 (January 24, 1980): 226–230.

Argues that medical practitioners cannot ethically participate in the administration of lethal injections.

Dow, Barbara. Physicians ponder role as the agent of death: practice of execution by lethal injection confronts medicine once again. *American Medical News* 30 (September 4, 1987): 9ff.

Reexamines the role of the physician in execution by lethal injection.

Entin, J. L. Psychiatry, insanity, and the death penalty: a note on implementing Supreme Court decisions. *Journal of Criminal Law and Criminology* 79 (Spring 1988): 218–239.

Comments on the justification of exempting the insane from capital punishment.

Ewing, Charles P. "Dr. Death" and the case for an ethical ban on psychiatric and psychological predictions of dangerousness in capital sentencing proceedings. *American Journal of Law and Medicine* 8 (1983): 407–428.

Considers the validity of psychiatric predictions of dangerousness in capital case sentencing. Opposes such predictions as unethical.

Kaplan, Stanley M. Death, so say we all. *Psychology Today* 19 (July 1985): 48–53.

Examines the high level of stress experienced by many jurors in capital cases.

Malone, Patrick. Death row and the medical model. *Hastings Center Report* 9 (October 1979): 5–6.

A discussion of the ethical issues of lethal injection and physicians' attitudes toward the process.

Reid, Dee. Low IQ is a capital crime. *The Progressive* 52 (April 1988): 24ff.

Discusses the execution of mentally deficient convicts.

Salguero, Rochelle Graff. Medical ethics and competency to be executed. *Yale Law Journal* 96 (1986): 167–186.

Explores ethical issues and codes to be considered by psychiatrists evaluating or treating inmates whose competency to be executed is in question.

Sargent, Douglas A. Treating the condemned to death. *Hastings Center Report* 16 (December 1986): 5–6.

Opposes psychiatric treatment for incompetent inmates on the grounds that a recovered inmate would then be executed.

Schwarzschild, Henry. Homicide by injection. *New York Times*, Dec 23, 1982: 15.

Opposes execution by lethal injection.

Sherrill, Robert. In Florida, insanity is no defense. *The Nation* 239 (Nov 24, 1983): 539ff.

Discusses Florida cases in which the mentally incompetent received the death sentence.

Showalter, C. Robert, and Richard J. Bonnie. Psychiatrists and capital sentencing: risks and responsibilities in a unique legal setting. *Bulletin of the American Academy of Psychiatry and the Law* 12 (1984): 159–167.

Advocates an increase in psychiatric input during capital sentencing, recognizing the difficulties involved.

Surfin, Ron. "Everything is in order, Warden": a discussion of death in the gas chamber. *Suicide and Life-Threatening Behavior* 6 (1976): 44–57.

Describes California's gas chamber and death there.

Weihofen, Henry. A question of justice: trial or execution of an insane defendant. *ABA Journal* 37 (1951): 651–654ff.

Examines justifications for not executing the mentally incompetent.

Weisbuch, Jonathan B. The public health effects of the death penalty. *Journal of Public Health Policy* 5 (1984): 305–311.

Discusses capital punishment's effect on the public health.

GOVERNMENT DOCUMENTS

GENERAL

Bureau of Justice Statistics. *National Prisoner Statistics–Capital Punishment.* Washington, DC: US GPO, 1950– .

Annual statistical report on the death row population and executions in the United States.

Federal Bureau of Justice. *Crime in the United States–Uniform Crime Reports.* Washington, DC: US GPO, 1930– .

Annual statistical report on crime in the United States.

Zimring, Franklin C., and Michael Laurence. *Death Penalty.* Washington, DC: National Institute of Justice, 1988.

Information on the death penalty prepared by the Department of Justice's research institute.

UNITED STATES CONGRESS

House Hearings

Committee on the Judiciary. *Sentencing in Capital Cases: Hearing Before the Subcommittee on Criminal Justice on H.R. 13360.* 95th Cong., 2d sess., July 19, 1978. Washington, DC: US GPO, 1978.

Committee on the Judiciary. *Capital Punishment: Hearings Before the Subcommittee on Criminal Justice on H.R. 2837 and H.R. 343.* 99th Cong., 1st and 2d sess., November 7, 1985; April 16, May 7, June 5 and July 24, 1986. Washington, DC: US GPO, 1987.

Committee on the Judiciary. *Death Penalty: Hearing Before the Subcommittee on Criminal Justice.* 100th Cong., 1st sess., July 18, 1987. Washington, DC: US GPO, 1989.

Senate Hearings

Committee on the Judiciary. *To Establish Constitutional Procedures for the Imposition of Capital Punishment: Hearing Before the Subcommittee on Criminal Laws on S. 1382.* 95th Cong., 1st sess., May 18, 1977. Washington, DC: US GPO, 1977.

Committee on the Judiciary. *To Establish Rational Criteria for the Imposition of Capital Punishment: Hearing on S. 1382.* 95th Cong., 2d sess. Washington, DC: US GPO, 1978.

Committee on the Judiciary. *Capital Punishment: Hearings on S. 114.* 97th Cong., 1st sess., April 10, 27 and May 1, 1981. Washington, DC: US GPO, 1981.

Committee on the Judiciary. *Prison Violence and Capital Punishment: Hearing Before the Subcommittee on Criminal Law.* 98th Cong., 1st sess., November 9, 1983. Washington, DC: US GPO, 1984.

Committee on the Judiciary. *Death Penalty Legislation: Hearing on S. 239.* 99th Cong., 1st sess., September 24, 1985. Washington, DC: US GPO, 1986.

Senate Reports

Committee on the Judiciary. *Establishing Constitutional Procedures for the Imposition of Capital Punishment.* Washington, DC: US GPO, 1978.

Committee on the Judiciary. *Establishing Constitutional Procedures for the Imposition of Capital Punishment, together with minority views to accompany S. 114.* Washington, DC: US GPO, 1981.

Committee on the Judiciary. *Establishing Constitutional Procedures for the Imposition of Capital Punishment, together with minority views of S. 1785.* Washington, DC: US GPO, 1983.

Committee on the Judiciary. *Establishing Constitutional Procedures for the Imposition of Capital Punishment, together with minority views on S. 239.* Washington, DC: US GPO, 1986.

Committee on the Jucidiary. *The Federal Death Penalty Act of 1988: Report (to accompany S. 32).* Washington, DC: US GPO, 1988.

BROCHURES AND PAMPHLETS

Bedau, Hugo Adam. *The Case Against the Death Penalty.* New York: American Civil Liberties Union, 1984.

A concise pamphlet summarizing the position of opponents to the death penalty.

The Death Penalty: The Religious Community Calls for Abolition. Washington, DC: National Coalition to Abolish the Death Penalty. n.d.

Statements by 29 religious denominations urging abolition of capital punishment.

Gunterman, Joe, and Trevor Thomas. *This Life We Take: A Case Against the Death Penalty*. 5th ed. Sacramento, CA: Friends Committee on Legislation Education Fund, 1987.

Reviews the current status of capital punishment and argues against the sanction.

Zehr, Howard. *Death as a penalty*. Elkhart, IN: Mennonite Central Committee U.S. Office of Criminal Justice. n.d.

Abolitionist moral, theological and practical arguments against the death penalty.

AUDIOVISUAL MATERIALS

Bill of Rights in Action: Capital Punishment. BFA Educational Media, 1976, 16 min, 16 mm.

A dramatization of the sentencing phase of the trial of a convicted murderer. Presents arguments for and against the death penalty.

Capital Punishment. BFA Educational Media, 1976, 23 min, 16 mm.

Lawyers argue over the sentencing phase of a trial involving a convicted murderer: Does the death penalty comprise cruel and unusual punishment under the Eighth Amendment? Is it an effective deterrent against crime?

Capital Punishment. Prentice-Hall Media, 1981, 27 min, two 35 mm filmstrips and two sound cassettes.

Discusses the legal and political history of the death penalty and debates the issues involved.

The Chair. Drew Associates and Time-Life Films, 1970, 54 min, 16 mm.

Believing that his client became rehabilitated while confined for nine years to death row, an attorney pleads to the parole board for the murder's sentence of execution to be commuted to life imprisonment.

Changing Views on Capital Punishment. Educational Enrichment Materials, 1977, 15 min, 35 mm.

Deals with such issues as why many people favor capital punishment, the deterrent effect of the death penalty on crime and whether the United States should have a national policy on the use of the death penalty.

Crime and the Criminal. Learning Corporation of America, 1973, 33 min, 16 mm.

Edited from the Columbia Pictures motion picture *In Cold Blood,* this film recounts the real life episode of mass murder depicted in Truman Capote's book. It considers how the criminal is different from the rest of society and questions the use of the death penalty.

Cruel and Unusual Punishment. CB Communications, 1972, 15 min, 16 mm.

Shows the preparation for and procedures of an actual execution and the effect on those involved. Deliberates the use of capital punishment from the viewpoint of inmates, correctional employees, governors and execution squad members.

Day's Last Rainbow. University of Southern California, Division of Cinema/TV, 1980, 12 min, 16 mm.

Examines life on death row as experienced by two black inmates—one resigned to dying, the other determined to live.

Dead Wrong—The John Evans Story. American Educational Films, 1984, 45 min, video.

The true story of Evan's life of crime and eventual execution in the electric chair. Uses footage of an interview taped before his death.

The Death Penalty. BBC-TV. Time-Life Films, 1976, 60 min, 16 mm.

Interviews with murderers, friends and relatives of murder victims, policemen, church leaders and executioners. Presents the pros and cons of the death penalty.

The Death Penalty. Dallas County Community College, 1979, 29 min, video.

This program explores complex and controversial questions about the death penalty. It captured the International Film and Television Festival 1980 Silver Award.

The Death Penalty: Cruel or Just Punishment? Current Affairs Films, 1980, 16 min, 35 mm.

Examines efforts by various states to create capital punishment laws which are acceptable to the Supreme Court on constitutional grounds. Surveys the public response to the death penalty.

The Death Penalty: What is Fair? Random House, Educational Enrichment Materials, 1984, one 35 mm filmstrip and one sound cassette.

Focus is on the arguments advanced by the supporters and opponents of the death penalty. A brief history of capital punishment in the United States is presented.

Death Row. BBC-TV. Time-Life Films, 1973, 49 min, 16 mm.

Examines the broad spectrum of opinion on capital punishment, from the man-on-the-street to those on death row.

Death Row and the Death Penalty. Journal Films Inc., 1984, 14 min, video.

Includes interviews with death penalty advocates and opponents and shows scenes of an actual execution.

Death Watch. International Telemedia, 1981, 53 min, video.

George Kennedy introduces the viewer to the world of life on death row. Six inmates who are awaiting execution at Arizona State Prison are interviewed.

11 Months on Death Row. Journal Films Inc., 1978, 17 min, video.

Examines the death penalty through the eyes of a man who spent 11 months on death row.

Executioner's Song. U.S.A. Home Video, 1982, 127 min, video.

An adaptation of the Norman Mailer book about the last nine months of convicted murderer Gary Gilmore's life.

License to Kill. Cinema Guild, 1985, 28 min, 16 mm.

Presents both sides of the debate on capital punishment through interviews with lawyers, jurists, crime victims, civil rights advocates and condemned criminals.

Life on Death Row. National Educational Television. Indiana University, Audio-Visual Center, 1968, 9 min, 16 mm.

Presents the thoughts and feelings of several men on San Quentin's death row. Artist sketches show the prisoners, the views from their cells and the last execution at San Quentin.

The Sentence. K.S.M. Concepts, Inc., 1983, 10 min, video.

In a dramatization, graphically demonstrates execution in the electric chair. The dilemmas of the extent of the man's guilt and the morality of capital punishment are presented.

The Thin Blue Line. Errol Morris. HBO Home Video, 1988, 101 min, video.

Documentary about 1977 shooting of a policeman in Dallas County, Texas. The man convicted and sentenced to death for the crime, Randall Adams, appeared to be innocent. Following the film's release, Adams, imprisoned 12 years on a commuted sentence, was finally freed.

Thy Will Be Done. CTV Television Network, 1976, 25 min, 16 mm.

Examines the issue of capital punishment and considers pros and cons of the debate.

CHAPTER 7

ORGANIZATIONS AND ASSOCIATIONS

This chapter is a listing of organizations that are a source of information and educational materials on capital punishment. These organizations include government agencies, professional associations, foundations and private advocacy groups. Also identified are religious organizations active in the debate over the death penalty.

National organizations are accompanied by a brief synopsis of their involvement in capital punishment issues and the types of information they make available. Similar abstracts are not provided at the state and local level or for the religious groups as the services and activities of these organizations are subject to change. For the most part, the private and religious groups advocate the elimination of capital punishment.

There is broad political support for the death penalty, evidenced by the fact the federal government and most states now have capital punishment laws, but there is no coordinated movement on behalf of the sanction.

NATIONAL

American Civil Liberties Union
Capital Punishment Project
132 W. 43rd St.
New York, NY 10036
(212) 944-9800

Project within the ACLU which coordinates efforts to block or repeal capital punishment. Publishes and distributes a range of resources on the issue.

American Civil Liberties Union
Legislative Office
122 Maryland Ave. NE
Washington, DC 20002
(202) 544-1681
Public interest law organization which opposes the death penalty. Source of information on legislative developments.

Amnesty International
322 Eighth Ave.
New York, NY 10001
(212) 807-8400
International human rights organization. Furnishes statistics, information and materials on capital punishment throughout the world.

Bureau of Justice Statistics
633 Indiana Ave. NW
Washington, DC 20531
(202) 307-0765
Justice Department bureau responsible for collecting, preparing and disseminating statistical information on the criminal justice system at the federal, state and local level. Maintains information on death sentences and executions.

Capital Punishment Research Project
P. O. Drawer 277
Headland, AL 36345
(205) 693-5225
Maintains extensive records on capital punishment in the United States.

Center for Constitutional Rights
666 Broadway, 7th Floor
New York, NY 10012
(212) 614-6464
Engages in advocacy and educational programs in opposition to the death penalty.

Defense for Children International
210 Forsyth Street
New York, NY 10002
(718) 965-0245
Provides information on juvenile offenders and the death penalty.

Friends Committee on National Legislation
245 Second St. NE
Washington, DC 20002
(202) 547-6000
Abolitionist advocacy group active in legislative matters.

FRIENDS OF SOLACE
6 Dudley Heights
Albany, NY 12210
(518) 432-7821
Information on the abolitionist group's work and activities on behalf of the families of murder victims.

Information Clearinghouse on Criminal Justice
P.O. Box 4090
San Rafael, CA 94913
(415) 454-6852
Information resource on the imposition of the death sentence on allegedly innocent persons.

International Human Rights Program
222 S. Downey Ave.
Indianapolis, IN 46206
(317) 353-1491
Conducts public education and advocacy work in opposition to capital punishment.

Law Enforcement Against Death
11 Leicester Rd.
Belmont, MA 02178
(617) 489-1708
Source of information on law enforcement and the effectiveness of the death penalty as a deterrent.

Martin Luther King Center for Nonviolent Change
449 Auburn Ave. NE
Atlanta, GA 30312
(404) 526-8929
Opposes the death penalty based on a belief in nonviolence. Engages in research and education.

NAACP Legal Defense Fund, Inc.
99 Hudson St., 16th Floor
New York, NY 10013
(212) 219-1900
Public interest law and education organization active in efforts to halt capital punishment. Maintains statistics and information on the death row population and executions.

National Bar Association
1225 11th St. NW
Washington, DC 20001
(202) 842-3900
Major national professional association for attorneys. Source of information on the legal aspects of capital punishment.

National Coalition to Abolish the Death Penalty
1325 G St. NW
Washington, DC 20005
(202) 347-2411
Coalition of religious, community, human and civil rights, public interest law and professional organizations. Provides information and materials on the abolitionist movement and arguments against the death penalty.

National Committee Against Repressive Legislation
236 Massachusetts Ave. NE # 406
Washington, DC 20002
(202) 543-7659
Advocacy group which opposes capital punishment legislation.

National Conference of Black Lawyers
126 W. 119th St.
New York, NY 10026
(212) 864-4000
Provides legal assistance in death penalty cases. Source of information on capital punishment and racial minorities.

National Council on Crime and Delinquency
20 E. Jackson St., # 300
Chicago, IL 60604
(415) 956-5651
Source of information on crime and the death penalty.

National Criminal Justice Reference System
P.O. Box 6000
Rockville, MD 20850
(800) 732-3277
Information clearinghouse operated by the National Institute of Justice. Specialists answer inquiries drawing on an extensive computerized database of books, reports, articles and audiovisual materials.

National Execution Alert Network
1419 V St. NW
Washington, DC 20009
(202) 797-7090
Network of concerned abolitionist groups and individuals who track and monitor pending executions. Source of information and resource materials.

National Institute of Justice
633 Indiana Ave. NW
Washington, DC 20531
(202) 307-2942
Part of the Department of Justice, the NIJ is the primary federal sponsor of research on the criminal justice system. Publishes its findings in various reports and studies. Operates the National Criminal Justice Reference System.

National Lawyers Guild
55 6th Ave.
New York, NY 10013
(212) 966-5000
Source of information on capital punishment and the law.

National Legal Aid and Defender Association
1625 K St. NW, Suite 800
Washington, DC 20006
(202) 452-0620
Source of information on legislation, legal actions and court cases related to capital punishment.

National Urban League
500 E. 62nd St.
New York, NY 10021
(212) 310-9122
Maintains information on the death penalty and racial minorities.

The Sentencing Project
1156 15th St. NW, Suite 520
Washington, DC 20005
(202) 463-8348
Abolitionist advocacy and education organization.

Washington Legal Foundation
1705 N St. NW
Washington, DC 20036
(202) 857-0240
Public interest law organization which advocates retention of the death penalty. Publishes working papers, studies, monographs and other materials.

RELIGIOUS

American Baptist Church
National Ministries
P.O. Box 851
Valley Forge, PA 19482
(215) 768-2487

American Friends Service
  Committee
1501 Cherry St.
Philadelphia, PA 19102
(215) 241-7123

Episcopal Church
Office of Social Welfare
815 Second Ave.
New York, NY 10017
(212) 867-8400

Jewish Peace Fellowship
29 Ridge Terrace
Central Valley, NY 10917
(914) 928-6409

Mennonite Central Committee
Office of Criminal Justice
107 W. Lexington Ave.
Elkhart, IN 46516
(219) 293-3090

National Council on Islamic
  Affairs
P.O. Box 416
New York, NY 10017
(212) 972-0460

National Interreligious Task
  Force on Criminal Justice
100 Witherspoon St.
Louisville, KY 40202
(502) 569-5810

Pax Christi USA
348 E. 10th
Erie, PA 16503
(814) 453-4955

Presbyterian Church (USA)
Criminal Justice Program
100 Witherspoon St.
Louisville, KY 40202
(502) 569-5810

Southern Christian Leadership
  Conference
334 Auburn Ave. NE
Atlanta, GA 30303
(404) 522-1420

The Synagogue Council of
  America
4101 Cathedral Ave. NE
Washington, DC 20016
(202) 244-6343

Union of American Hebrew
  Congregations
Commission on Social Action
838 Fifth Ave.
New York, NY 10021
(212) 249-0100

Union of American Hebrew
  Congregations
2131 Elmwood Ave.
Rochester, NY 14618
(716) 244-7060

Unitarian Universalist
  Service Committee
1176 Warren
Topeka, KS 66604
(913) 296-5491

United Church of Christ
110 Maryland Ave. NE
Washington, DC 20002
(202) 543-1517

United Methodist Church
Board of Church and Society
100 Maryland Ave. NE
Washington, DC 20002
(202) 488-5657

United Methodist Church
Board of Global Ministries
475 Riverside Dr., Room 332
New York, NY 10115
(212) 870-3832

STATE AND LOCAL

ALABAMA

Alabama Prison Project
410 S. Perry St.
Montgomery, AL 36104
(205) 264-7416

ALASKA

Alaskans Against the Death
Penalty
303 Kimsham
Sitka, AK 99835
(907) 747-8775

Anti-Death Penalty Info Network
P.O. Box 100804
Anchorage, AK 99510
(907) 272-9164

ARIZONA

Office of the Public Defender
Attn: Appeals Division
45 W. Pennington
Tucson, AZ 85701
(602) 791-3373

ARKANSAS

Arkansas Coalition Against the Death Penalty
209 W. Capitol, Suite 214
Little Rock, AR 72201
(501) 374-2660

CALIFORNIA

American Civil Liberties Union
1663 Mission St. #460
San Francisco, CA 94103
(415) 621-2493

American Civil Liberties Union
633 S. Shatto Place
Los Angeles, CA 90005
(213) 487-1720

Amnesty International
Western Regional Office
3407 W. 6th St. #704
Los Angeles, CA 90020
(213) 388-1237

Death Penalty Focus of
California
P.O. Box 412
Whittier, CA 90608
(213) 693-4536

East Bay Justice Project
3020 E. 16th Street, Apt. 1
Oakland, CA 94601
(415) 832-4460

Northern California Coalition
to Abolish the Death Penalty
1251 Second Ave.
San Francisco, CA 94122
(415) 681-6750

Southern California Coalition Against the Death Penalty
980 N. Fair Oaks Ave.
Pasadena, CA 91103
(818) 798-7213

COLORADO

Colorado Coalition to Abolish the Death Penalty
P.O. Box 300552
Denver, CO 80203
(303) 349-9450

CONNECTICUT

Connecticut Civil Liberties
Union
32 Grand St.
Hartford, CT 06106
(203) 247-9823

Connecticut Network Against
the Death Penalty
144 South Quaker Lane
West Hartford, CT 06119
(203) 872-7205

DELAWARE

ACLU of Delaware
903 French St.
Wilmington, DE 19801
(302) 654-3966

DISTRICT OF COLUMBIA

Amnesty International
Middle Atlantic Office
608 Massachusetts Ave. NE
Washington, DC 20002
(202) 547-4718

NAACP
1025 Vermont Ave. NW #820
Washington, DC 20005
(202) 638-2269

FLORIDA

ACLU of Florida
225 NE. 34 St., #208
Miami, FL 33137
(305) 576-2336

Florida IMPACT
106 W. Jefferson
Tallahassee, FL 32301
(904) 222-3470

Florida Clearinghouse on
  Criminal Justice
121 E. Georgia St., Suite 6
Tallahassee, FL 32301
(904) 222-4820

Gainesville Citizens Against the
  Death Penalty
P.O. Box 13332
Gainesville, FL 32604
(904) 372-4396

Tampa Bay Coalition to Abolish the Death Penalty
P.O. Box 41532
St. Petersburg, FL 33743
(813) 345-2721

GEORGIA

ACLU of Georgia
88 Walton St.
Atlanta, GA 30303
(404) 523-5398

Southern Prison Ministry
910 Ponce de Leon Ave. NE
Atlanta, GA 30306
(404) 874-9652

Amnesty International
730 Peachtree St., Suite 982
Atlanta, GA 30308
(404) 876-5661

Southern Prisoners' Defense
  Committee
185 Walton
Atlanta, GA 30303
(404) 688-1202

Clearinghouse on Georgia
  Prisons and Jails
P.O. Box 437
Atlanta, GA. 30301
(404) 522-4971

Team Defense
P.O. Box 1978
Atlanta, GA 30301
(404) 688-8116

HAWAII

ACLU of Hawaii
33 S. King St. #412
Honolulu, HI 96813
(808) 545-1722

ILLINOIS

Amnesty International Midwest
53 W. Jackson, Suite 1162
Chicago, IL 60604
(312) 427-2060

Illinois Coalition Against the
Death Penalty
20 E. Jackson, 16th Floor
Chicago, IL 60604
(321) 427-7330

Lutheran Social Services of Illinois Justice Ministry
880 Lee St.
Des Plaines, IL 60016
(312) 635-4627

INDIANA

Indiana Public Defender
Council
309 W. Washington St.,
Suite 401
Indianapolis, IN 46204
(317) 232-2490

Hoosiers Opposing
Executions-North
1325 Greencroft Dr.,
Apt. 350
Goshen, IN 46526
(219) 533-0756

Hoosiers Opposing Executions
1710 N. Talbott
Indianapolis, IN 46202
(317) 925-8819

IOWA

American Friends Service
Committee
4211 Grand Ave.
Des Moines, IA 50312
(515) 274-4851

Iowa Civil Liberties Union
409 Shops Building
Des Moines, IA 50309
(515) 243-3576

KANSAS

Kansas Coalition Against the Death Penalty
1176 Warren St.
Topeka, KS 66604
(913) 296-5491

KENTUCKY

Kentucky Coalition Against the Death Penalty
712 E. Muhammad Ali Blvd.
Louisville, KY 40202
(502) 637-9786

LOUISIANA

ACLU of Louisiana
921 Canal #1237
New Orleans, LA 70112
(504) 522-0617

Loyola Death Penalty
Resource Center
348 Baronne, Suite 421
New Orleans, LA 70112
(504) 522-0578

Pilgrimage For Life
916 St. Andrew St.
New Orleans, LA 70130
(504) 522-5519

MAINE

Maine Civil Liberties Union
97A Exchange St.
Portland, ME 04101
(207) 774-5444

MARYLAND

ACLU of Maryland
The Equitable Building,
  Suite 405
10 N. Calvert St.
Baltimore, MD 21202
(301) 576-1103

American Friends Service
  Committee
317 E. 25th St.
Baltimore, MD 21218
(301) 366-7200

Let Live
P.O. Box 5206
Hyattsville, MD 20782
(301) 277-7177

180

MASSACHUSETTS

Amnesty International-USA
  Northeast Region
58 Day St.
Somerville, MA 02144
(617) 623-0202

Massachusetts Citizens Against
  the Death Penalty
Old South Church
645 Boylston St.
Boston, MA 02116
(508) 460-1439

MICHIGAN

American Friends Service
  Committee
1414 Hill St.
Ann Arbor, MI 48104
(313) 761-8283

Michigan Coalition Against the
  Death Penalty
300 N. Washington, Suite 52
Lansing, MI 48933
(517) 482-4161

Michigan Committee Against Capital Punishment
524 S. Walnut
Lansing, MI 48933
(517) 484-9497

MINNESOTA

Minnesota Coalition Against the Death Penalty
1021 W. Broadway
Minneapolis, MN 55411
(612) 522-3702

MISSISSIPPI

Mississippi Coalition Against the Death Penalty
1133 Cloister St.
Jackson, MS 39202
(601) 352-6347

MISSOURI

Criminal Justice Task Force
American Friends Service
  Committee
438 N. Skinker
St. Louis, MO 63130
(314) 862-5773

Criminal-Victim Services of the
  Kansas City Catholic Charities
P.O. Box 411776
Kansas City, MO 64141
(816) 444-7878

Missouri Coalition Against the Death Penalty
P.O. Box 1022
Jefferson City, MO 65102
(314) 635-9127

MONTANA

ACLU of Montana
P.O. Box 3012
Billings, MT 59103
(406) 248-1086

Montana Coalition to Abolish
  the Death Penalty
910 Ronald
Missoula, MT 59801
(406) 542-2310

NEBRASKA

Nebraskans Against the Death Penalty
P.O. Box 81455
Lincoln, NE 68501
(402) 474-6575

NEVADA

ACLU of Nevada
P.O. Box 40967
Reno, NV 89504
(702) 786-8260

Rising Son Ministry, Inc.
1829 E. Charleston #100
Las Vegas, NV 89104
(702) 383-8282

NEW HAMPSHIRE

New Hampshire Civil Liberties Union
11 S. Main
Concord, NH 03301
(603) 225-3080

NEW JERSEY

ACLU of New Jersey
2 Washington Place
Newark, NJ 07102
(201) 642-2084

New Jersey Coalition Against
  the Death Penalty
687 Larch Ave.
Teaneck, NJ 07666
(201) 836-5187

People Against Legalized Murder
P.O. Box 594
Cape May Court House,
  NJ 08210
(609) 465-7157

South Jersey Committee Against
  Capital Punishment
P.O. Box 724
Ocean City, NJ 08226
(609) 398-4350

NEW MEXICO

Coalition for Prisoners' Rights
P.O. Box 1911
Santa Fe, NM 87502
(505) 982-3691

Committee to Stop Executions
P.O. Box 4811 Coronado Station
Santa Fe, NM 87502
(505) 983-3695

NEW YORK

ACLU of New York
132 W. 43rd St.
New York, NY 10036
(212) 382-0557

New York State Coalition to
    Abolish the Death Penalty
362 State St.
Albany, NY 12210
(518) 436-9222

Long Island Coalition Against
    the Death Penalty
22 Stratton Lane
Stony Brook, NY 11790
(516) 589-6200

New York State Defenders
    Association
11 N. Pearl
Albany, NY 12207
(518) 465-3524

New York State Coalition
    for Criminal Justice
362 State St.
Albany, NY 12210
(518) 436-9222

People Against the Death Penalty
P.O. Box 81
Fayetteville, NY 13066
(315) 443-2011

NORTH CAROLINA

Death Penalty Resource Center
P.O. Box 1070
Raleigh, NC 27602
(919) 733-9490

North Carolina ACLU
P.O. Box 28004
Raleigh, NC 27611
(919) 834-3390

North Carolina Prison and
    Jail Project
P.O. Box 309
Durham, NC 27702
(919) 682-1149

Office of the Appellate Defender
P.O. Box 1070
Raleigh, NC 27602
(919) 733-9490

OHIO

Ohio Coalition to Abolish
    the Death Penalty-Cincinnati
123 E. 13th St.
Cincinnati, OH 45210
(513) 421-8327

Ohio Coalition to Abolish
    the Death Penalty
612 American Blvd.
Columbus, OH 43223
(614) 445-6136

Ohio Public Defender
  Commission
8 E. Long St.
Columbus, OH 43215
(614) 466-5394

Ohioans to STOP Executions
P.O. Box 10444
Columbus, OH 43201
(216) 455-3664

Progressive Prisoners' Movement
462 ½ Granville St.
Newark, OH 43055
(614) 344-7313

OKLAHOMA

Oklahoma Coalition to Abolish the Death Penalty
P.O. Box 799
Oklahoma City, OK 73101
(405) 524-2296

OREGON

Oregon Coalition to Abolish
  the Death Penalty
245 SW. Bancroft, Suite B
Portland, OR 97201
(503) 221-1054

Oregon Criminal Defense
  Lawyers Association
44 W. Broadway #403
Eugene, OR 97401
(503) 686-8716

PENNSYLVANIA

Allegheny County Death
  Penalty Project
5132 Friendship Ave.
Pittsburgh, PA 15224
(412) 434-5011

Northeast Pennsylvania Coalition
  Against the Death Penalty
550 Madison Ave.
Scranton, PA 18510
(717) 342-4117

Centre Region Coalition to
  Abolish the Death Penalty
P.O. Box 502
State College, PA 16804
(814) 238-1983

Pennsylvania Council to Abolish
  the Penalty of Death
125 S. 9th St.
Philadelphia, PA 19107
(215) 592-1513

Western Pennsylvania Coalition Against the Death Penalty
P.O. Box 6893
Pittsburgh, PA 15212
(412) 391-6458

RHODE ISLAND

Rhode Island Civil Liberties Union
212 Union St., Room 221
Providence, RI 02903
(401) 831-7171

Rhode Island Justice Alliance
P.O. Box 28610
Providence, RI 02908
(401) 421-7833

SOUTH CAROLINA

South Carolina Coalition Against
the Death Penalty
P.O. Box 11513
Columbia, SC 29211
(803) 254-0282

Southeast Regional Coordinator
AI-USA Death Penalty Project
6248 Yorkshire Dr.
Columbia, SC 29209
(803) 777-3898

SOUTH DAKOTA

South Dakota Peace and Justice Center
P.O. Box 405
Watertown, SD 57201
(605) 882-2822

TENNESSEE

Death Penalty Resistance Project
of Tennessee
P.O. Box 120552
Nashville, TN 37212
(615) 256-7028

Southern Coalition on Jails
and Prisons
P.O. Box 120044
Nashville, TN 37212
(615) 383-9610

TEXAS

ACLU of Houston
1236 W. Gray
Houston, TX 77019
(713) 524-5925

Capital Punishment Clinic
University of Texas Law School
727 E. 26th St.
Austin, TX 78705
(512) 471-5151

Dallas Coalition Against the
Death Penalty
P.O. Box 3850, Station A
Dallas, TX 75208
(214) 426-5333

Texas Civil Liberties Union
1611 E. 1st St.
Austin, TX 78702
(512) 477-5849

UTAH

ACLU of Utah
450 S. 900 E, Suite 310
Salt Lake City, UT 84102
(801) 521-9289

The Rocky Mountain Defense
  Fund
175 E. 400 S, Suite 400
Salt Lake City, UT 84111
(801) 355-0320

Utah Coalition Against the
  Death Penalty
P.O. Box 3441
Salt Lake City, UT 84110
(801) 364-2318

Salt Lake Legal Defender
  Association
424 E. 500 S, Suite 300
Salt Lake City, UT 84111
(801) 532-5444

VERMONT

Vermont Coalition Against the Death Penalty
21 Fairground Rd.
Springfield, VT 05156
(802) 885-3327

VIRGINIA

Virginia Association Against
  the Death Penalty
6 N. 6th St.
Richmond, VA 23219
(804) 648-2237

Virginia Coalition on Jails and
  Prisons
4912 W. Broad St., Suite 205
Richmond, VA 23230
(804) 353-0093

People Abolishing the
  Death Penalty
8319 Fulham Court
Richmond, VA 23227
(804) 262-3900

Virginia ACLU
6 N. 6th St.
Richmond, VA 23219
(804) 644-8022

WASHINGTON

Inland Northwest Death
  Penalty Abolition Group
411 S. Washington
Spokane, WA 99204
(509) 838-7870

Washington Coalition Against
  the Death Penalty
1720 Smith Tower
Seattle, WA 98104
(206) 624-2180

WEST VIRGINIA

West Virginians Against the Death Penalty
Alderson Hospitality House
P.O. Box 579
Alderson, WV 24910
(304) 445-2980

WISCONSIN

ACLU of Wisconsin
207 E. Buffalo St., Suite 325
Milwaukee, WI 53202
(414) 272-4032

Casa Maria Catholic Worker
P.O. Box 5206
Milwaukee, WI 53205
(414) 344-5585

WYOMING

Wyoming Church Coalition
1215 Gibbon
Laramie, WY 82070
(307) 745-6000

Wyoming Coalition Against
the Death Penalty
P.O. Box 15566
Cheyenne, WY 82003
(307) 632-3174

APPENDIX

APPENDIX A

———

ACRONYMS

ABA	American Bar Association
ACLU	American Civil Liberties Union
AMA	American Medical Association
NAACP	National Association for the Advancement of Colored People
NAACP LDF	NAACP Legal Defense and Education Fund
NCADP	National Coalition to Abolish the Death Penalty

APPENDIX B

FEDERAL COURT SYSTEM

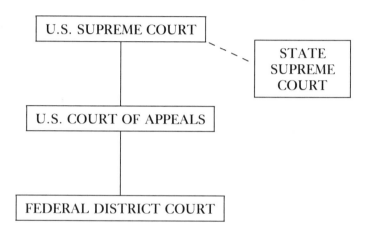

The federal court system is organized into three tiers. District courts are the federal trial courts. Each state has at least one federal district court. These courts hear both federal cases and appeals from state courts involving questions of federal law.

The next level, the U.S. Court of Appeals, handles appeals of the decisions of the District Courts. The United States is divided into 12 circuits, each of which takes appeals from several districts. The focus in the appeals court is on whether the trial court correctly interpreted the law. Findings of fact ordinarily are presumed complete and are not reviewed at the appellate level.

The U.S. Supreme Court is the court of last resort for the nation. Its decisions are binding on all federal and state courts. The Supreme Court hears limited appeals from the lower federal courts and from the highest state courts where a federal question is presented. The Court has the authority, through the power of judicial review, to strike down legislation it deems unconstitutional.

APPENDIX C

STATE CRIMINAL COURT SYSTEM

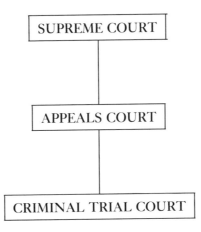

Each state has its own unique court system. Generally, these systems conform to the three-tier division found in the federal court system. Criminal cases are heard in local trial courts. In some jurisdictions, more serious offenses are tried in statewide criminal courts rather than at the local or county level.

The appellate level of courts is the first stage where appeals of trial court rulings are heard. The appellate courts normally are concerned with issues of law. The decisions of the trial courts on issues of fact almost always are considered final.

The state supreme court is the highest court in the system. It reviews appeals from the lower courts, most often in connection with state constitutional issues. A state's supreme court is the final authority on its constitution. If federal questions of law are involved, state court rulings can be appealed to the federal court system.

APPENDIX D

STATUS OF CAPITAL PUNISHMENT BY STATE

Executions since the reinstatement of capital punishment in 1976 through Jan. 18, 1990. Total = 121.

Texas	33
Florida	21
Louisiana	18
Georgia	14
Virginia	8
Alabama	7
Nevada	4
Mississippi	4
Utah	3
North Carolina	3
Indiana	2
South Carolina	2
Missouri	2

Death Sentences Carried Out

- Capital punishment used
- Law passed, but no one executed
- No capital punishment

Source: NAACP Legal Defense and Educational Fund Inc.

Copyright © 1990, The New York Times; Reprinted with permission.

APPENDIX E

___

EXECUTIONS SINCE 1977

EXECUTIONS BY YEAR SINCE 1977

Year	Count
1977	1
1978	–
1979	2
1980	–
1981	1
1982	2
1983	5
1984	21
1985	18
1986	18
1987	25
1988	11
1989	16
TOTAL	120

EXECUTIONS BY STATE SINCE 1977

Texas	33
Florida	21
Louisiana	18
Georgia	14
Virginia	8
Alabama	7
Nevada	4
Mississippi	4
Utah	3
N. Carolina	3
Indiana	2
S. Carolina	2
Missouri	1

INDEX

Index

197

Index

Index

Index

200